d0u8le

Shooting the Pacific
&
Your Eye-D Please

Two novellas by

Neil Sonnekus

LASAVIA
PUBLISHING

Published by Lasavia Publishing,
Auckland, New Zealand
www.lasaviapublishing.com

ISBN: 978-1-991083-42-5

Shooting the Pacific

'This has been the most boringest day of my life!'

Tiny girl in a tutu, scolding her father for picking her up late
after a ballet competition at Auckland Grammar.

Chapter 1

Franks got a text from Rat that said: Taniwha St, GI.

He started the Holden Commodore with its restless horses and left the Auckland docks. The song 'Blackbird' by Fat Freddy's Drop was playing on the radio. They were his ex-wife's favourite band, but he didn't want to go there now – if ever. He headed south on Tamaki Drive, through Mission Bay. That's where their daughter, Ally, used to have 'such fun' before she became a nose-in-the-air teenager. It was a perfect day for the beach. Hot. Muggy. Then he was clopping up St Heliers Bay Road, past all those toff houses. Took a left into West Tamaki, along the edge of equally lah-dee-dah Glendowie. Then a right down into Taniwha Street, Glen Innes, where Rat was ambling along as innocent as an ice pick between your eyes.

Franks stopped and Rat got in with his lousy teeth, bad breath and jacket. Rat knew the streets, so Franks and everything he represented paid Rat for that knowledge. All very hush-hush, of course. Franks offered Rat a smoke because the informer had a habit to maintain and was therefore always broke. But then Franks was always broke too, and he was employed, so where was the justice?

'Hey John,' Rat said, lighting up.

'What's happening?'

'Ah, you know, the usual vomit-inducing odour of infanticide, P-abuse and corruption in the mildest of places.'

'"Mildest"?'

'Yeah. I'm still working on it,' he said a little nervously 'That and the Chinks.'

Franks gave him a look and Rat said, 'Sorry, I forgot you're sensitive about that.'

'You must be the most considerate snitch I've ever known,' Franks said, making sure no one was following or watching them as he cruised along and Rat pontificated.

'I always think of it like this,' Rat said a little shakily. 'If demons hadn't colonised my veins in Theology III, if they hadn't sucked out my soul and spat it out onto these sweet streets, I would never have met an angel like you.'

'Of course, Rat.'

'No fuzz without us fizz, ay.'

'Yeah, yeah. What have you got for us today?'

'Something quite big, I'm afraid.'

'Why afraid?'

'Sorry, that's just a figure of speech,' Rat said a little more nervously than usual, his eyes darting this way and that.

'Okay, so what is it?'

'I've got an address for you.'

'What about it?'

'I've heard Eric Schultz is scheduled to visit there in the next hour, and it's right here in GI.'

Schultz was on the run for having raped and killed a woman in Christchurch shortly after being granted parole for good behaviour. He'd done ten years in the clink for exactly the same crime, so the cops wanted to do more than just talk to him. They also didn't want anyone from the public to approach him, even if he was instantly recognisable. Apart from all the other tats on his face, the one that stood out on his forehead, inked in beautiful Script font, was mesmerisingly blatant. It said HATE. Anybody stupid enough to confront him ran the serious risk of ending up like that poor woman in Canterbury.

'Why're you so jumpy?' Franks said.

'Can you imagine what would happen to me if one of my lot were to rat on me?'

'Fair enough. What's the address?'

Rat gave it to him.

'If he's not there within an hour, it means there's been a change of plan. But the address is solid, bro. You can put it in your notebook. All the beauties go there some time or other.'

'Okay,' Franks said, giving Rat a stuffed envelope, which he put in his grubby jacket pocket.

'See you later,' Rat said, getting out and heading for the public toilets of Point England, where he would probably shoot up, Franks thought.

He drove to the address, parked two houses away, and continued doing what he'd done with Malone and their new rookie, Jiaping Wu, down at the docks. He waited. Watched. The shit part of the job. Waiting and watching.

Smoked. Waited.

Franks and Malone had grown up in houses like the weatherboard one he was watching now, houses that had been erected for returning servicemen. Houses that were now being replaced by multiple units on single properties. But they hadn't known each other back then. Malone's father had been a respected member of the local *hapū*. Franks' old man had not been a respected member of anything. He'd been too busy dodging the cops or spending time 'away', or 'inside'. Which didn't mean people didn't love him – they did, even if he was absent most of the time. He was what people called a character. Was it this memory that was agitating Franks, he wondered. He had a restless, churning feeling in his guts. Lit another cigarette.

Come on, he thought, exhaling.

Someone finally came out just after the hour, but it wasn't Schultz. The man was wearing a typical outfit of white sneakers, black socks that stayed halfway up his calves, long black shorts, a black singlet with a red 10 on it, plenty of tats, and a navy-blue NY peak cap. He got into an old, souped-up Japanese car – low, noisy, tinted – which screamed gangster. The man put on his sound system, the bass causing the surrounding houses' windows to rattle, and thumped away. The hour was over by twelve minutes now, his guts were screaming, and he thought he should call Malone. Just then his phone rang. It was Jiaping. That was always a good thing because he was nuts about her, regardless of what she told him to the contrary.

'Hello, Officer Wu,' he said in their official flirt mode.

She said something, but the line was scratchy.

'Sorry, you're breaking up. Can you say that again?'

'John, I need help,' she said.

'Where are you?' he said, getting the address, chucking the smoke, keeping the lights off, but summoning the horses. He needed all of them because Jiaping wasn't the kind of cop – or woman – to call for help if something wasn't seriously wrong.

Chapter 2

Franks screamed to a halt outside an abandoned warehouse next to a noisy Mount Wellington foundry, unlocked the box in the foot-well, grabbed his Glock and got out of the car. He had a moment in which he thought he should call for back-up and put on his bulletproof vest, but by then the first bullet had screeched into the front right mudguard. The American training – *'move!'* – instantly kicked in. He changed direction and crabbed to the rear mudguard as the second bullet hit, closer this time, and then he was scrambling around to the other side of the car, hopefully out of the line of fire. Unless it was a trap and there was another shooter on the other side of the car, in which case he was toast.

But there wasn't. Just silence. Heat.

And the noise from the foundry drowning out the pistol shots. Better call for back-up and put on that vest. Crouching, he opened the passenger door and leaned over to the radio, but then he saw a figure – hoodie, jeans, trainers – running towards an alley next to the warehouse behind him. No time to call or put on a vest. Franks gave chase, shouted 'Hey! Stop!', halted at the corner, looked around, pistol at heart height, saw the figure running towards a wall that was too high to cross. This was simple. The arsehole couldn't go anywhere and Franks had him covered, but then you always learned something new in this business, his boss Smith always said. The figure headed towards a corner of the wall, jumped onto a discarded table, leapt, and, using his momentum and the 45-degree angle of the two walls, scrambled up, caught the top of the wall, pulled himself up and flipped over.

Gone.

Franks knew he could do the same, but he'd be a sitting duck, so he ran back the way he'd come, decided the vest would take too much time, and went to a door that was hanging open on a single hinge. He stepped inside, out of the line of fire, and let his eyes get used to the gloom. It was boiling in there, in every sense. There was another door on the other side of the warehouse. Franks crossed the heavy air, the empty space, waiting for a bullet to rip into him, but nothing happened. Now he had to prepare himself for broad daylight again. When he was ready, he stepped out, instantly moved to the side, and almost shot a seagull that suddenly took off right next to him.

Fuck!

The yard had hip-high weeds and crunching broken glass underfoot, and the glare was something not to behold. He headed towards the next open door, the next abandoned warehouse. This one was full of deserted work benches, stripped machinery, the smell of dust and old grease. As he waited for his eyes to adjust again, he saw a dry-wall office in the furthest corner, then something halfway between it and him, sticking out behind a torn tarp, which was hanging from a hook. It was the toe of a trainer. He was about to start reading out rights, but the figure had clearly sensed his intention and started running towards the office.

'Hey! Stop or I'll shoot!'

But the figure ignored him. Franks gave chase and the man slammed the door behind him, but it bounced back open again. Franks saw him running to the right, to another exit. He entered the office, covering right, aiming right. Then the training kicked in: *Expect the unexpected. What if it's a trap?* Too late. A figure was coming towards him from the left so he swivelled. But before he could compute that it was Jiaping who'd been pushed towards him, pointing her pistol at him, her arm tied to a support, mouth taped up, eyes wide with terror, he shot her plumb in the heart.

Chapter 3

A few weeks or maybe months later – everything had become a bit of a blur after that little incident – Franks was in his usual haunt, drinking his usual midday beers. If he'd been intense, lean and unshaven in the past, now he was just unshaven, heading for unhealthily podgy, thanks to the endless takeouts and beers he consumed on a daily basis. It was a delicate balance, staying within the law he had left with a dishonourable discharge before he picked up the last vestige of sanity in his life, his daughter, Allyson: fifteen going on twenty-one. This was when they mostly spoke as he drove her over to her mother's house. After that he would go to the two-bedroom flat he'd bought, line up the cheap whiskies and beer chasers, and drink himself into oblivion.

He liked it here in the Bar None, which he half-owned, even though he'd paid for all of it. It was where his ex-partner's wife, Pat Malone, served him, and where Morris usually joined him at lunchtime. In fact, here he came now, out of the eternal rain with his dark skin and blue eyes, his gold necklace, watch and rings. They had been two very different types of undercover cop, Franks going for the nondescript, worn look, and Morris very much the too-flashy-to-be-a-cop type. That had been then. They had had each other's backs, no matter what, and that was all that mattered when your life depended on it. It had also created a bond that went way beyond ideology.

'Hey,' Morris said.

'How's it going?'

Morris looked up at the weatherman droning on about the rain on the TV above the bar and said, 'If we aren't being flooded by rain, we're being flooded by fucking P.'

'Yeah,' Franks muttered.

'Not that you give a shit anymore, do you?'

'Nah.'

'Sit here and flirt with my wife while I try to keep the country clean of meth dealers.'

'Why does it feel like I've had this conversation before?'

At which point Pat passed them on her way back from a customer and asked Morris whether he wanted his usual double espresso, which was rhetorical so he didn't even bother answering.

'Give me a short one please, darling,' Franks said, just to wind up Morris.

'Fucking wanker,' he replied.

'Morris dear,' Franks continued, 'don't you think coffee is the last thing you should be drinking if you've got an ulcer?'

'Mind your own fucken business,' Morris said, poker-faced. 'Loser.'

'You're hurting my feelings,' Franks said, only half taking in the televised deluge and the weatherman's drone.

Pat brought him his beer and took the double whisky to the person half behind him as he took a slug and became aware that there was a bit of a problem with the customer. She – obsidian hair, trim – thought she had her purse in this bag, but it must still be in the other one.

'What am I supposed to do with a drink that's already been poured?' Pat asked loudly enough for Morris and Franks to hear. She didn't like this woman; there was something off about her.

'I'll do two hours' dishes,' the woman said.

Morris looked as miffed about this turn of events as his wife did, and was about to say something when Franks offered to put it on his tab.

'I'll repay you, I promise,' the woman said as Pat purled.

'You don't have to,' Franks said. 'It's on me.'

'He's here every day this time,' Pat said disapprovingly.

'Thank you,' the woman said to Franks.

'No worries,' he replied and drowned the last of his short one. 'See youse.'

Chapter 4

Every working day Franks drove to the Methodist Church on Mount Eden Road, where Ally waited for him, as she did now, using her portfolio bag to cover her blonde head from the rain instead of just taking her bloody raincoat along. She took art classes in the community centre behind the church, which could be reached by a side street, Ngauruhoe, but she'd insisted he drop her off in the main road.

'Why? Are you embarrassed by me? Is my car not smart enough for you?'

'No, Dad. I would just like a little independence. Do you mind?'

'Of course not, sweetheart.'

Blonde head? Ally had shiny black hair, like her mother, but she'd dyed it white and he didn't like it. When she got in and greeted him, he asked her what the hell she'd done to it and she replied, 'Dyed it, and hello to you too.'

Franks grunted and Allyson told him he reeked.

'I'm within the limit.'

'You still smell.'

'How are you otherwise?'

'I'm okay,' she said.

Franks negotiated the ultra-cautious Auckland traffic – give them a drizzle and they caused traffic jams to avoid the drudgery of insurance claims – so everything was down to a crawl right now, which didn't do much for him, or his restless horses. The only thing he had left from his cop days was the Commodore he'd bought, patchwork panel-beating and all.

'How was your class?'

'Cool.'

'What's that supposed to mean? Good, bad, indifferent?'

'We're doing a nude study,' she said, staring out the window, channelling some Hollywood starlet, offering nothing further.

'And? Was it an old woman, a young woman, a Pakeha, an Islander?'

'It was a man.'

'Nude?'

'Come on, Dad. I've seen a willy before.'

'Where?'

Allyson switched to wounded-actress mode and said: 'It was at school, back in 2023…'

'Very funny.'

'It's true. But I've been wondering,' she said, back in Ally mode.

'What have you been wondering, sweetheart' Franks said, still pissed off about the hair thing.

'Do you think I'm a good artist?'

'Of course I think you're a good artist.'

'Even though you haven't seen my work for over six months?'

'I *know* you're a good artist,' he said as the traffic eased and he headed for the turnoff to her mother's house in Sandringham.

'Every parent thinks their darling is a genius.'

'Well, what do you think?'

'I think I'm a really crap artist.'

'So why do you carry on doing it? For my and your mother's sake?'

'No, Dad. I do it for a very obvious reason.'

'And what is that, Allyson?'

'I like the model.'

'You're a laugh a minute,' he said as he stopped outside the house that used to be all of theirs but was now occupied only by his ex-wife, Ngaio, and their daughter.

'I know,' she said, opening the door. 'Anything you would like me to convey to your ex?'

'No.'

Ally got out, started walking away and then came back to the window.

'By the way, I dyed my hair because I was tired of being a blackhead.'

Franks gave her a false smile and she returned it with an even falser smile so he gave her a grotesque grin, which she bettered. This went on for a while and was their way of saying they were still father and daughter.

Chapter 5

Now life became simple again. He drove to his unkempt flat in Mount Roskill, sank the first shot like it was water, and did pretty much the same with the first beer. That was *much* better, *much* simpler. If there was a sun you could watch it set, but there wasn't a sun and the boy next door was being told, once again, to turn his dense electronic music down.

'Jake?'

'Yeah?'

'Please put that crap a bit softer.'

'It isn't crap.'

'Okay, but it's too loud. Please put it softer, honey.'

'All right,' Jake grumbled.

Poor guy. His mother had an industrial-strength voice, but how could he, Franks, not have seen it was a set-up? The decoy had been set and he'd walked into it eyes wide shut. He'd chased blindly because he wanted to protect Jiaping; instead he'd shot her, killed her. Every night he saw her shock, the desperation in her eyes as he asked her who it was. But she couldn't talk – because of the pain, because the notoriously elusive Mr Li had put a dollar coin in her mouth and then taped it shut. So Franks had had to get rid of that too, but by then her eyes were fading as he tried to keep her with him, holding her cold, tiny hand, which opened and gave him her winning Lotto ticket worth $6 million.

Another whisky, another beer.

How did he know it was Li who'd done it? Because he'd seen that dollar trick with Morris on another occasion. Rat had told them their missing colleague, Peter, was being held by a certain Mr Li in yet another warehouse, this one in Onehunga. They drove there and approached the structure with extreme caution: armed, bulletproof vests, the works. But the rolling door was open and they'd looked in from either side of it.

Peter was on his knees, hands tied behind his back. Li, an elegant dresser, stood over him, next to an Islander with a pistol dangling at his side. That was bad enough, but there were two other bulky Islanders standing around in the light too.

'You've got a very simple choice Peter,' Li said. 'You either tell me who's working with you, or Israel here kills you.'

Peter said nothing, grim but determined, and Franks indicated to Morris that they should burst in and arrest the lot. But Morris shook his head, pointing to a spot beyond the men. There were three more Islanders beyond the circle of light, all armed with semi-automatics. Morris and Franks would have had no chance and, instead of just Peter being dead, they'd all be dead.

'Come on Peter,' Li said. 'You've got a wife, young children. I pay well. Ask these guys.'

Peter wavered for a second before he braced himself. Li sighed and nodded at Israel, who shot Peter point blank through the head.

Franks started hyperventilating as they watched Li spinning a dollar coin in the air before catching it and putting it in the dead Peter's mouth, after which one of the hoods taped it up. This was Li's simple but very effective way of showing people what happened if they messed with him.

Then a phone was ringing and Franks couldn't work out why no one seemed particularly perturbed by the sound. Was this some sort of game? A set-up? Why weren't Mr Li and his hoods reacting to it? But it eventually dawned on Franks that he wasn't at the warehouse or in a dream anymore: it was his own phone ringing in real time.

Here. Now.

Chapter 6

It was morning. He'd fallen asleep on his couch again, and it was still raining lightly outside. Once he'd finally managed to find the device, he said, 'Franks.'

'John, it's Smith. I need to talk to you.'

He got up, splashed his face with cold water and drove to town, where they met outside a trendy coffee bar in upmarket Newmarket. Smith was standing in his usual grey suit beneath his black umbrella. Good old Smith. He'd been Franks' boss and maybe even a bit of a father figure: he was your quintessential, quietly spoken, decent, old-school Kiwi. Franks had often said outrageous things, just to see how Smith would react, but a ten-metre tsunami wouldn't ruffle the man. You could trust him with your life.

'Why here?' Franks said.

'Because I need some fresh air ...'

'And no one can hear us, right?'

'Yes. How's Ally?'

'I didn't know this was going to be social. I would've brought some photographs.'

Smith guided them away from Broadway Street, past the fish smells of the Asian markets, giving Franks a pursed look.

'She's dyed her hair blonde.'

'They all go through that,' Smith said.

'I didn't know you were such an expert on teenagers.'

'I might not have kids but I've got eyes, ears, nephews, nieces ...'

'Fair enough. So, what do you want to know?'

Smith stopped. 'I want to know what's going on.'

'Nothing's going on. I resigned and that's that. You know why.'

Smith started walking them again.

'Morris tells me you bought a bar.'

Franks gave a so-what shrug.

'Nothing wrong with that. I just wonder where you got the money if you took a dishonourable,' Smith said.

Franks said nothing.

'John, this is not social. It's bad enough that I lost Peter and now you, my best player. But I need to know if there's some new department. I can't afford crossed lines here. This thing is too delicate. You know that.'

'I'm not working for anyone.'

'Not even the other side?'

'Well, actually, I've just joined an international syndicate,' Franks bullshitted. 'We have branches in Seattle, Manila, Johannesburg, Shanghai, Auckland ...'

'At least that would explain where you got the money.'

Franks said nothing.

'Or are you going to tell me you won the Lotto?'

'Yes.'

Smith stopped again and just looked at Franks until he realised he was being serious. Then he burst out laughing and said, 'Go away.'

Chapter 7

There was a woman talking about the endless downpour on the TV set above the counter at Bar None as Franks ordered a bottle of beer instead of his usual jug.

'What's the occasion?' Pat asked.

'Business.'

'Okay,' she said, walking away with that extra sway of the hips when Morris wasn't around. She clearly wasn't getting any sex from her husband, though he gave her plenty of lip when she flirted with others, including Franks.

Morris came in, smelling of rain, tobacco and cologne, and Pat started preparing his double espresso. Franks asked him why he'd told Smith about buying Bar None.

'He's worried about you. We're all worried about you.'

'Well, I'm deeply fucking touched.'

Franks had bought the bar with the unwritten agreement that Morris and Pat had fifty percent ownership and therefore shared its running profits. This was because Morris couldn't own a business as a cop, and he and Pat were the only two people Franks cared about anyway, apart from Ally.

'So, has your little hustler been around yet?'

'What do you mean?'

'I'm talking about that tart who got a double Scotch off you yesterday.'

'I gave it to ...'

Franks stopped. Morris was looking at something or someone behind his ex-colleague's ear. Franks swung around. It was the woman with the very black hair.

'Hi,' she said. 'Can I buy you a drink?'

'No thanks, I've already got one.'

'Can I pay for it?'

'No, and I told you the drink was on me.'

Morris had a disapproving look about him for some reason and Pat had an ugly look about her for another.

'Is there nothing I can do for you?' the woman said.

'Not that I can think of,' Franks lied.

'When last did you have a good, home-cooked meal?' she asked.

Chapter 8

Franks didn't have another beer and drove to Mount Eden, not to pick up Ally but to meet an estate agent at a huge, old-style bungalow beneath the burnt-out volcano of Maungawhau. The man went on about the flow of this and the sunny aspect of that, and it was the kind of house Franks wouldn't have been able to afford over three lifetimes in the force. But now he said he would take it, cash.

Then he drove to the Methodist Church in the same suburb, where Ally was waiting for him. When she got in she gave him a peck on the cheek and said, 'Hello, Pops.'

'Hi sweetheart.'

'What's up?'

Franks asked her what she meant.

'You don't smell so strong, and you're smiling. Are you cutting down?'

'No, but I've just bought you and your mother a new house.'

'But we've got a house.'

'Yeah, but this is a nice big one in a nicer area. This one, in fact. Within walking distance of your art school.'

'Okay,' Ally said, sounding dubious.

'I suppose a "gee, that's amazing" or "thank you" is completely out of the question.'

'I'm not sure about this, Dad.'

'Amazing how women are born suspicious.'

'That's probably because their fathers give them reason to be,' Ally said.

Franks snorted at female ingratitude and soon stopped outside her mother's bungalow, an abode which had been working-class when they'd bought it but was now considered gentrified.

'Love you,' Franks said.

'But is it enough?' she said, back in actress mode, before heading towards the front gate.

'Hey?'

Ally stopped and looked back at him.

He pulled a face at her.

She gave him a mock-contemptuous 'Pfft', turned, and opened the gate.

Chapter 9

He'd forgotten what home-cooked food smelled like and told himself to drink the beer she'd given him slowly, because his first instinct was to swallow it down in one go and then refill. Her name was Tracy, and she was making a stir-fry of chicken and vegetables that had none of the greasy smells of a takeaway joint. The steamed rice smelled good and dry, nutty. She was wearing a loose top and track pants, and her Kohimarama apartment was exactly the opposite of his. That is, tidy verging on sterile, very upmarket, with a view of Rangitoto and a hint of the Pacific beyond.

He wasn't mad about her girly music, but cut it out as best he could.

'What?' she asked.

'Sorry?'

'Why are you looking at me like that?'

It wasn't an accusatory question, just enquiring, slightly teasing even.

'You know that feeling you get when you meet someone and after a while you start thinking you've met them before?'

'No?'

'Well, I'm starting to get that feeling.'

'But you *have* met me before,' she said, pouring some soy sauce over the intoxicating smells of onion, garlic, capsicum, white flesh, green vegetables.

'I meant before we met in the bar.'

'Gosh, where do you think we might have met?'

'I don't know. Maybe I'm just having a flashback to my old dope days.'

'What kind of a cop are you?' she teased.

'A very experienced kind of cop.'

She paused briefly to take a sip of wine, the outline of her body visible beneath the loose clothing.

'Maybe we met in a previous life,' she smiled.

'Yeah, maybe that's it,' he said, warming to her.

Chapter 10

Ally had also done some cooking and set the table, complete with two lit candles. She heard her mother pull into the driveway, stop, the car door opening and closing, footsteps coming in through the open front door, stopping.

Ngaio looked tired after a day's work, but her heart warmed instantly when she saw her daughter, smelling the beef and vegetable roast she'd made, taking in the low light.

'Hello, darling. What's the occasion?'

'You're a hard-working woman.'

'That's nice. How was your day?'

'Dad's bought us a house.'

'He's trying to make me feel guilty,' Ngaio responded instantly, putting down her bag, kicking off her shoes and sitting down at the table, relieving her feet.

'That's exactly what I thought,' Ally said.

'What would you know about my guilt?'

'Nothing. It sort of came naturally. Do you think he's trying to' – Ally made air quotes with her fingers – 'buy you back?'

'I very much doubt it.'

'Would you take him back?'

Ngaio gave her precious daughter a look that said she wasn't going to indulge that thought, so Ally looked at one of the other chairs and said: 'This, dear guest, is what is called the parental evasion. Or simply: silence.'

Ngaio sighed.

'They will not let you into their world,' Ally continued. 'No matter how hard you try to find out what happened, they will not budge. They "don't want to hurt your feelings. You're too young to understand." Et cetera, et cetera.'

Chapter 11

Back in his flat, where Ally rarely stayed, and after more whiskies and beer chasers on home turf, Franks started thinking about that scene with Li again as Jake's mother once again asked him whether he thought that was music.

Yeah.'

Okay, but it's too loud.'

Jake turned the music down and the thugs had brought a black bag, filled it with stones, and zipped Peter's corpse up in it. The crew were chatting as if they were going about their normal business when Morris noticed one casting a glance in their direction as a car drove past behind them. The man casually mentioned something to one of his colleagues in Tongan, who then said something to Li in Mandarin. He didn't say anything for a while, then told the Mandarin speaker: 'We've got company. Two of you go out the back and capture them. If they offer resistance, kill them.'

Morris had enough te reo Māori and therefore Tongan to whisper, 'They're onto us. Let's go.'

As they moved away, Franks accidentally kicked an empty paint tin and then there was no reason to be discreet. It was time to get the hell out of there as quickly as possible.

They ran like lunatics towards the parked Holden, which was about twenty metres away, as the thugs started opening fire. But they stopped almost as quickly as they'd started. Franks looked back in all that panic and saw Li standing in the middle of the group: he had told his thugs to stop.

Morris and Franks cleared out in the Commodore, which had a flat tyre and a couple of holes in it, and drove as if possessed. When they were sure they were out of harm's way they stopped just beyond the Aotea Sea Scouts building and got out.

'Fuck! *Fuck!'* Franks screamed.

'There's nothing we could have done!' Morris shouted.

'I know. But what are we going to tell Angie!'

'That he died doing his job.'

'*Fuck,*' Franks said again. Then, 'You're bleeding.'

'Shit,' Morris said, looking down at his arm, then at Franks.

'You too!'

'Where?'

'Your leg.'

'Oh Christ,' Franks said, and they started laughing half hysterically, high on guilt and adrenaline beside the Manukau Harbour's choppy waters.

Chapter 12

Another day, another jug of beer, another pack of smokes.

Franks sat at the bar, wondering what that conversation with his former boss had been about. Then again, it was none of his business anymore, no matter how 'delicate' Smith had said it was, no matter what lines were going to be crossed. He, Franks, was just going to sit here every day, at his bar, and do what? Keep within the limit, drive his precious daughter home, and that was it. Listen to the music, both there and here. 'Love is a Terrible Thing' by Marlon Williams was playing over the speakers. No shit, he thought. He didn't hear Pat talking to another desperate customer further down the bar (things got more respectable as the day wore on), nor did he see Tracy appear next to him.

'Hey,' she said.

'Ah,' Franks said. 'What're you drinking?'

'Nothing. I'm not really a drinker.'

'It didn't look like that last night.'

'I make exceptions,' she said.

'I'll take that as a compliment,' Franks replied.

'It is. I just came to thank you for not trying to get into my pants.'

'Well, the thought did cross my mind.'

'That's fine. You're a man. But at least you didn't try, or become forceful.'

'Are you sure you don't want a drink?' Franks asked.

'No, I get too morose.'

'Well, I can relate to that.'

'Thanks again,' she said.

'What for? You did the cooking.'

'It was good to have some company again,' she replied, clearly dealing with some inner stuff, adding: 'I've got to go.'

'Okay, cheers?' Franks said, watching her leave and seeing Pat glancing up from her drunk male customer with a disapproving look.

Odd behaviuor, Franks thought about Tracy. Strange woman. But then all women – and men – were strange. You thought you knew them, then it turns out you only knew them in a particular set of circumstances. Change those and everything changes.

Took another slug of beer, lit another cigarette. Got a feeling he was being watched from behind, but when he finally turned to look, there was no one. Just a lot of empty tables that would slowly fill up at lunchtime and then empty out again before nightfall, when the serious drinking began. Probably just a throwback to his active days. Subconsciously, you were always on the lookout for someone who might want to put something in your back, like a knife or a bullet. He missed those days, but then he went and blew it – and now he needed to go for a leak.

He went into the men's, which reeked of chemicals and that pervasive smell of male urine, and still felt like he was being watched. And was. It was his ex-informer.

'Rat? What the hell are you doing here?'

'Hi, John.'

'What's up?'

'Certainly not my dick, if you know what I mean. But I want to give you some advice,' the rodent said.

'What for? You know I'm not in the force anymore, so I'm not paying.'

'This is free advice.'

'Why?'

'You've been good to me over the years, John.'

'Okay, so what's this "advice"?'

'Don't think just because you've left the force it's all over.'

'What are you talking about?'

'I'm saying mind your back, bro.'

Just then the only other Bar None customer stumbled in and Rat started washing his clammy hands until the older man was in a cubicle, struggling to undo his trousers and muttering to himself. Rat took a bulging brown envelope from his jacket pocket, put it on a low wall, and left with a nod of his greasy head.

Franks knew exactly what was in the bulging envelope, and it wasn't a book, money, or drugs. It was cold, and it was hard – and it was loaded.

Chapter 13

The bloody rain wouldn't go away and Ally was not waiting outside for Franks, as she usually did, come rain or shine.

Franks stopped outside the church and waited for Ally, thinking about what was in the envelope. Why had Rat given him an unmarked Glock 17? That could be a service pistol. Might it have been Peter's? Was one of his former cases about to be released on parole? Sure, he had enemies; that was part of being an undercover cop, even an ex-undercover cop, which was why your back still itched at times. But what was Rat up to? He didn't strike Franks as someone brimming with altruism, so what the hell?

He was so deep in thought that he didn't notice a middle-aged woman coming towards him, under an umbrella and wearing the multi-smudged overall of an art teacher.

'Hello John,' she said.

Franks started and desperately tried to remember her name.

'Hi, uh, um …' What was it? He knew it started with a C. Carrie? Catherine? Claire? 'Clarissa.'

'Christa,' she corrected him gently. 'How's it going?' she asked with a South African accent, meaning she wanted to know how he was in general but not too much about things like his divorce from Ngaio, or his drinking.

'Fine,' he said. 'Fine. And you?'

'Good, thanks. But I'm wondering how Ally is?'

'What do you mean?'

'Well, she hasn't been in class for the last two weeks.'

'Why didn't you let us know?' Franks said, feeling a creeping sensation along his shoulder blades.

'I thought she might be sick. You know, with all this rain everyone's getting the flu, so I'm checking with you now.'

'Jesus.'

'Is everything alright?'

In other words, are you and Ngaio still having post-marital problems that might be affecting Ally?

'I don't know. I'll call her mother.'

'Okay. I have to get back to class. Please let me know if she's okay.'

'Right. Thanks, Claris … uh, Christa.'

She nodded and made her way back to Ngauruhoe, the side street that led to the community centre's entrance.

First you're given a gun and told to watch your back, then you're told your daughter isn't attending art classes. Was there a connection? He didn't have a good feeling. It was too much like the past. It tensed the upper part of his back. Badly.

He started dialling Ngaio's number but, lo and behold, there Ally was, coming around the corner onto Mt Eden Road, bright and breezy, as if all was sunshine and roses. Franks cut the call to his ex-wife.

'Hi, Dad,' she said, getting into the car.

Franks greeted her, switched on the ignition, merged into the traffic.

'How come you're late?' he asked.

'Oh, you know: the creative process.'

'Right,' Franks said tensely.

'Dad, are you okay?'

'Yeah, I'm fine,' he lied. 'Have you and Mum seen the new house yet?'

'No, we can only go tomorrow night. She's very busy.'

'I'm sure,' he said bitterly.

'You seem very tense, Dad,' she said.

'I'm fine,' he snapped.

Chapter 14

More rain. There was almost something vengeful about it, but Ally didn't mind it at all. If others didn't like being alone at home, she loved it, even though some might argue she'd had no choice but to get used to it. Her parents had both worked for as long as she could remember; that's just the way it was. They did it so that she could get the kind of schooling (including extra art classes) only rich parents could afford, they'd said. That didn't prevent them from breaking up, but never mind. Her phone rang and she saw it was her mother.

'Hi, Mum.'

'Hello, sweetheart. Are you okay?'

'Yeah, fine,' Ally said, more interested in the text convo she was having with her friend, Frances, except that her mother sounded a little concerned. 'Why?'

'Your father tried to call me today.'

'Maybe he's missing you,' Ally fished.

'I very much doubt that. Are all the doors locked?'

'Yeah,' Ally said, not knowing or caring whether they were locked or not: her parents were so paranoid.

'Have you had something decent to eat?'

'Yeah,' Ally lied.

'Okay, sweetheart. I'll see you in about an hour.'

'Sure.'

'Look after yourself.'

'Will do,' Ally said, rolling her eyes.

'Love you.'

'Love you too, Mum.'

Ngaio rang off and Ally felt a twinge of love but also resentment towards her mother, who had something about the martyr about her: keeping a secret from Ally as if she was doing so to protect her from some earth-shattering truth. As if she wasn't old enough to know the truth about something, anything, Ally thought, biting into her Whittaker's peanut slab.

Chapter 15

As it happened, Ngaio was sitting in an office opposite a truth that would have outraged Ally. She was facing the married man she'd been having an affair with for the last two years.

Ngaio had fallen for the younger Tom, the 'son' part of McAllister & Son Attorneys, slowly but surely. At first she'd just been his legal secretary, then he'd invited her out for working lunches and they'd slowly started to realise they had something in common. She had a husband whose job had rendered him emotionally and physically dead. Tom had a beautiful wife who ticked almost all the boxes. Beautifully groomed and from a good family, the perfect blonde mother who drove the boys to their top-notch school in the brand-new Range Rover her husband had bought her as a birthday present. But she was perfectly dull too, according to Tom. Deadly dull, in fact, especially where it mattered for men. That is, in bed.

The working lunches got longer and finally ended up in motel rooms. It was exhilarating, but with the distant knowledge that it had very little to do with the real world. She had a teenage daughter who insisted on living her own life (but with the unconscious proviso that her parents stuck together). He had two young sons who made him puff up with pride just mentioning them. Then again, he said he wanted to start a new life with Ngaio, her daughter and his two boys, but whenever it came to the mechanics of that statement there was this anniversary and that rugby match to attend. Endlessly. And, smitten as she was with this silver-tongued young lawyer, Ngaio couldn't bring herself to tell her daughter about it, let alone her husband. Something, probably maternal instinct, told her to protect Ally insofar as she could be protected in the circumstances. Or was she protecting herself from seeing the anger and hurt it would cause their daughter?

It wasn't a very rational time and it couldn't last and it couldn't stop except by some sort of intervention, and that had come from, of all people, John. If he wasn't an astute detector of emotional, middle-class matters, he was a very connected man and someone had whispered something in his ear about seeing Ngaio and Tom entering a motel. He'd proceeded with all the thoroughness of a criminal investigator. He'd gathered all the evidence he needed and then told Ngaio he wanted a divorce – and why. She was shattered, as was their daughter, who was told they had irreconcilable differences but still loved her very much. She didn't believe a word of it. Franks hadn't taken the legal route, which would have meant they'd have to sell the house and split the proceeds. Instead, he insisted that Ngaio and Ally stay in the house until their precious daughter was finished with school, after which they could deal with legalities. He would move out (and feel very sorry for himself).

'I've got a little surprise for you,' Tom said, getting a boyish glint in his eyes.

'What is it?' Ngaio smiled.

'I've bought us a flat in town.'

'Just like that?'

'Yes. Would you like to see it?'

'I would,' Ngaio said, thinking Tom had a way of spending much more than even he could afford.

Chapter 16

Franks shakily reached for his first Scotch of the night while the woman next door asked her son to please put 'that noise' a little softer, for crying out loud.

'Okay, okay,' Jake grumbled and Franks, having downed the first whisky, smiled.

But that didn't last long. Soon the horrors were back, this time starting with a piercing scream. He and Morris were standing out in the sunshine at their late colleague Peter's place, when it came. Franks was in a moon boot, Morris's arm was in a sling. They automatically went into reaction mode – but it was only Sally, Peter's daughter, being chased by his son, Peter Jnr. The kids were vaguely aware that their father wouldn't be coming home again. Sally ran past the portrait of her late father on the mantelpiece, past everyone from the department attending the memorial service, including, of course, good old Smith. She came running out onto the deck, followed by Peter Jnr, and Franks caught her, hobbling, telling her to 'slow down, young lady.'

Peter Jnr said he'd touched her and now she was infected and she was going to die, so there!

'No! Never!' Sally replied when her ginger-haired mother came out onto the deck.

'Peter? Sally? Inside. Now.'

The kids instantly quietened down and left, leaving Angie to face Franks and Morris. She was in her late twenties, a fiery redhead, and she was seething with anger and sorrow.

'So are you two cowboys proud of yourselves?'

'Angie ...' Franks started.

'Don't you "Angie" me, you dickhead,' she said.

'There was nothing we could do,' Morris replied, trying to keep his tone sympathetic and low.

'I know that, arsehole. But do you know what else I know?'

Smith had become aware of the conversation outside and was casting concerned looks in their direction, with Pat looking on, while the only thing 'the boys' could say to Angie was exactly nothing.

'I know that in a way I'm actually glad he's dead,' Angie continued. 'Do you know why? Because it means I can take my kids away and start a new life somewhere. Away from the force, away from macho fuckheads like you. Do you hear me?'

They could only nod as tears started forming in her eyes.

'I don't know what it is with you men that you want to be dead heroes, but I think I'd prefer a live coward for my children. You … fucking arseholes.'

She turned and walked back towards the living room. Smith came towards her and put his arms around her as she burst into tears. Smith made all the appropriate comforting sounds, stroking her back, giving them both a pursed look as he did so.

That was probably the shittest part of the job, and maybe all of it was shit, Frank thought. But it was the only shit he knew and he missed it, so he downed another Scotch and reached for another beer.

Chapter 17

The arrangement was that Ngaio dropped Ally off at school in the mornings and Franks picked her up from art classes and took her home in the afternoons. That way they didn't cross paths, which is what he'd insisted on. Ally would catch a bus to Mt Eden Road with Frances, whose parents lived in that upmarket suburb, so it all worked out very nicely.

But now Franks was waiting to see if she was going to pitch at all, given the latest information he'd received. He was hungover and hanging for a drink, but he first had to sort this thing out. He'd always insisted that he'd rather hear unpleasant truths from Ally than deal in secrets and lies, and she had clearly lied to him about her last art class. He thought they were clear they could talk about anything, even 'willies', but something had changed.

Here she came now in her school uniform, with Frances, on Mt Eden Road. They stopped, chatted a bit, laughed, and said goodbye. But it was her friend who took Ngauruhoe Street towards the community centre, while Ally continued along Mt Eden Road, in the same direction Franks would normally drive, but away from where he'd park. North. Franks got out and started following her at a distance, wondering what she would say if she suddenly turned and saw him. If that happened she'd have a hissy fit about privacy, which was her agreed-upon right. He'd just say he was going to visit an old copper mate, and where was she going anyway? But she didn't see him because she was intent on where she was going, even speeding up a little.

She crossed the Mt Eden and Stokes roads intersection and continued along the noisy main road until she took a street to the left, then the first right, heading towards a block of flats that wasn't half as upmarket as the rest of the suburb. This was part of an integrationist policy, of which Franks approved, but he didn't like the fact that his daughter was going up the stairs of a three-storey block, all the way to the top. What the hell was she doing? He kept his distance and, when he got to the top floor, slightly out of breath, waited sixty tormenting seconds before peeking around the corner.

Nothing.

All the old fears and instincts were kicking in. Best not to think about them. Just do what you can, methodically. So he knocked on the first door and waited, impatiently, nerves screeching. Open the bloody door. But the inhabitants were probably at work. Just because you don't work doesn't mean others don't.

Next door. Knock. Wait. Ah, there was movement behind the frosted glass. A young woman, a young mother with her baby, opened the door.

'Sorry,' Franks said. 'Wrong number.'

'Are you okay?' the woman asked.

'Have you seen this girl here?' Franks asked, showing her a photo of Ally inside his wallet.

'Why do you want to know?' the woman asked, instantly suspicious, whereupon her baby started crying, probably at the sight of an unshaven, hungover and freaked-out ex-cop.

'I'm her father.'

'You look like a cop,' the woman said, then to her child: 'There, there, my angel.'

'I'm an *ex*-cop, but she's still my daughter.'

'I think she visits two doors down,' the woman said, still unsure about this wild-eyed man.

'Who lives there?'

'Some Chinese people, I think.'

'Thank you,' Franks said and moved away, but the young woman kept watching him, as if to protect another woman, even though she didn't know Ally from a bar of soap. But then her phone rang inside her flat and, with a last suspicious look at Franks, she went inside with her crying baby.

Franks knocked and waited.

Nothing.

Count to five, breathe.

Nothing.

Another five.

Ah, someone was coming to the door, opened it.

An older teen. Chinese.

'Where is she?' Franks said.

'Sorry. Who are you?'

Franks pointed the pistol at the boy's third eye and said: 'I'm her father. Where is she?'

The boy froze, kept his hands in plain sight and said in a very measured tone: 'She's inside.'

'You lead the way.'

The teen retreated, keeping his hands very visible as they moved along a dark passage towards the lounge. They rounded the corner into the cramped space, and there Allyson was – not bound, not wide-eyed like Jiaping was, not bleeding – just studying a board with a lot of chess pieces on it.

'What the hell do you think you're doing?' Franks asked.

'What the hell does it *look* like I'm doing?' Ally hissed.

Chapter 18

The air inside the Commodore was charged, to say the least.

'How am I supposed to trust you again?' Franks asked, livid.

All he got was a sulky teenage silence.

'Is this the model you like?' he tried.

More sulking teenage silence, staring at the traffic and the rain.

'Is he?' Franks insisted.

'No,' Ally answered icily.

'Where did you meet him?'

'Where everybody meets.'

'And where might that be?'

'Online, obviously.'

'Christ, haven't you heard about Grace Millane?'

'Yes.'

Franks couldn't believe he was having this conversation.

'How long has this been going on?'

Silence.

'Allyson ...'

'Six months.'

'Six mon ...? Well, thank you very much for telling me.'

'Pleasure,' she said cuttingly.

Franks couldn't stomach the Auckland traffic when it rained. Everybody drove like old farts – or Asians, as Morris would say. Christ, he needed a drink!

'Why didn't you tell me?' he said again.

Ally stared at the rain for a long time before she gave her classic teenage answer: 'I don't know.'

'Great!' Franks said, seething.

Chapter 19

Ngaio picked Ally up at home and they drove to Mt Eden in the downpour so that they could look at the house Franks had bought them. The agent had left a key in a lockbox for them and the house was easily twice the size of their current bungalow. Ally was overawed. She had grown up in various flats and then their two-bedroom abode in Sandringham, but this was on a completely different scale. It reeked of old money.

'So what do you think?' Ally half whispered in the large living room with its ornate fireplace.

'It's very big,' Ngaio stated the glaringly, annoyingly obvious, as usual.

'So?'

'I'd need an army to help me with this.'

'Maybe you could sell it and buy another smaller place and keep the balance.'

'Maybe I like my own place.'

'Why?'

'You were born there, for starters.'

'But look at the fantastic garden.'

'Are you going to help me with it?'

She could always twist things to make her feel guilty, Ally thought.

'Ally?'

She knew that tone. It meant something important was coming, a different direction, something that had nothing to with the here and now. Maybe her mother was about to tell her why her father had left them.

'I have to go away for a few days.'

'Have to or want to?'

'I need to be alone for a while, sweetheart.'

'How long?' Ally asked, feeling desolate.

'A week.'

'So I have to spend my hols with El Creepo?'

'He had every reason to be angry with you. So do I.'

Ally pursed her lips.

'Please?' Ngaio asked.

'Okay,' Ally said, close to tears.

'So, what do you think?' Ngaio asked, indicating the room they were standing in, the house and, by implication, the suburb.

'I think the life of a teenager is just one big ball of bloody fun,' Ally said.

Chapter 20

The kid next door was playing his music loudly again.

'Jake?' his mother said. 'Please turn that music down.'

'I thought this is your kind of music?' he said.

'It is, love, but I don't want to upset the neighbours.'

'Okay,' Jake grumbled and turned it down.

Franks smiled and thought he should acquaint himself with this youngster, whose taste in music was certainly varied, therefore occasionally even overlapping with his. He was listening to 'Once in a Lifetime' by Talking Heads, a band that was as much to Franks' taste as the shot of Scotch he chased with a beer.

Time for the horrors again. This was because he only had a past, no future, and the song got him thinking about the time he, Morris and Smith were involved in a bust in the middle-class suburb of Greenhithe across the bridge on the North Shore. He and his partner had dressed up (or down, depending on your politics) as Jehovah's Witnesses and had sat in the boiling-hot car with Smith.

The house they were targeting was two properties away, and looked as ordinary as any other house in that area, except that its curtains were drawn. That didn't necessarily mean anything, even though the sun and the humidity were drenching them with sweat. But, according to the information they had, it meant something that the curtains were drawn. The innocuous-looking house they were targeting was a P-lab, so the property behind it had ten armed Special Ops men poised – helmets, bulletproof vests, semi-automatic rifles – waiting for a lightly perspiring Smith to give them orders. Their commander confirmed they were in place.

'Okay,' he said to Franks and Morris. 'Go for it.'

They got out of the unmarked car and approached the house, complete with their *Watchtower* magazines, benevolent smiles – and hidden pistols. They walked up to the door and Morris knocked. At first nothing happened, but after another knock there was a slight movement behind the peephole. They made quite a sight, radiating the light and goodwill of Jesus – but ready to do hell and damnation. The door opened a crack.

'Good morning, sir,' Franks smiled. 'How's your day been?'

'Not interested, bro' the huge Islander said, starting to close the door.

'Well, we're interested,' Morris said, wedging his foot into the door before giving it a shove.

The man saw Franks pistol and ran into the living room, shouting that the cops were here; they had to get out. But by then Smith, keeping an eye as a passing pedestrian, had whispered into his sleeve and told the boys at the back to move in, 'Go!'

The men in the lounge room – which had no furniture in it, just trestles, funnels, Bunsen burners, plastic containers full of chemicals and large glass beakers – rushed for the back door, but they were confronted by ten barrels pointing at their torsos, so the game was up. They raised their hands, quickly.

Franks and Morris came into the lounge.

'Get down on the floor, motherfuckers!' Morris shouted. '*Down!*'

The men lay flat, keeping their hands in plain sight.

'Put your hands behind your heads!'

They complied.

'Where's Mr Li?' Morris barked.

'He's not here, bro,' one said.

'Well, where is he, "bro"?' Morris continued.

'He's overseas,' the man said.

'Bullshit!' Morris barked, putting the barrel of his pistol against the man's head. 'Where is he?'

The man kept quiet and Morris cocked his pistol, but Smith came in and told him to relax. Morris complied, reluctantly, and straightened out as Smith told the troops to cuff the men and take them to the station for processing. Then he told Franks and Morris to check the rest of the house while he made all the necessary calls to the likes of forensics to come and do the necessary follow-up.

If the house and its appliances aspired to upper-middle-class respectability, then its present occupants showed very clearly what they thought about that. In three of the four bedrooms mattresses lay on the floor, the sheets crumpled, open suitcases standing around, along with empty takeaway containers. In the master bedroom the single mattress had been shoved against the wall and there was a *Chinese Herald* next to it. What a life, Franks thought, covering each room with the usual caution, then jerking cupboards open, pointing.

Nothing.

The toilet reeked of unflushed piss. The bathroom had large tiles and even larger mirrors. It also had one of those freestanding, pseudo-marble baths, and a shower that wasn't enclosed. These had never made any sense to Franks: surely they wet the floor around them? None of his business anyway, but if he ever won the Lotto he'd have a proper bloody cubicle. See-through, but enclosed.

The house was empty. The three of them walked back to the car in the cloying air, deciding they'd wait until forensics came. But something was bothering Franks. He felt like he did when he walked out of a room and something was missing. It wasn't a conscious thing, but he'd taught himself to make that feeling conscious, because it usually meant he'd left something behind, like his car keys. What was it, he wondered as they got to the car. *Think,* he told himself. Do a replay. What stuck out? Then he remembered. Two things. When Morris had asked one of the suspects where Mr Li was, one of the others had looked in the direction of the passage, meaning there might be someone there. It might not be Mr Li, but it was someone. And why would any Islander read a *Chinese Herald*? He and Morris may have checked the house, but maybe they hadn't checked it well enough. Maybe there was someone in the ceiling. Maybe that unflushed toilet wasn't about saving water or just a lack of male consideration, maybe it was more like stopping in mid-action and leaving in a hurry.

'Chief, I want to go back into the house,' Franks said.

Smith knew and trusted his agent well enough not to ask him why, and nodded. Franks walked back towards the house, then went in.

Softly.

The freestanding bath, Franks thought. A slight person could easily have wedged himself in between it and the wall if he'd just used the toilet when they'd burst into the living room. Franks now knew there was still someone in the house – he could feel him – and he'd have to go through the same routine of checking each room again. But this time he'd start with the bathroom, minding his back. It still looked exactly as it had a few minutes ago, of course, but it confirmed to Franks that a slight man could fit in there.

Now for the rest of the house.

He checked each room again, opening cupboards, working his way towards the master bedroom, where there were two full-length mirrored doors covering the walk-in wardrobe. Franks could feel him in there.

'If you don't come out in three seconds I'm shooting,' Franks said, instantly moving away in case the man shot where the voice was.

'One.'

He moved.

'Two ...'

One of the doors slid open and the Chinese man stood there, hands in plain sight. Only it wasn't a man.

'Walk to the centre of the floor and lie down on your stomach.'

The small woman complied. Franks approached her.

'Put your hands behind your back,' Franks said.

She did as she was told.

Franks took out his cuffs with his free hand, opened one, and, as he tried to click it around the woman's wrist, she swivelled in a corkscrew blur, kicked, and Franks' pistol went flying. She produced a jagged knife and lunged at Franks, who managed to evade the blade by bending backwards, but there was no more space for retreat. He had an extra .38 in his calf holster, but didn't have time to get to it. The woman lunged again, and Franks again managed to avoid the blade, which went into the mattress. But he didn't avoid her elbow. Having missed the stab, her return action included hitting Franks square on the jaw. Lots of power for such a small frame, hitting him with the hardest part of the body. Franks was stunned, and tried to go for the .38 as he saw her bending to pick up his pistol. It was all a blur, happening elsewhere, to someone else. He was going to die in someone else's master bedroom. What a joke. She started pulling the trigger but didn't complete the action because Morris splashed her brains all over the mirror of the wardrobe door.

Chapter 21

Ally and Jeff were sitting in the park across the road from a shopping centre, studying a game she didn't know was famous. She had reached a compromise with her father: she and Jeff could meet for chess in a public space, nowhere else.

So here they were, studying Nigel Short's 'the Famous King March' against Jan Timman in 1991, having completed move 30, a point where Short with a slight advantage could opt to exchange rooks and probably win, but it would be a long, drawn-out game. It lacked a killer move. Ally and Jeff were close to the end of their allotted time.

Franks parked the Commodore and watched them from afar, taking note of Jeff's large motorbike near a tree, while Ally was trying to work out what white's next move should be.

'What would you do now?' Jeff asked.

'I don't know. It looks like everything's ground to a halt.'

'What about king to h2?'

'What about it? It's on the other side of the board. It's limited, like all kings are.'

'True. Rook goes to c8 and what does white do?

'I don't know. Its queen is still stuck.'

'What about king to g3?'

'It still seems pointless and far away.'

'Try it anyway,' Jeff said.

Ally did.

'Now black goes back to e8,' Jeff continued, 'realising he can counter-attack with his bishop. So what now?'

Their time was up. Franks got out of the car and approached them.

'I don't know,' Ally said, frustrated.

'How about king to f4?'

'What is it with you and this useless king?'

'Do it anyway while black's bishop goes to c8, threatening white's rook.'

'Yeah. He's going to win. Slowly ward off the attack and then massacre white,' she said, making the move.

'What about king to g5?'

'What about it?' Ally said once again.

'Black resigned.'

'What?'

Jeff saw Franks first, as Ally was furiously trying to compute the move before picking up that something was happening. She looked up and saw her father.

'Hello,' Franks said.

Ally wouldn't even grace his presence with a greeting.

'Jeff?' Franks said. 'I'm sorry about yesterday.'

'That's okay, Mr Franks.'

'"Mister"?' Ally spat with contempt.

'I'll be in the car, Miss,' Franks said.

'Ms,' Ally replied.

'Sorry. *Ms,*' he said and headed back towards the car while Jeff smiled.

'What are you smiling about?' Ally wanted to know.

'Have you got it yet?' he responded.

'How am I supposed to think with that *idiot* around?'

'Look.'

Ally took a long hard look, finally saw the light of Nigel Short's stalking brilliance, and said: 'King to g5 and mate is unavoidable.'

'That's right,' Jeff said.

'How utterly beautiful.'

Chapter 22

Ngaio had hated asking Ally if she could spend some time by herself – it sounded so selfish. But she knew Ally'd be okay with her father – as much as they scrapped with each other they were more similar than they cared to admit. And she knew she could trust Franks on that score too. For all his faults, he wouldn't let anyone, including himself, mess with her.

All Ngaio wanted was a few days to work out what she was doing, find some kind of equilibrium. So she'd rented a reasonably priced room in the Hokianga with a good view and a small, semi-private beach. Walking along that coast now at dusk, she couldn't believe how naive she'd been to think Tom McAllister would ever leave his wife and start a new life with her, Ally, and his two boys. How had she not seen that money and enthusiasm didn't equate with maturity, that all he'd really wanted was some kind of mother figure to help him deal with his personal baggage of aloof parents? She knew Ally would simply have said the man's an arsehole, get rid of him, his kids are brats anyway – which got her smiling and teary for her beloved daughter. If she were to ask Ally what she should do her daughter would say, 'Simple. Tell needy dick, who looks a bit like Dad anyway, to get lost.' So she started dialling his number.

'Hi,' he said in that intimate tone he used with her.

'Have you got a moment?'

'Always,' he lied.

'I'm leaving you. And the company.'

There was a long pause.

'Don't do this to me,' he said in that pained, boyish way that had worked a hundred times before.

'Go and talk to your wife, Tom, not me.'

'Listen ...'

'It's over, Tom. There's nothing more to say. I'll clear my desk when I get back and you're not in the office. Goodbye.'

Ngaio rang off and felt young again, free.

She would have to find another job, of course; she had a mortgage to pay, regardless of what John had just done. She was glad he'd won the Lotto, but what had possessed that man to go and buy a small mansion? Was it just to get 'Ms Precious' closer to her art classes and her friend Frances, which meant she could apply to go to a posher school? Was he also twisting the resentment knife? Why couldn't he just offer to pay off the existing house if he wanted to be expansive? Had he been drunk at the time? Probably. She knew he was drinking even more heavily than ever. That bloody job. That was a mistress, too, but it was legal. Legal! She was sick and tired of the word. If he'd never cared much for money, which was admirable in a way, then he'd also never cared much for talking, which was the main reason her attention had wandered. Tom could talk, John couldn't, or rather, he wouldn't. Didn't. And if he didn't talk much to their daughter either, he was always there for her. Which of course got her wondering how Franks and Ally were doing. She already missed her, always missed her, and she still had a few days to go.

Time for a maternal check-in.

Chapter 23

The rain seemed intent on going on forever, and it didn't help much that Franks was playing 'Fragile' by his favourite musician, Sting. Ally's mood inside his now-tidy flat was the final nail in the coffin. She could cast a mood like no one else he'd ever met, and she was doing so right now. This was partly because he'd thought it would be a good idea if she met Tracy and saw that he was human too. Big mistake. Ally had taken one look at the trim young woman and proceeded to act as if she didn't exist. He had told Tracy he'd order takeaways (couldn't cook to save his life), but she'd offered to come over and make them a Thai curry. Now they were sitting in a silent little triangle, with the rain coming down outside, the music mooning on inside, the cutlery clinking, and the air so thick you'd need a steak knife to slice it.

'So, what do you think?' he asked his daughter.

'What do I think about what? The Kardashians? The Middle East crisis? The slowing of the Chinese economy?'

'No, Ally. The food.'

Ally gave her perfect teen shrug.

'Well, I think it's very good. Thank you, Tracy.'

'No worries,' she replied, and made the fatal mistake of asking Ally what she intended doing after school.

'Oh, I was thinking of becoming a sex worker,' Ally said, channelling a dead-eyed actress.

'Ally ...' Franks warned.

'It's okay,' Tracy said, but the onslaught was about to take a verbal form.

'You know, of course,' Ally said, 'that my father has a bit of a thing for women with black hair. I mean his ex-wife, my mother, has black hair. The woman he had an affair with had black hair, like you. So you're one in a line, but at least I can say one thing about him: he doesn't discriminate on racial grounds. My mother is Māori, that other woman was Chinese, and you seem to be a Pakeha.'

'Ally, that's enough,' Franks said.

'Or maybe you're just after his millions.'

'I don't know what you're talking about,' Tracy said.

'He's rolling! He won the Lotto! He never has to work a day in his life again! He bought his ex, us, a mansion. He would have bought his China doll a house too, if she hadn't died. Maybe he'll buy you one as well. You see, he doesn't know what to do with his money – except drink.'

'Allyson, you stop that right now,' Franks said, eyes flashing.

By now Ally had reached her objective.

'Okay,' she said, with another teenage shrug, whereupon her phone rang and she left the table without excusing herself.

'Hello, mother,' she said pointedly.

Chapter 24

When Franks eventually saw Tracy off, he wondered how he was going to make it through the night without a drink. Ally had gone off to the spare room with her smartphone, and Franks made himself a cup of coffee. He waited for the horrors to kick in, while Jake next door put on a high-speed funk number.

'Jake?' his mother said.

'Yeah?' he said sceptically.

'How come you're playing that?'

'I thought it was from your time?' Jake said.

'It is. What's it called again?'

'"Can't get enough".'

'That's right,' she said. 'Band called Supergroove.'

'Yeah.'

'I was still in my teens then. God we were wild.'

'Tell me about it?'

'Not right now, honey. And you better turn it down. I mean, we don't want to get kicked out, do we?'

'Nah, I suppose not,' Jake said reluctantly.

It was the same song Pat had played after they'd held a party to celebrate their Greenhithe bust.

Of course, after such a successful haul everyone needed to let off a little steam, celebrate, and that's what Morris had said they were going to do. He would provide the venue in upmarket Glendowie – his and Pat's home – which was just a few hundred metres away from Glen Innes, but there the similarity ended. He liked mentioning that he'd grown up tough in GI, but also liked to show that he, too, could cross the road and be equal to the rich. Then again, he was the first to admit that this was only because he'd inherited a packet from a well-to-do uncle in faraway Ireland. As for the drinks and food, the department could provide that, and did.

Everybody was there. Well, almost everybody. Franks and Smith still had to arrive, but all the Special Ops boys were there, single or with their partners, and the office crew, including surveillance. There was also a host of young women no one knew, but that the single Ops boys wanted to get to know. ASAP.

Pat was playing hostess and DJ, the booze was flowing, so was the talk, and the only little problem, as far as Morris was concerned, was that Chink woman. Who the fuck was she, why was she here, and who'd had the gall to invite her? Maybe he should walk over and tell her the story about those three portraits of his beloved son, Rawiri, on the mantelpiece. The first showed Rawiri looking as happy as any ten-year-old could be with his father, showing off their catch of snapper with their friends John, Ngaio and a younger Ally. The second showed a teenage Rawiri in skateboard gear, peak cap back-to-front, eyes a little dreamy, but with his father gripping his neck, seeming to say his son might have a few strange ideas, but he was still his son. The last portrait showed Rawiri as a neck-tatted twenty-year-old, eyes glazed, almost tired before their time, with a black band through the photograph. Rawiri was dead, and he, Morris, would like to tell that smug-looking bitch what P had done to his son and who had supplied it to him: the Chinese.

Franks entered and Morris watched as Pat made a beeline for his partner, virtually wrapped herself around him and gave him a full wet kiss on the mouth, keeping her crotch tightly against his.

'Hey handsome,' she said. 'Where've you been?'

'Taxi duties,' Franks said, disentangling himself, catching Jiaping's eyes across the room, sticking out like a sore thumb, sitting alone, drinking a fruit juice.

'Oh, that,' Pat said.

'Yeah.'

'How's Ally?'

'You know, fifteen going on twenty-one.'

'Well, I'm sure she's still as pretty as her father.'

'Yeah, yeah,' Franks said, humouring her.

He liked Pat, felt a little sorry for her when she'd had a couple of drinks, like now, but that was it. He and Ngaio and Morris and Pat had been friends forever and that was all it would ever be, as far as he was concerned.

'Congratulations on your bust,' Pat said, pressing hers against him.

'Thanks, but if it wasn't for Morris, I wouldn't be standing here. And we didn't get the main man anyway.'

'I'm sure you will eventually. But why don't you grab yourself a drink in the meantime?'

'I think I'll do that.'

'You can grab me too, if you like.'

'Yeah, sure Pat,' he said, catching Jiaping's eye again.

'I mean it, babe. That man of mine is so busy chasing Chinks he can't think of anything else. Not with me anyway. He's changed, and not for the better.'

'Sorry, I need a drink,' Franks said and Pat replied with an 'Okay,' saw a Special Ops boy with a tight butt pass her and followed him into the kitchen.

Franks moved towards Morris, who said, 'Hey boss, how're you doing?'

'Just great. You?'

'Fine. Grab yourself a drink, and a bit of snatch.'

'Who are those women? Where'd you get them?'

'I rented them. The boys need a little distraction, a little release. So do you.'

'I'm fine,' Franks lied.

'I think I better go and rescue one of the boys from Pat,' Morris said grimly and moved towards the kitchen.

Franks headed for the drinks table, passing a group of men as one delivered the punchline to a joke: 'So she said, "I'm fucked if I know!"'

They all burst out laughing and Franks caught Jiaping's eye again as he passed the group of women, a blonde saying she'd do *anything* for money, which was followed by raucous female guffaws.

Franks got his beer and headed towards Jiaping when the music suddenly went softer and Morris shouted across the crowd: 'Hey, John?'

Franks looked back over the room, past the group of women, the men, and saw Smith had arrived, still in his office attire. Morris waved Franks over to join them. Franks gave Jiaping a mock-apologetic look and she gave him a smile as he waded across the room and shook Smith's hand. The three of them went into Morris's study with its photographs of the two young families at Franks' bach, those times when they were two young couples who were happy and Rawiri was still alive and Franks and Ngaio were still together.

'So what is it with that ... woman out there?' Morris asked Smith.

'What woman?' Smith wondered.

'Didn't you see that slant-eye out there?' Morris asked.

'I was told she's joining us,' Smith said. 'I didn't have a say in the matter. She's your new rookie.'

'I don't like it,' Morris said. 'She could be a plant – or worse.'

'You mean internal affairs?'

'Yeah, or the triads.'

'No, she's clean. Comes highly recommended. Be nice to her.'

Smith pointedly looked at Morris but said: 'Both of you.'

'They don't understand nice,' Morris retorted. 'But let's get you a drink in the meantime,' he said, and they all left the room.

Franks wended his way back to Jiaping, while the boys and the girls were getting nicely juiced up on the booze on the dance floor. When he reached her, he asked her what she was smiling about – a good or bad opening line, depending on the situation – and she said, studying the landscape of his face, 'It's good to be alive.'

Franks needed a drink even more now as Jake's mother once again told him to put that noise down. The ex-cop needed a shot – badly. So badly that he didn't notice his daughter standing in her doorway, watching him sweat, willing himself clean, doing it for her, as something seemed to dawn in her teenage consciousness: pity.

Chapter 25

He was up first thing next morning, just like before everything had gone to the dogs, and packed the few things he needed for his week away with Ally, who slept with all the determination of a teenager. When she was woken with a mug of tea, she did so moodily and it didn't help when he said, 'Good morning, Ms Sunshine', either. She dragged her feet, literally and figuratively, brushing her teeth, eating breakfast, packing her bags, refusing to even grace his 'Try not to take forever,' with a reply, before getting into the car and disappearing behind her sunnies, mobile and earphones.

Franks felt better for not having drunk the night before and felt even better when they got onto the highway, heading south, out of town. Soon they were turning off to the Coromandel. Hell, there were even patches of sunshine through all this interminable, rainy gloom. They were heading to the ramshackle bach he'd spent his youth in and then inherited – there'd been almost nothing else to inherit – and where he'd made some memories of his own with Ngaio, Ally, Morris, Pat and Rawiri. They'd spent long, seemingly endless summers at the shack, fishing, diving, barbecuing, talking, drinking, watching their children grow up at the speed of light. That, of course, had all gone haywire when Rawiri had died and he and Ngaio had split, but right now he felt good, even with Ally listening to her music while texting Frances and/or Jeff and not taking the slightest interest in the beauty of the Hauraki Plain they were passing through. Franks listened to nothing except the sound of the Commodore's engine and the wind whistling past his side mirror. He felt so good that he smiled at Ally in the rear-view until she became aware of him and indicated: What? Nothing, he shrugged, smiling. Ally frowned and returned to her other world, but when they stopped for takeaway coffees she saw a cute little dog on a leash, and that seemed to cheer her up – for a while at least. Soon she was ensconced behind her social-media armoury again as they approached the town of Thames and the ranges looming over it. Next they headed for Coromandel and then over the spine of the mountain to behold the Pacific in all its glory. That had given Franks a thrill as a child, and it still did. When they approached the turn-off to Black Rock he decided he'd take the longer, scenic route instead of the short cut along the dirt road they had travelled so many times before. Halfway to the rock, lost in the beauty of the sea and the memory of a young Ally getting excited as they approached it, jutting high and dark over the sea, he asked her what she thought of the scenery.

'What?' she said.

'Could you take off your earphones for a second?'

She did so, reluctantly, and repeated her question.

'I said, don't you think it's beautiful?'

'Dad, I'm a teenager. We don't do scenery.'

'Right.'

They got to the bach with its view of the endless ocean and the black mass of jagged rock to one side, a feature Ngaio had never really liked. Ally got out, stretched, and said sarcastically, 'Ah, the great outdoors …'

'Great view, fresh air,' Franks added.

'Connectivity,' Ally smiled.

'Oh, I didn't tell you: no social media.'

'I thought you said this was going to be a holiday,' Ally said, mortified, as her phone started ringing.

'You can talk to your mother. That's it.'

It *was* her mother, not Jeff as she'd hoped.

'What?' Ally grumbled.

Chapter 26

After a day or two they settled into a routine that was more or less agreeable to both parties. Ally would go to the nearby beach – in the opposite direction from Black Rock – and hang out with other teenagers or listen to music (or talk to Jeff by text) until sunset. Franks would go fishing or potter around the nearby shed, read, then usually fall asleep on the deck. The weather, for a change, had decided to play along and the days were mostly sunny. At night he would either cook the catch of the day or they'd eat out at the restaurant in the nearby town.

One night, sitting at a fire, Ally said, 'I've been thinking.'

Franks refrained from making any smart-arse comment and asked her what she'd been thinking about.

'Why do we spell bach the way we do? I mean, when we talk about the composer Bach, we don't say batch, we say Bach; yet when we talk about a b-a-c-h, we say batch. It doesn't make sense.'

'I've never thought about that,' Franks said. 'Where did you hear about Bach?'

'Jeff told me his music is very good for chess.'

'And is it?'

'No. It's terrible.'

'Why?'

'I don't know … Not much of a melody, or a beat. It sounds like a documentary about ants or something.'

'Tell me about him?'

'Well, he's second-generation …'

'I meant Bach.'

'Oh, him. I don't know anything about him. I think he was Italian or something.'

'Does the name Bach sound Italian to you?'

'No, it sounds more … Scottish.'

'*Scottish?*'

'Yeah. Loch. Bach?'

'Fair point. But it's German.'

'Oh. Okay. Are you still listening to that ex-Police man?'

'Of course.'

Ally pulled a face.

'At least he's still going, whereas most of the musos you listen to are here today, gone tomorrow.'

'And Mum still listens to Fat Freddy's Drop,' she said.

Their music made her lower back ripple and her lips purse with pleasure, and that's how Franks had first seen her, and fallen for her. Big time. She wasn't all that impressed with this slightly pissed man, but he was persistent and charming enough to persuade her to have a swim with him at the public pool the next day. As it turned out, he wasn't going to show her how well he could swim, he was going to show her how well he could dive.

'Why didn't you tell me you'd been a national champion?' she berated him.

'I didn't want to show off,' he grinned.

Ally kept a framed, faded newspaper photograph of John and Ngaio in her bedroom. In the photo, Ngaio was standing at the side of the pool, her smooth brown skin glowing in a white bikini, while, close-by, John's bullet-straight body was parting the water, head first.

But diving wasn't exactly a lucrative sport and, when Ngaio became pregnant, Franks decided to do exactly the opposite of what his father had done. If the old man had had his fingers in one too many pies, his son became something the old man despised. A copper. Franks had had no regrets and by the time he was thirty-two he was an undercover cop. To celebrate, the small family had gone to the bach. Ally was about ten at the time. He told her and her mother to come with him, he wanted to show them something. They followed him, puzzled. He took them to the top of Black Rock and stripped down to his old Speedo. Ngaio asked him what he was doing and he said he was going to dive. She became half hysterical and Franks told her this was where he'd learned to dive. Ngaio didn't like heights and refused to even look down, but Ally forced herself. She saw a small dark pool, surrounded by jagged rocks and churning water.

'Trust me,' Franks said.

Ally nodded, digging her nails into her mother's palm, while Ngaio turned away.

'Don't worry, love,' Franks said. 'If anything happens to me, you're covered.'

'That's not the point, you idiot. I want you alive.'

'Well, that's what I'll be,' he said, and balanced himself on the tip of the rock, the seagulls shrieking, the ocean heaving, smashing against the jagged rocks below. Ally watched as her father took a deep breath, exhaled, and dived out wide, spreading his arms like an albatross, or a god, or something. He plummeted down, quickly, cleaving the water.

Then, nothing.

Just the noise of the gulls and the wind and the waves. Ally stared into that abyss for what felt like an eternity, her stomach small and tight and awful. Then her father emerged, smiling, waving wetly.

'He's okay,' Ally said.

'Bastard,' Ngaio grumbled.

Anyway, that was all ancient history now, and he really needed a drink. Day three and only two beers allowed at a time. Another painful sunset.

On the fourth night, Ally asked whether she could at least play one game of online chess a night with Jeff. Her father acquiesced. She'd become a picture of health. No city zits, nothing. She even sounded quite upbeat when she had her daily chat with her mother, who was heading back to Auckland.

Franks did his best not to think about the past, and so the days became a pleasant (if slightly tense) blur, as holidays do. Towards the end of the week he was sitting on the deck again, staring out at the sea, slightly hypnotised by the slow swell and breaking of the waves, the gulls shrieking, flapping, the sun beating down. He'd always dreamed about this kind of existence, but he'd wanted to earn it, he thought drowsily. He hadn't wanted guilt money; he'd wanted sweat or brains money. How could he ever get over what he'd done to Jiaping, that single shot still ringing in his ears?

It took him two seconds – too long – to compute that he wasn't remembering that fatal gunshot; he'd just *heard* one, now, in the present. *Move*, the training kicked in and he was rolling and then running into the house as the next shot rang out and he realized he shouldn't run inside the house, but rather away from it, towards that patch of grass between the bach and Black Rock, overlooking the Pacific. Ally was standing there with his smoking rifle in her hands – the only other thing his old man had left him: the bach legal, the rifle not.

He walked towards her, firmly but not hurriedly.

Don't ever panic someone with a firearm.

'Allyson, give me that gun,' he said in as calm a voice as he could.

'Why have you got a gun in the shed, Dad?'

'Because there are still people out there who would like me dead. Now give it to me.'

'I quite like the feel of it.'

'Allyson, you don't make jokes with guns around.'

'I know.'

'What did you think you were doing, anyway?'

'I thought I'd try my hand at shooting the Pacific.'

Keep them talking.

'What's that supposed to mean?' he said.

'Maybe I can get you to tell me what happened this way.'

'What are you talking about?'

'You and Mum splitting – what else?'

'First give me the gun.'

'No. Why did the two of you split?'

'Sweetheart, that's between your mother and me.'

'What about me?'

'You know we love you very much.'

'Then why didn't you stick together?'

'Allyson, give me that gun.'

'Why didn't you?'

Be calm, reasonable, but firm.

'Sweetheart, that really is between the two of us. Now give me that gun.'

'Will you tell me if I do?'

'No, I will not, my love. Give me that gun.'

'"My love." That's rich.'

'It's true, sweetheart. You know we love you.'

'And if you have to choose between telling me and being shot?'

'You know what happened to me; death would be quite a relief, Allyson. Give me that gun.'

Ally wavered.

The shot that rang out wasn't aimed at Franks, but rather at one of three bottles perched in a nearby hollow. That had been the deal. To save face, she had negotiated that, if she gave him the gun, he'd show her how to use it.

'That's very good, sweetheart,' Franks said, standing behind her. 'Just keep breathing naturally. As if you're walking to school.'

'That's an unfortunate image.'

'Okay, like you're playing chess with Jeff.'

'That's much better,' she said, squeezing the trigger.

The second bottle shattered.

'Is there anything you're bad at?' Franks asked.

'Yes,' she said, after smashing the last bottle. 'I'm really bad at art.'

Chapter 27

Back in the city, the drinking resumed. So did the horrors. Franks wondered what Rat had meant by 'it's not all over' that day he'd given him the gun in the Bar None toilet. He'd been very useful as an informer, and Franks drifted into thinking about the last time Rat had helped them.

They'd met in the usual Auckland CBD alley, and he told them where they could find two of Li's accomplices, who could then tell them where Li was – or so the thinking went. Rat then asked Morris for a small advance.

'Not a fuck. You get your retainer.'

'Ah, have a heart, Morrie. I just need a drink or two.'

'Or three or four. No.'

'Here's twenty bucks,' Franks said.

'Bless you, John,' Rat said, pocketing the money. 'You can deduct it from my next payment.'

Morris disapproved but they moved on to Union Heights, flat number 27 and, indeed, two of Li's accomplices were sitting with the door wide open in the heat. One a slight Chinese, the other a large Māori. They were playing cards and suddenly there were two cops who closed the door behind them and pointed their pistols at them.

'Where's Mr Li?' Morris asked the Chinese man.

He said in Mandarin that he didn't speak English. Morris shot the man stone dead and shocked not only his colleague in crime, but Franks too.

'Jesus Christ!' he shouted. 'Are you out of your fucking mind?'

'Where is Mr Li?' Morris said, ignoring his partner and pointing the pistol at the other man.

'I don't know, bro' the man said, keeping his hands in plain sight.

'Are you sure about that?.'

The man said nothing.

'Where's Mr Li?'

'I told you. I don't know, bro.'

I'm not your fucking bro. If you don't tell me in three, you're dead.'

'How do I know you won't shoot me if I tell you?'

'I give you my word,' Morris replied.

The man showed what he thought of that kind of promise and Morris said: 'One …'

'This is so wrong,' Franks said.

'Are you going to get all touchy-feely on me too?' Morris said.

'I honestly don't know,' the man muttered. 'Mr Li moves a lot. Most of the time he isn't even in the country.'

'Two …'

'Morrie, we need to take this guy in.'

'What for? So one of Li's fancy lawyers can get him out and none of us is any the wiser?'

'Those are the rules.'

'Fuck the rules.'

'Come on. You don't mean that.'

'Maybe I should kill you as well.'

'Stop talking shit,' Franks said. 'Let's take him in.'

'Fuck that,' Morris said, glancing at him before he said 'Three'. In that moment the man went for his gun. Franks shot him in the shoulder, pushed Morris away, and the man's weapon dropped to the floor. Still, it took Franks a long time to convince an enraged Morris not to kill the man, who lay whimpering and bleeding next to the dead Chinese man.

Chapter 28

Ngaio was feeling a little better about herself and much better now that her darling Ally was back. They were standing in the kitchen, cutting potatoes and peeling carrots.

'So what was it like?' Ngaio asked her daughter, expecting the worst.

'Awesome.'

'Oh?' Ngaio said, a little surprised but also unable to prevent herself from feeling a little jealous. 'Why?

'Well, Dad was very good with the booze. Strictly two beers a night.'

'Good. And?'

'He taught me how to shoot.'

'I don't like that,' Ngaio said.

'I'm very good at it.'

'That doesn't mean it's right.'

'But even when I pointed it at him, he wouldn't tell me why the two of you split.'

'That's very noble of him, but then he's quite an honourable kind of guy – in his own twisted way.'

'What do you mean?'

Ngaio just shook her head.

'I mean,' Ally continued, 'I don't really blame you for kicking him out for having an affair with that other ...'

'I didn't kick him out. He left.'

'This is news to me,' Ally said.

'And he didn't leave because he was having an affair with Jiaping.'

'Then why did he leave?'

'Because *I* was having an affair.'

Ally was gobsmacked.

'Mother, you're messing with all my stereotypes,' she finally said.

Ngaio was close to tears.

'Why?' Ally finally managed to squeeze out.

'Take this knife,' Ngaio said.

'What for?' Ally said, confused.

'I want you to cut me.'

'Are you out of your mind? I'm not going to cut you.'

'I just want to show you that I also bleed, Ally.'

'Of course you do,' Ally said, her mouth bone dry.

'I also have needs,' Ngaio said.

Ally could barely speak but had to ask the question.

'And were your needs met?'

'For a while.'

'And now?'

'Now I'm just your mother,' Ngaio said, her large brown swimming in tears. 'And I love you very much.'

Chapter 29

Smith had called in Morris and Franks, and he was not happy. Nor were they. They might have been partners who trusted each other with their lives, but that didn't mean they didn't have differences – differences that had grown ever since Rawiri had OD'd. So they sat in their chief's office, waiting for him, seething. Smith eventually came in, but remained standing.

'Okay, what happened?' he said calmly.

'John here got all liberal on me,' Morris said.

'I didn't know it was our job to kill suspects,' Franks retorted.

'Suspects? They're not suspects. They're fucking vermin. Do you really think they were going to tell us anything?'

'I thought there was a better chance of them telling us something alive than dead.'

'Well one of them is still alive, thanks to you, John,' Smith interrupted. 'Well done.'

'And do you really think he's going to tell us the truth about Li?' Morris pressed.

'We'll just have to wait and see, won't we?' Franks replied.

'Maybe if your precious daughter died of P you'd be singing a different tune,' Morris said to Franks.

'Morrie, I'm very sorry about Rawiri, but it's not only the Chinese who are dealing in P, for fuck's sake.'

'Well I still say the only good Chink is a dead Chink.'

'Okay, calm down you two. Morris, I won't have that kind of language in here. John is right. This man could tell us where Li is.'

'He's probably in China by now,' Morris grumbled.

'Maybe, but he'll be back. It's in his interest to be back.'

'Maybe he's got bigger fish to fry than little old New Zealand.'

'Maybe. Maybe not. But you can't just go around killing suspects. I've had the minister, the mayor, and the press down my throat the whole morning.'

'So where is this … man?' Morris asked.

'He's in a safe place.'

'Hey, what's with the secrecy?' Morris persisted. 'Am I suddenly a suspect around here?'

'No. John doesn't know where he is, either. And the two of you are supposed to be partners.'

Morris grunted while Franks continued raging. Silently.

'Go on,' Smith said. 'Kiss and make up, you two.'

After what seemed like an eternity in that charged space, Morris said, 'You're right. I'm sorry, bro. You actually saved my life last night.' He offered his hand to his friend and partner. 'But I'm fucked if I'm going to kiss you,' he added.

Chapter 30

Now that he was back at home, Franks reasoned he could drink at full throttle again, and did, while his neighbour asked Jake to put his electronica a bit softer, please.

'Okay, okay. I'll try to find something you like.'

'It's not the contents, sweetheart. It's the volume.'

Franks lifted a shot glass to the boy as his mobile started ringing and downed a shot.

'Franks,' he said.

'Hi,' a woman replied.

'Who is this?'

'Gee, am I that unimportant in your life?'

'Oh, hi Tracy. Sorry, I just didn't get round to saving your number under your name. Bad admin.'

'That's okay. What was your holiday like?'

'Well, it started off like the past, the present and the future walking into a bar.'

'How's that?'

'It was tense.'

Tracy gave a little laugh that would only sound false in retrospect.

'But it got better. We really bonded, as they say.'

'That's good,' Tracy said. 'I like her.'

'So do I.'

'She's got spunk.'

'That's no lie. So, what's up?'

'Well, I've had this crazy idea.'

'Tell me about it,' John said, thinking if she did all the talking he could drink.

'Well, I really need a holiday and I've decided I'm going to Rarotonga for a week, and I was wondering if you'd like to come along with me. I mean, I know you've just been on holiday, but would you like to come? We could go Dutch. No strings attached.'

Rarotonga. He'd never been to Raro. And what was he going to do with the days ahead, except drink and, oh shit, fetch Ally after her so-called art classes? But then Ngaio could get her. After all, he'd just looked after their daughter for the last week.

'That *is* a crazy idea,' Franks said, 'but I like it. I'll just have to make sure I can sort Ally's transport. I'll get back to you.'

'Great. It could be a lot of fun.'

They said goodbye and he downed a beer, wondering what Ngaio would think about him going away again, if she thought anything about it – or him – at all. So he started texting her. He would only call her when there was an emergency, and so far the only emergency they'd had was a fake one.

Tracy rang off and turned her music back on again. Soft background music, the kind that, along with low lights, helped create an aura of erotic possibilities. She was dressed, if that was the word, in a negligée that didn't leave much to the imagination, even though it was a particularly predictable kind of imagination.

She wasn't alone. There was a man standing over her, looking down at her sitting on the couch in her living room, her legs suggestively crossed.

'Hook, line and sinker,' she said, reaching out to the man's bulging crotch and slowly teasing the zip down.

'Well done,' Morris said.

Chapter 31

They landed at the Avarua international airport and were given the customary garland of flowers, then headed to the kind of place Franks could now afford but which made him feel deeply uncomfortable. It was a luxury resort that gave the impression that the Islanders were there merely to serve foreigners' whims, the kind of place Ngaio quietly resented.

Tracy told him she owned a gym and he asked her how she'd acquired it as they settled down to a seafood buffet overlooking the moonlit Pacific.

'It used to be my husband's, before he died,' she said.

'Sorry.'

'That's okay. So now I'm … comfortable. In fact, I've decided this holiday is on me.'

'No way,' Franks said.

'I'm not prepared to have an argument about this, and you can just keep your male arguments for some other woman, okay? I'm paying, and that's it.'

'Right,' he replied, thinking he was still basically a working-class copper who just happened to have a lot of money, which wasn't strictly his anyway.

'Excuse me,' she said, and went to the euphemistic bathroom. He was surrounded by couples who seemed to be on honeymoon, and he'd far prefer to be at the bach with, well, not necessarily anyone, but he felt at home there, easy. He and Ngaio had had great times there, they had 'made' Ally there, which they'd teased her about when she was old enough, before they'd split.

Tracy came walking towards him and he got that feeling again.

'What?'

'You know, I'm more than convinced now that I've seen you before,' Franks said.

'Well, it's quite possible. I mean, we live in the same city. We might have passed each other on the beach, in the supermarket, anywhere. These things happen.'

'I don't know,' John said. 'You're not the kind of person I'd just pass.'

'Is that a compliment?' she smiled.

'It's not an insult,' he smiled in return.

She had booked the short holiday and they would stay in separate rooms. Franks gave her a goodnight peck on the cheek and went to his room, noticing it had a door connecting to hers. There was plenty of booze in the fridge so he continued the assault on his liver. He wasn't going to sleep and he wasn't going to get that image of shock on Jiaping's face out of his head, so he just lay there, impervious to the light breeze stirring the curtains, the sound of the pounding reef, and the beauty of the shimmering Pacific beyond. But he must have fallen asleep anyway because now he was tied up, on his knees, and Li was asking him whether he would work for him. 'Fuck you,' Franks said. 'Think about your wife, your daughter,' Li said. 'Who says I won't kill them after I kill you? They probably know too much.' The man was evil, he thought, knowing he'd have to compromise. He didn't want to face eternity with the knowledge that a single hair on his daughter's (or ex-wife's) head had been hurt, let alone her life taken. 'Okay, I'll work for you,' Franks said. 'Good,' Li replied, and shot him between the eyes anyway.

He woke in a sweat, teeth grinding, moaning. There was someone in his room and his first instinct was to move, but it was Tracy, standing at the foot of his bed.

'Are you okay?'

'Yes,' she said, sounding vulnerable. 'I just had a nightmare.'

'I know those.'

'I'm sorry I woke you,' she said, and started walking back to the interleading door.

'Hey,' John said.

Tracy stopped.

'Come here.'

Chapter 32

The next morning they had a relaxed breakfast, ate lots of fruit, smiling about what had transpired that night, and then went for a stroll along the private beach. Franks felt like a huge weight had been lifted from his shoulders, though he knew it wouldn't last. But what the hell, one was allowed to live in the moment too, so he said to a somewhat thoughtful Tracy: 'I'll race you to that line of palms.'

'No,' she said, smiling sadly.

'Why not?' he wondered, puzzled.

She shrugged, but in a way that said she was embarrassed about it more than that she was indifferent to his request.

'Is this a woman thing?'

'No.'

'Come on. You're a gym instructor, and you were pretty athletic last night.'

Tracy gave him a look that said she knew something he didn't.

'What?'

'John, I don't know how to say things nicely or diplomatically so I'm just going to tell like it like it is.'

'Okay. Sure. Anything.'

'I've got cancer. I'm not supposed to run, or gym, or do what we did last night. Except that you were pretty persuasive – and wonderful.'

Franks took it all in, sighed, and put his arms around her. She wept as the sea gently lapped at their feet.

Chapter 33

He'd just dropped her off at Kohi Mansions, back in rainy Auckland, when his phone rang. It was Ngaio.

'Hi,' he said, keeping his voice neutral.

'Ally's left.'

'What do you mean she's left?'

'She's left home. I got here and she was gone. She left a letter.'

'What does it say?'

'She said she was going to stay with a boy called Jeff and his family. Do you know them?'

'I know him. I'll call her.'

'She won't answer. I've been trying since six o'clock. Texting like mad. Nothing.'

'I'll go talk to her.'

'Thanks, John.'

He didn't know what to say to that without getting emotional, one way or the other, so he said nothing and rang off.

Chapter 34

This time he didn't have his pistol out and it wasn't Jeff who opened the door but, presumably, his grandmother. She was tiny, and had wary eyes.

'Hello, could I speak to Jeff, please?'

She said something, but what it meant only she knew.

A female voice enquired loudly from inside the flat, and the grandmother replied even more loudly. This could mean anything, but after another awkward pause, Jeff appeared.

'Hi, Jeff. I believe Ally is here. Is that right?'

'Yes. Do you want to speak to her?'

'If that's okay, yes, please.'

'Okay, I'll ask her.'

Jeff disappeared down the passage and Franks waited as the old woman looked him up and down. Asking permission to see your own flesh and blood, he thought. A young girl peeped around the corner and looked at him, smiled, waved. Franks returned the gesture, missing the Ally of that age. The girl's grandmother addressed her sternly and she disappeared. What was Ally up to? Was she actually going to refuse him? Jeff finally appeared and said Ally would see him.

'Thank you,' Franks said, starting to like this boy.

He followed Jeff down the passage, smelling the wok-fried food and spices – another world – and then saw the rest of the family sitting around a table in one half of the living room, the TV blaring. A half-asleep grandfather, the grandmother, the smiling parents, the inquisitive, mischievous-looking daughter. Franks said good evening and the parents returned his greeting in English. He thanked them for letting him see his daughter. They said it was a pleasure and the grandfather asked his wife something in Mandarin. She replied in a short, sharp volley and he said, 'Ah.'

Jeff showed Franks into the small bedroom. Ally was sitting on one of two narrow beds and he sat down on the one opposite her.

'Hi, sweetheart,' he said.

Silence.

'What's up?'

After another long silence she said, 'I thought of committing suicide, but then it would have been messy and the two of you would eventually get over it. You'd have to. Mum could run off with someone else and learn to love their children, and you could probably do the same.'

Let them talk.

'But then I thought I could do the same too. I could find someone I love and have my own children – or maybe not find someone and not have children, and that would be cool too. But I'd continue playing chess with people like Jeff.'

'Ally, you can't stay here.'

'Why not? Because it's against the law?'

'It's not against the law, but ... we don't even know these people.'

'*I* know them. They have given me only kindness and good food and I'm very partial to that, which comes as a bit of a shock to my teenage system, but there you have it.'

'Allyson, you need to go home.'

'Dad, if you love me as you say you do, you'll let me stay for a while. That's what I want. I feel safe and wanted here. I want you to pay the Chens some rent and, one day, when and if I become a nicely adjusted adult, I'll repay you.'

Franks gave his daughter a long look, sighed and called his ex-wife.

'Is she alright?' Ngaio asked.

'Yes, she's fine. But she's staying.'

There was a silence that could have meant a million things.

'She'll call you,' he said, looking at Ally, who nodded.

He rang off. Ally didn't reward him with a smile, instead allowing him to give her a kiss on the cheek.

After he'd spoken to the Chens and left, she put her favourite photograph next to her bed, the one where her young mother stood by the pool while her father's body split the water like a bullet.

Chapter 35

Now that that little problem was out of the way, he could return to his old routine. What else was there to do? Everything was more or less back to normal, except that Ally wasn't at home with her mother. Ngaio. He'd been so angry about her infidelity that he'd left and thrown himself into his work instead of – he now realized – asking her why she'd done it. But then he'd seen Jiaping and become distracted. Seriously distracted. Typical male again. But why not? Life went on, and Jake next door had put on something nice and upbeat.

'Jake?'

'Yeah?'

'Who's that?'

'Fat Freddy's Drop.'

'What's it called?'

'"Wandering Eye",' Jake said.

After a pause his mother said, 'That's what your father had.'

'Yeah, I know.'

After their chat at the post-bust party, Franks had asked Jiaping out. They went for a drink in Mission Bay, where the rich lived and the poor often made a noise with their souped-up sedans and motorbikes, just to remind all and sundry that they were still around. After their drink at the De Fontein bar, they walked along the boulevard, where a potpourri of languages could be heard under a near-full moon. Rangitoto loomed across the glassy water as a stark reminder that one day another volcano would erupt in Auckland, also known as Tamaki Makaurau. It could happen any time, like losing a wife, or a colleague, or a son, or your own life.

'So, tell me your story,' he said.

'It's a very common migrant's story,' she replied as they started walking on the beach. 'My parents came here looking for opportunity, worked hard, clung to their traditions, knowing we probably wouldn't. But they got us into good schools, we became Kiwis, and here I am. A copper making a living. How about you?'

'Why a copper?'

'Can you see me in an accountancy firm?'

'Not really, no. So you're actually an accountant?'

'Qualified, yes. And no, I'm not from internal affairs, just in case you were wondering.'

'I wasn't.'

'And you?'

'No, I've never been very good with numbers.'

'I meant why did you become a copper?'

'Oh. Well, my parents were Mr and Mrs Franks before my mother discovered I had a half-brother and half-sister too. The old man also spent quite a bit of time inside, so he wasn't exactly an angel. I suppose that's why I became a cop – in reaction to him.'

Jiaping asked him about his ex-wife and daughter, so he told her about them in his brief, factual way, while she looked up at him with a face full of moon.

'And may I add,' he said, 'that I think you're absolutely beautiful.'

'That's what my partner always says,' she replied teasingly.

Franks laughed, half despairing, half amused.

'Well, tell him he shouldn't be talking about your looks.'

'Who says it's a him?'

'Her, they, whatever.'

'They know they shouldn't be talking about my looks,' she said, working the ambiguity to the max, 'but it's very normal, even though I don't agree with them – or you.'

'And do *they* normally just let you go out at night with another man?'

'I could have said it was work,' she replied.

'That would be fibbing,' John said, stopping.

'Just a little white lie from a yellow woman,' she smiled, increasingly lovely – and likeable.

'You know,' John concluded, 'I don't think you have a partner!'

Jiaping smiled and left him dangling for a good couple of seconds before saying, 'And I don't think you're over your ex-wife.'

Chapter 36

The next heavily hungover day, Franks was at the Bar None at opening time and started drinking with a vengeance again. Pat told him he was drinking too much and the text from Tracy didn't help much either: *Im goin away 4 awhile will call when i get bak*. He was pretty pissed by the time Morris arrived, asking him why he wasn't going to pick up Ally. He said his services were no longer required, slurring.

Pat, who had always had a soft spot for Ally, said: 'It'll pass.'

At which point Franks' phone rang.

'Talk of the devil,' he said.

'Hi Dad,' Ally said cheerfully. 'How are you?'

'I'm just fine thank you, love. How are you?'

'You sound pissed.'

'That's a distinct possibility. So, what's up?'

'I thought maybe you could take me to Mum's, but you clearly can't.'

'Do you want to go home?' Franks said, suddenly happy.

'No, I just wanted to get some stuff.'

'Take a taxi. I'll pay.'

Morris interjected. 'Where is she? I'll take her.'

'Don't worry,' Ally said, 'I'll get Jeff to take me on his motorbike.'

'You are *not* getting on to any goddamned motorbike!' Franks shouted, causing some of the other patrons to look up.

'Tell her I'll take her,' Morris insisted.

'Says the man who's pissed at three in the afternoon,' Ally snorted, hearing Morris in the background. She'd never told her father that she'd become increasingly uncomfortable around the man with his leering silences, much as she still loved Aunty Pat.

'Ally, Uncle Morrie says he'll take you to … Ally? … Shit! She's cut me off!'

'Where is she?' Morris asked.

'The hell with her,' Franks said. 'Give me another beer, Pat.'

'I think you've had enough, John,' Pat said.

'Christ, can I not even get a drink in my own fucking bar!'

'Maybe you should go for a little walk or something, bro,' Morris said.

'Well fuck you all. I'll go and drink somewhere else.'

And with that he stumbled out of the Bar None.

Chapter 37

He couldn't drive, so he walked, or rather, staggered, in that eternal drizzle, looking out for another bar where he could maybe get a drink. He was faintly aware of the fact that people were looking askance at this man who was talking to himself, cursing the world, but then he passed a pavement blackboard that penetrated his foggy skull. It took him a second or two to register that it wasn't a menu, so he stopped, paused, and turned around, which felt like it was taking as much effort as one of those massive tourist ships in Auckland harbour. The sign on the fold-up blackboard said, in simple white chalk letters:

NOW AND ZEN ADVICE

Franks chuckled. Everybody was so bloody serious these days! He could hear children playing. He was standing outside a creche of some sort, swaying. Well, he was going to find out who the joker was, and staggered up the stairs.

Inside, he asked a receptionist who had written 'that thing' outside and she said it was Alan. Well, could he see this Alan? He wanted to thank him for having a sense of humour. The receptionist could smell the booze on him but kept her Kiwi reserve and said he could wait in the adjacent court. She'd call Alan.

'Court?' Franks wondered, seeing both a court of justice and a tennis court at the ASB stadium.

'Basketball court.'

'Ah, right,' John said, and stumbled through.

This was stupid, he thought, maybe he should leave, but just then a man entered the indoor court and walked towards him. Alan was about fifty, bald, bearded. He was wearing a golden earring, a white singlet, a host of tats, a Samoan lavalava skirt, and jandals.

'Can I help you, mate?' the man said. Bloody Australian.

'I don't know. Can you?'

Alan did the last thing Franks would have expected. He smacked him, hard and loud.

'Jesus! What was that about?'

'I'm helping you.'

'Right,' Franks said sarcastically, his cheek stinging.

'So why do you need help?'

'Can't you smell?' Franks replied.

Alan smacked him again, just harder this time.

'Don't you get smart-arsed with me, mate.'

'Sor-ry,' he replied sarcastically.

'What do you think this is? A church or something?'

'What do you mean?'

'Do you think you can just come here when there's nowhere else to go?'

'Look, my wife ...'

Alan slapped Franks again and said: 'Shut up, sit down and wait.'

The man walked away and Franks did as he was told, muttering, 'Such a charming manner.'

Alan stopped, turned, and gave his visitor a look that said he wasn't beyond picking up his miserable carcass and slapping him again. Franks raised his palms in a placatory manner, his face still stinging.

Chapter 38

The rain kept gushing down as if it had been sent to punish the City of Sails, while Franks added to the deluge by opening the first beer bottle and, instead of pouring it down his throat, emptied it down the kitchen drain. This he did five more times before the phone rang.

Ally.

'Hi sweetheart. How are you?'

'I'm okay, thanks. Have you got a leak?'

'No. Why?'

'It sounds like water's running into a bucket in the middle of your living room or something.'

'Nah, I'm just pouring some stuff down the drain.'

'What stuff?'

'Just stuff.'

'Like the blood of your latest victim?'

'Very funny,' he smiled. 'But blood has a much thicker texture. You should know that.'

'True. So what is it? Booze?'

'Yeah.'

'Wow.'

'It's nothing.'

'No, it's not. I'm impressed.'

'Thank you, sweetheart.'

'I mean it took me absolute *ages* to get over the firewater,' Ally said in crusty, aged-actress mode.

Franks laughed in the way one does when your child is sticking a love-knife into your heart, then said: 'So how was the bike ride?'

'He's very careful, Dad.'

'Good.'

'I mean, he'd have to deal with you if he messed up, wouldn't he?'

'Am I that bad?'

'Nah. Gotta go. Dinner time.'

'Thanks for the call. Have you spoken to your ...'

But she'd rung off already.

Time for the whisky to chase the beer down the drain and then wait for the shakes to start, along with Jake's music next door, while the rain just kept on coming down.

Chapter 39

Today, the wording on Alan's blackboard read:

CITY ZEN ADVICE

($100 a slap)

He was a regular joker, the Aussie. Franks was facing him, having been told to take off his shoes, as if he were in a *marae*. Alan was barefoot too, in his colourful lavalava. The first profundity he let loose was, 'Where's my money?' Franks brought out the requisite cash.

'So do you think I've got the answer to everything?' Alan asked.

'No.'

'Good. Because I don't. But one thing I do know is that you have to be in control of yourself. And why is that? Because if you're not in control of yourself, then someone or something else is. It's not rocket science. Does that make sense?'

'Yes.'

'Of course it does. You know it, everybody knows it. Yet we insist on acting against what we know. So go away and think about it.'

'But what about my wife?'

'She's welcome to come and see me any time. But you can go now. In fact, don't come back.'

'What do you mean?'

'I mean: don't, come, back.'

'Why?'

'Because I deal with brats who've had no chance in life, not spoilt brats who are too lazy to do their own thinking.'

'I'll pay you double.'

Alan looked at Franks for a few seconds, then said: 'Do you want me to hit you again?'

Chapter 40

Franks sat down with a pot of coffee, a packet of smokes and his four walls, and waited for the horrors, dreading them. No. He was prepared for them. Let them come. You just had to live from one second to the next, each one a small triumph, even when it's an obstacle. This is your space. You can sweat, curse, scream, cry, anything. So he sat. It was raining, and what did rain consist of? Water. That wasn't so bad. It was life. Too much of it, however, was not good. Just like everything else. And then a bluesy sound wafted in from next door.

'Jake?'

'Yeah?'

'What's that music?'

'It's still Fat Freddy's Drop.'

Silence. Rain.

'Why'd you ask?'

'It's quite nice,' his mother said.

'Yeah, it's called "Rain".'

'Are you DJ-ing the weather now?'

'Yeah, kind of.'

It wasn't all bad, Franks smiled a little desperately. He just had to make it through the night, which sounded like a song he might have heard once. If there was no one else, there was always good music. Rain. Get into the music and the pain, bro. Just get into it. Just you and you alone. And the harmonica. Deal with it. It's doable.

But then he saw the shock in Jiaping's eyes after he'd shot her. What the hell was he supposed to do with that? The only thing was to reach for the nearest bottle, but there was no bottle, so what was he supposed to do? Think, Alan had said. Think what, for Christ's sake? Maybe … if you think about what happened *before* that event instead of after it, you'd get somewhere. Okay. So what happened before?

He and Morris had parked their cars next to each other at the incoming-goods section of the docks, where he and Jiaping had joined Morris in his car. And what did they do? They waited, they watched. They watched Li's men waiting for the goods to come through. Big, bulky Islanders. Li wasn't there, of course. So they waited some more. The part of the job they didn't tell you about in the recruitment drives. The waiting. The tedium.

'Who wants some coffee?' Jiaping eventually asked.

The two men placed their orders and Jiaping went in search of a coffee stall. Morris's disapproval was clear as they watched her go. Soon after Li's consignment arrived, his men signed for it and started packing it into their truck.

'Look at those poor bastards,' Morris said. 'Little cogs in a one-point-five billion-buck machine.'

Franks said nothing. After a while Jiaping approached with their coffees, a newspaper and a big smile.

'I don't trust this woman,' Morris muttered.

'Why not?'

'Because she's a Chink, and a woman.'

'I think you're being paranoid,' Franks said. And racist, he thought.

Jiaping passed their drinks through the front window then got in the back, still smiling. They sipped their coffees, watching the men talk, joke, pack. Then, once Morris's coffee was finished, he started getting out of the car.

'Where're you going?' Franks said.

'For a crap, if that's okay.'

Franks cringed inwardly and apologised to Jiaping about his partner's manners. She just smiled.

'He's a bit of a rough diamond, but I trust him with my life.'

Jiaping sipped her coffee, and smiled.

'What?'

'As a trained accountant, I just wonder where he got his big house and fancy jewellery,' she said.

'He inherited,' Franks said defensively. 'At least, that's what he tells everyone.'

'Hmm,' she said, smiling.

'You know, it's very disconcerting when you just smile at everything.'

'Wouldn't you smile if you'd just won the Lotto?'

'Yes sure, but ... have you just won the Lotto?'

She nodded, still smiling, as he tried to absorb that news.

'Can I be your friend?'

She shook her head, grinning.

'You should be very careful who you tell about that!'

'I know,' she said, as he received the text from Rat.

Ah, I've got to go and do a little grey work because some of us still have to earn our daily bread, you know,' Franks said.

'What's grey work?'

He told her about Rat and how the accounts department had to be creative about that part of their budget, and she'd nodded as Li's men got to the end of their packing.

Now, with Jake's local music in his ears, he poured another coffee, lit another smoke, felt like he was close to something. But he just couldn't put his finger on it. It was like a word or name that eluded you, on the tip of your tongue, but you just couldn't remember it. Then let it go, he told himself. It'll come to you. You know that. Okay. It's gone, he thought, still listening to 'Rain'. Christ, even that sounded familiar. Had he heard it on the radio before? Maybe. Or at the Bar None? Possibly. No, it was at Morris's house. That time they'd celebrated their Greenhithe bust with the rest of the staff. He was making his way towards Jiaping, when Morris, standing with the newly arrived Smith, turned down the music and called him across the room. He tore his eyes away from Jiaping and looked back across the room, back across the group of women and men, and saw the two men ... But wait a bit ... that woman who said she'd do *anything* for money, the blonde woman in the group he'd just passed ... It was – *shit!* – Tracy.

The music had blurred her accent, and the hair colour had changed her appearance, but it was Tracy one hundred percent. Ally's instinct had once again been spot-on: Tracy was a gold digger. He wondered whether she'd even gone away, as she said she was going to when she texted him. Maybe he should go and see whether she had, in fact, left town.

Chapter 41

Franks stopped outside Kohi Mansions and saw that a light in her apartment was on, which didn't necessarily mean she was in, or even in town. He would sit here in the rain and wait, and maybe something would transpire. Bloody rain. Wait your life away, watching, smoking.

Why would she go away? Probably just didn't want to see him. Or make herself elusive. And if she did go away, maybe it was to target someone else. Who said you couldn't multitask at deception? Or maybe she really did just go away for the sake of going away. One never knew, and all you could do was try to find out.

Wait.

But lo and behold, half an hour later she came out of her building, dressed for a certain kind of night-time action. Track shoes, tights, waterproof hoody. Going out for a jog on Tamaki Drive. He started following her in the Commodore. After about five minutes she was doing more than just jogging, now that she was warmed up, Franks realised. She leapt onto a wet bench, sliding along the top of its backrest, hit the pavement again. Up onto the low wall holding back the sea, and along it, attracting the interest of one or two late-night strollers. And when the low wall was interrupted by steps leading down to the beach, she didn't just jump over but did a mid-air swivel, landing on the wet wall and carrying on. Up ahead was one of those quaint Edwardian toilets and she was running straight towards it, as if she wanted to wipe herself out against its wall, but she leapt towards it and almost got to the roof before she did a backwards somersault, landed back on her feet, and started jogging in the direction she'd come. All very impressive, Franks thought, but hardly the kind of activity you'd expect from someone dying of cancer. No wonder she didn't want to go running with him on the beach in Rarotonga: it would look too much like that day he'd chased her and she'd scaled the wall, with him even stupidly thinking she was a man. Someone, moreover, who knew how to use a gun, so much so that she'd made sure she *didn't* hit him.

He'd been such a complete idiot that he'd even started convincing himself he might be falling for her. What a moron.

Dick brain.

Chapter 42

Ally, meanwhile, sat pondering the profundity of chess. She wasn't all that mad about losing to Jeff all the time, but she had to concede there was a certain, well, magic to the game. You've got these rules, but within those rules there are endless possibilities. At first you think things can only go one way, and then you discover that, no, they can go two or even more ways. Endless ways. No game is ever the same. Amazing. This is much better than say, basketball, she thought. Or art. There was even a famous artist, according to Jeff, who said that all chess players were artists. That was about as stupid as the TV series *The Queen's Gambit*. What a load of emotional rubbish, she thought. She was completely with Bobby Fischer who said he wasn't interested in psychology, he was interested in good moves.

Chapter 43

Franks showered, brushed his teeth, washed his hair, shaved – as if that was going to somehow cleanse him, absolve him, destroy his desire for a drink. His doorbell rang and he put on a pair of jeans and instinctively tucked the pistol Rat had given him into the back of them. He looked through the peephole and saw a distorted Tracy. Opened the door, all senses alert, but keeping a cool exterior, he hoped.

'Hi,' he said.

'Can I come in?'

'Sure,' he said, though it was the last thing he wanted her to do.

Tracy stepped in and took a look around. She'd changed her outfit and was now dressed comfortably, as if she'd been travelling.

'Don't I even get a kiss?'

'Yeah. Sorry,' he said, giving her a perfunctory peck on the left cheek.

'You've cleaned up.'

'Yeah. Going for a job interview tomorrow.'

'Cool. Where?'

'Can't talk about it.'

'Ah, one of those.'

'Yeah.'

'Where's Ally?'

'She doesn't live here.'

'Oh, I thought ... Where does she live?'-

There were certain lines that had to be drawn, and this was one of them. He wasn't going to tell her where Ally was even if she put a gun to his head.

'Does she live with her mother?'

'No. She boards. Sacred Sisters.'

'Nice.'

'Not for her. She hates it.'

'Well, I wasn't mad about boarding school either. Hated it, in fact. But I really like her.'

You lying bitch, Franks thought, but said, 'Yeah, so do I.'

'I should hope so,' Tracy smiled.

'So, when did you get back?' he asked.

'I've just come here, straight from the airport.'

'Cool,' he said, amazed at how people could lie with such ease, such straight faces. 'Where'd you go?'

'Out of town. Family stuff. Short trip. Long story. Very boring.'

Just fudge it and move on, that's how they do it. Habitual liars.

'So aren't you going to offer me a drink or something?' she asked, looking at his naked torso.

What he really wanted to offer her was something much more violent than that, but instead he said, 'Listen Tracy, I'm not very good the day before an interview. I need to be alone.'

'Is there anything I can do to change your mind?' she asked suggestively. 'I mean, something that would maybe relax you a little, because you seem really tense.'

'No.'

Tracy gave him a changed look. 'I've heard you can be quite a cold bastard when you want to.'

'And where would you have heard that?'

'I do have a drink at the Bar None occasionally.'

'Right. And you and Pat talk.'

'Maybe.'

Franks said nothing, waited.

'Well,' she said, 'it looks like I'm not welcome here.'

'It's not like that,' he said, not meaning a single syllable.

'Have a nice romantic fling with a woman, discover she's got cancer, and then start a slow process of extracting yourself.'

He almost admired the way she was playing her part, and said, 'It's not like that at all.'

'Then what is it like?' she asked, tears welling up in her eyes.

By God, she was good, he thought, in an Antarctic kind of way. 'I just told you.'

'I think I'd rather hang out with people who truly care for me,' she said, complete with slight tremor in her voice, wiping away that annoying tear on her cheek.

'If that's what you want,' he replied.

Franks looked down and saw she was wearing the same pair of trainers she'd worn the day she'd lured him into the warehouse, where he'd shot Jiaping. No. Where he'd killed her.

'Goodbye,' she said, looking like she believed her own fake tragedy.

'Cheers,' John said icily.

He would never have thought that someone like her would work with the likes of Li, but then greed was always pro-green – as long as that colour refers to money and nothing else. Tracy turned and walked out the door, slamming it shut behind her.

Chapter 44

Ally lay awake, trying to solve the world's problems, along with a chess conundrum or two, while Jeff's little sister, Hope, lay on the other narrow bed in the room, sleeping the sleep of angels. Still, Ally started when her phone suddenly started buzzing.

'Dad?' she whispered.

'Hi sweetheart, were you sleeping?'

'No. Beauty has always evaded me,' she said, going into tragic-actress mode.

'Nonsense. You're the most beautiful girl in the world.'

'And you're not biased in any way, are you?'

'No,' John chuckled drily – and a little forced, Ally thought.

'So what's up?'

'Sweetheart, I want you to stay out of school for the rest of the week, okay?'

'This is a new approach. Why, pray?'

'Because I think your life might be in danger.'

'You're not serious.'

'I'm very serious, Allyson. Dead serious. Please do as I say, and be careful. Will you?'

He was always serious when he called her Allyson, so she said, 'Okay, Dad. Are you okay?'

'I'm fine. Love you.'

Ally replied that she loved him too.

Chapter 45

Ngaio had started her new job at another legal firm and would have been excited under normal circumstances, but these weren't normal circumstances. It was bad enough that she hadn't been able to finish her legal studies long ago, but, more to the point, now her baby was gone. She knew she wouldn't sleep that night and, when Franks called, she hoped he might at least tell her where Ally was. Instead, he told her about the whole sordid affair with Tracy – the shooting at the warehouse, the supposed cancer (but not the sex), the lies, the questions about Ally's whereabouts – and said he thought 'that woman' might retaliate by harming Ally. Therefore, it was better that Ngaio didn't know where Ally was.

'Do you think I'd tell anyone where my daughter is?'

'People will do anything to get out of pain.'

'Do you think I'm not prepared to die for our daughter?'

'Sorry, no. I know you would if you had to. But I don't want you to die. Nor her. We're dealing with the people who shot Peter because he wouldn't comply. Life means nothing to them.'

It was a kind of backhanded declaration that he still had feelings for her, but she still wanted to know where Ally was.

'I'm not telling you over the phone.'

'Then come tell me here, or I'll come to you.'

'Alright, I'll come over tomorrow morning.'

It was better than nothing, she thought.

'Come early. I've got a new job.'

'Well done. You can tell me about it in the morning.'

'Okay. Bye.'

She wanted to say take care and that she still loved him but wrote it off as just another habitual tick, and lay wondering how she was going to make it through the night.

Chapter 46

The only thing Franks wanted to do was go over to his ex's house, their house, take her in his arms and tell her he still loved her, wanted her – but he had to save face. And he had to think. He couldn't see the connection between Tracy and the elusive Mr Li. After two more coffees and even more cigarettes he thought maybe she'd been a high-class prostitute and Li was one of her clients. Maybe it was as simple as that. It often was.

He thought about the one night when things were so bad that he was about to swallow his pride and drive over to Ngaio's, but there'd been a knock on his door. He'd hoped it was her, or Ally, but it was too late for even Ally to be up. It was Jiaping. He let her into his mess of a life and she saw the empty beer bottles, the half-empty (as opposed to half-full) bottle of cheap Scotch, the flat that was really just a place where he slept. He said nothing, trying to avoid her eyes, and she didn't say anything either, but came and stood in front of him. Then she put her hand on his cheek and kissed him, tenderly, while Jake next door put on the most beautiful song Franks had ever heard. They'd started dancing to it, holding each other, scarcely moving, smiling at each other and at what was happening between Jake and his mother next door.

'What's that you're playing, sweetheart?'

'It's called "Phobos and Deimos,"' the boy said.

'What the hell is that supposed to mean?'

'They're the two moons of Mars.'

'I suppose only a jazz musician could come up with a title like that.'

'Yeah, like Dad.'

'Exactly.'

There was a pause.

'Who's the musician?'

'Guy called Callum Allardice, and the album is called *Cinematic Light Orchestra*.'

'American?'

'No, he's from Motueka.'

There was another pause.

'That's on the South Island, isn't it?'

'Yeah.'

An even longer pause.

'Lovely.'

By the end of that week there wasn't a drop of booze in the very tidy flat and Jiaping had unofficially moved in (while officially she stayed at home with her parents, who worried that she was doing so much night work). He'd told his daughter about her and Ally had tartly told him that not only did he have a weakness for women with black hair, he also had a much worse male weakness, which was the fear of being alone. It didn't help that Jiaping often gave him a look which said that, contrary to her actions and his statements, she knew he was still pining for his wife.

Chapter 47

At first Ngaio thought she was dreaming, but then she realised she was in that hazy state of semi-sleep and someone was knocking on her door. Could Franks have changed his mind? She certainly hoped so. More insistent knocking. She got up, put on her nightgown, gave her hair a brush and went to the front door. She could see the outline of the person outside the door – and it wasn't her ex. Franks was shorter, leaner, even when he'd gone to seed. But she knew that outline. It was an old family friend, one she hadn't seen in a long time, not before, during or after their painful break-up. Ngaio unlocked the door and said, 'Hi Morrie.'

'Can I come in?'

'Of course. How are you? Long time no see. What's up?'

Morris entered without kissing her on the cheek or letting her hug him and walked to the middle of her living room.

'I'm okay. Is Ally here?'

'No. Why?'

'Where is she?'

'She's ... out.'

'Bit late, isn't it?

'Why do you want to see her so late?'

'I need to talk to her.'

'About what?'

'Something. Where is she?'

'Morrie, I'm not going to tell you if you talk to me like that. What do you want to talk to her about that's so urgent at this time of the night?'

'Nothing,' Morris said. 'Let's go for a drive.'

'Now? What for?'

'I just want to show you something.'

'Morrie, you're acting all weird. I'm not going anywhere.'

'Sure?'

'Yes.'

'Okay,' Morris said, and hit her. Hard.

Chapter 48

The one moment you're happy with someone, the next you're burying them. Jiaping's funeral had been excruciating. Her parents hadn't known about him at all: Jiaping had been terrified of telling her folks she was involved with a non-Chinese man. Now they stood on the other side of the coffin as it was lowered into the gaping hole, her father angry, her mother just looking steadily at Franks, slowly recognising his pain, realising that he and Jiaping had been more than just colleagues. Standing on her other side was the ever-supportive Smith. Mrs Wu's eyes bored into Franks' so insistently that he looked away, to his partner standing next to him. Morris.

They weren't invited to the memorial service and Morris had had to do something urgent anyway. So Franks had sat in the Bar None, which was up for sale and which he decided to buy. Pat comforted him because she would really do anything for him. 'Anything,' she reiterated. But he was too far gone to pick up on any of that and she put him in a taxi and sent him on his miserable way, back to his flat of empty whisky bottles and squashed beer cans. Which was where he was now, but sober this time.

Stone cold sober. And tidied up.

He didn't sleep much, and when he did, he was haunted by images of Jiaping's shocked eyes, or her mother's searching ones, and then looking to his partner, Morris, for support. Morris, who hadn't been able, at one point, to stifle a yawn. That had annoyed Franks, but now it was doing something else to him. It was making him angry. Really fucking angry. Morris was, in fact, an insensitive piece of shit. And what if ... what if *he* had actually set up Jiaping's death? Was his hatred of the Chinese that intense? After all, they'd both witnessed Li putting that dollar coin in Peter's mouth in the warehouse, so what if *Morris* had actually orchestrated the whole thing and then made it look like the Chinese were behind it? Christ, it *was* him. Which meant that he and Tracy were in cahoots. Clever disguise. Make like you hate someone when you are, in fact, working with them.

Franks got up, dressed, washed, grabbed the Glock. It was all as clear and cloudless as the dawn outside. The mistake he'd made was to believe

Morris, who'd said that when he came back from the men's at the docks that day, Jiaping was gone, having been recognised and taken away by Li's workers. That was complete bullshit, just as it was no accident that the CCTV wasn't working that day. That could easily have been 'arranged'. What it would have shown was Morris and Jiaping leaving the docks together, ostensibly heading to a Mt Wellington warehouse for another job, where she'd have been overpowered, tied up, and told to call Franks. But for that, Morris would have needed an hour or so, and a decoy. And who would that be? Of course. Another lowlife Morris professed to despise. Rat. Rat who had been unusually jumpy that morning, who'd sent Franks off on a little wild-goose chase to supposedly capture the violent psychopath Eric Schultz. Give the devil his due, though, Schultz had later been arrested at the address Rat had given Franks, and was awaiting trial.

Time to talk to Rat and Mr Morris Fucking Malone.

Chapter 49

It wasn't difficult to get hold of Rat. All you did was text him and say you had a little gift for him, even if mornings weren't exactly his operating hours. Franks told him to meet him at the Point England toilets. Half an hour later, Rat skulked in, looking and smelling like he hadn't slept, eaten or washed for days.

Hi, John. What's the occasion?'

Nothing much,' Franks said, pointing the barrel of the Glock between Rat's eyes.

That's the pistol I gave you.'

That's right.'

I made sure it had no numbers on it.'

I did notice that, yes,' Franks said.

I do my best, bro. So what kind of gift do you have for me?'

That depends on what you tell me, Rat. It could be freedom, it could be lead.'

I don't have any relatives to pay for the lead, John.'

Do you think I care for the cost of a bullet?'

No, you've never been big on money, have you?'

Exactly. So if you don't tell me what I need to know you're going to be a wee bit heavier.'

Don't you think that's being a bit drastic, John?'

No, I don't, Rat.'

Yeah, I can see that.'

Sing.'

Would you mind taking that gun out of my face, bro. It's very unnerving.'

That's the whole idea.'

John, I'm just a junkie with a couple of leads. Someone who lost his moral compass in Theology III.'

I don't want your life story, Rat. I want the truth.'

Which one would that be, John?'

I'm not going to tell you what you did. *You're* going to tell me what you did.'

John, I haven't slept since that day.'

Yeah, P can do that to you.'

That's not what I'm talking about. I'm talking about what I did.'

What *did* you do?'

You know what I did.'

Yes, but I want to hear you say it.'

Rat, for once, was silent. Then he continued:

I have a habit to maintain. A really bad habit.'

I'm waiting.'

Morris told me to keep you distracted for an hour.'

Did he say why?'

No, but I put two and two together when I read about Jiaping Wu's death.'

So?'

I'm sorry. I'm truly sorry.'

Do you think that's going to bring her back?'

No, John. I don't. And I acknowledge that it must have been tormenting you too.'

Well, that's very kind and considerate of you, Rat. But tell me why I shouldn't just put you out of your misery?'

Oblivion doesn't seem like a bad option these days, bro. I mean, I'm getting kind of tired of being torn between the hounds of heaven and the angels of hell.'

Franks was tempted, sorely tempted. He could put a bullet between Rat's eyes and walk and no one would ever be the wiser. Or, if there were any witnesses who saw Franks leaving the toilets, he could always plant a knife and say he'd been attacked by a maniac high on P. He'd never done it before and wouldn't do it on principle, but if he had to do it in this case, he would.

Lie down on your stomach,' Franks said.

What?'

You heard me.'

Rat went down on his knees, slowly, then lay down flat.

We could take this in a completely different direction, John.'

We could indeed, Rat. But we're not going to. Put your hands behind your back.'

Rat did as he was told and Franks put his knee between the stinking man's shoulder blades.

You can't arrest me, John.'

I'm not arresting you,' Franks said, switching off his mobile, which had been on Record.

John, rather shoot me now than put me inside. I won't last a week in prison.'

My heart truly goes out to you, Rat.'

That's what I've always sensed about you, John. A man with heart. Problematic in the force, but... hey, who're you calling?'

The cops. They're not too far away.'

You realise, don't you, that every second you spend with me endangers your wife and daughter?'

Good point,' Franks said, and took out a cable tie and fastened Rat's wrists behind his back. 'Put your feet together.'

Rat complied and Franks tied his ankles together too.

Goodbye, Rat.'

These ties are hurting me, John.'

Better not move too much then, ay?'

Franks left and Rat shouted after him: 'What about my human rights?'

Franks walked towards the Commodore as fast as he could without seeming hurried as police sirens drew nearer.

'Don't you want to know about corruption in the mildest of places?' Rat shouted.

But his voice was drowned out by the weew!weew!weew! of the sirens.

Chapter 50

Ten minutes later, Franks screamed to a halt outside Ngaio's house in Sandringham and saw the door was slightly ajar. She wasn't inside, and the carpet looked freshly scuffed. There was a drop of blood on the wooden floor next to the carpet.

He drove to Morris and Pat's house in Glendowie and banged on the door, holding the Glock behind his thigh. No response, so he banged again. Pat opened, still in her pyjamas, looking shocked.

'Where's Morris?'

'He's not here, but ...'

'Are you alone?'

'No, but ...'

Franks forced his way past her.

'John, you can't come in. We've got a guest.'

'So?' Franks said, heading for the kitchen.

'He's been staying with us.'

'Have you started an Airbnb?' Franks asked.

'No, it's just that Morrie said he needs to stay with us for a while and that no one should know about him.'

'Why the hell would he ...?'

And then Franks saw why Morris would have said that. Saw it very clearly. Sitting at the breakfast table in the kitchen was none other than the elusive Mr Li himself.

'Hello, John,' he said. 'Take a seat.'

'Hello, Mr Li,' Franks said, pointing the pistol at Li's chest. Li didn't move. 'So that's why you didn't chase us that night you had Peter killed.'

'Why don't you sit down so we can talk?' Li said.

'Why don't you keep your mouth shut and put your hands on either side of that pole,' Franks said, producing more cable ties.

Li complied and held his hands on either side of the pole supporting the breakfast counter.

'Tie him up,' Franks told Pat.

'I'm sorry, Mr Li,' she said. 'I don't understand.'

'It's a misunderstanding,' he replied.

'John, what is going on?' she asked him.

'Morris has been working for Mr Li,' Franks said.

'But he doesn't even like them,' Pat said. 'Sorry,' she said to Mr Li, who didn't even bother to shrug.

'Well, he doesn't seem to mind their money,' Franks replied, at which point his phone started ringing. Morris.

'Keep an eye on him, stay out of his reach and don't give him anything he asks for,' Franks told an increasingly confused Pat. 'Your life depends on it.'

He went out on to the lawn, near the pool and barbecue where their children had played and they'd cooked, drunk, smoked, chatted, laughed.

'Where are you?' he said to Morris.

'I've got Ngaio, and if you don't get me two million dollars by the end of today, your little darling won't have a mother. Do you understand me?'

'Okay, I'll get the money, but let me first talk to Ngaio.'

'No.'

'I need to know she's still alive, otherwise there's no deal.'

There was a tense pause.

'Okay, but if she tells you where we are, she's dead. Capiche?'

'Yes, sure,' Franks said, hearing seagulls shrieking in the background before Ngaio came on the line.

'John?'

'Are you alright?'

'Yes, I'm fine.'

'Are you at the bach?'

'No.'

'Okay, I'm going to get Morris his money and you're going to be fine, okay?'

'Okay,' she said, sounding dubious, tentative, frightened.

'Tell him he'll have his money by the end of the day.'

'Yeah,' she said in that way they'd had of speaking volumes in monosyllables.

'Love you,' Franks said and rang off before Ngaio could say the same. Then he went inside to check that Li was still there and Pat was keeping an eye on him.

'Why don't you come sit here and we make a deal?' Li said.

'Why don't you shut your fucking mouth?' Franks said.

'I can make you a very rich man,' Li persisted.

'One more word out of you and I will make you a very dead man,' Franks replied.

Li shut his mouth with Pat looking more puzzled.

'You're doing a great job, Pat. I'll be back in a second,' Franks said, and walked out onto the lawn again, dialling Smith's number.

Smith was driving to work and listening to the news on the radio when his phone rang. He cut the news, dutifully pulled off to the side of the road, and said, 'John?'

'I've got Li. He's at Morris's house. They've been working together.'

'I'm on my way,' Smith said, unruffled as ever.

He was close to work and pulled in to get an official car so he could drive out to Glendowie, siren blaring, knowing Franks was thorough enough to keep Li safe.

Chapter 51

Franks headed towards the bank opposite the park where Ally and Jeff had played chess – and couldn't believe what he was seeing. Ally and Jeff were sitting there right now, in the park, playing chess. This, after he'd expressly told her not to go out. Jeff's motorbike was parked nearby. There was nothing Franks could do except try to keep an eye on them while he tried to convince the bank that they had to give him two million dollars – cash – *now*.

When he got inside that venerable institution, he of course had to confront the one thing he hadn't taken into account. He hadn't made an appointment with the manager, who was busy with a client, busy in that leisurely way people with jobs and money in general are. Franks was invited to sit down and have a cup of coffee while the assistant offered to see what she could do. He told her it was a police matter and very important, and she'd treated it with the same urgency as walking along the beach on a Sunday morning, while outside the window he could see his endangered daughter playing chess in broad daylight.

Shit!

Chapter 52

Ally had thought it was a much better idea to play chess out in the sunshine than in Jeff's parents' flat. He wanted to show her a famous game and she was just too happy for him to show her the game, any game. Jeff arranged the board so that Ally would be white and he would be black and took it to moves 8 of the match between Judit Polgar and Vishwanathan Anand, played in Dos Hermanas, Spain, 1999. At that point white's attacking knight was being threatened by a pawn.

'So here we have a Hungarian playing the then world champion, Vishwanathan Anand,' he said.

'That doesn't sound Russian.'

'It isn't. He's Indian.'

'Oh. What's the Hungarian's name?

'Jude Polgar,' Jeff fibbed about the first name. 'So what would you do as white now?' he wondered.

'Well, I'd get out of the way or maybe go to h6, since it's covered by the bishop.'

'Not bad. But that's not what Polgar did. He counter-threatened black's knight.'

'Okay,' Ally said after a moment. 'But then he'd lose a pawn?'

'That's right. So black took his knight and what do you think white did?'

'Took the black knight, obviously.'

'No. He took the pawn instead of the knight.'

'Stupid. And now he can lose that pawn too?'

'That's right,' Jeff said. 'And black pushes his d-pawn down the central line, threatening a fork for white's bishop and knight. What would you do next?'

'I'd try to move one of those players. Get out of the way. Or even better, take the black knight.'

'What about the exposed pawn?'

'It's a pawn,' Ally said somewhat condescendingly.

'The French player Philidor called pawns the soul of chess.'

'Has soul ever won a war?'

'Yes, it has in fact. But if you were to defend the pawn, would you do so with your queen or bishop?'

'Why hasn't the Hungarian taken the knight that was threatened a few moves back yet?'

'Maybe he's got a plan.'

'Okay,' Ally said, sighing a little dramatically, 'I'd probably cover the pawn with my bishop, so I can at least let my king castle.'

'Okay, but don't you think moving the queen to f3 would be a more active, threatening move?'

Ally looked at the situation for a while and then conceded that it was probably a better move, because the bishop could be the next move and firm up the defence of that soulful pawn, even though she still thought the pending fork of her bishop and knight was suicide.

'I suppose black now pushes his pawn and pins the bishop and knight?' she said.

'That's right. What would you do now?'

'I don't know. Probably sacrifice the bishop, so that white can at least have another bishop and knight.'

'What about a queenside castle, thereby threatening black's queen?'

Ally studied the move intensely, angry with herself for missing what seemed so obvious a solution, albeit a temporary one.

Chapter 53

Franks could see the manager and his client through the glass partition, and they seemed to be having a whale of a time, in banking terms, while outside Ally sat motionless.

How could he have been such a fool about Morris! Before last night he'd trusted the man with his life, and wife. Now he wouldn't trust him with a dollar. Christ, the man was holding his so-called best friend's wife hostage! What an idiot I am, Franks thought, furious with himself. How did he not pick up on all those snide comments, made in a jokey manner, of course? How could he have thought they were mates, brothers virtually, inseparable? Jiaping, though, had seen right through Morris and paid for it with her life. Even Pat had said he'd changed, and he hadn't taken it seriously.

And then Tracy. Another embarrassment. He'd fallen for her tricks like a sack of cement. 'Thinking with your willy,' as Ally had said, and she'd been right. How smoothly, cynically they'd operated. Now Morris was holding Ngaio in their bach, just to rub it all in. Franks knew they were at his bach as surely as he knew he was sitting here in a bank, fuming.

Christ, when were those two going to stop talking!

Chapter 54

'It doesn't solve the problem,' Ally said. 'If the pawn takes either the bishop or the knight, the black queen can still be protected.'

'That's right,' Jeff said. 'Anand chose to put his knight in the way, like this. So which piece would you move now?'

'I told you: the knight.'

'Well, Polgar moved the bishop back to d2 so that when the black pawn took his knight, the bishop could take it in return. Does this make any sense to you yet?'

'No ... I mean, let's see ... I suppose there is a kind of attack building against black's kingside,' she ventured.

'That's right. So Anand puts his bishop on g7 to triple-protect his knight – and to start looking dangerous. What would you do now?'

'I'd take the bloody knight, as I should have ages ago!'

Jeff just looked at her.

'What did he do?' she asked.

'Rook to g1.'

'That's ridic ... Okay, this is very strategic, very long-term.'

'Correct,' Jeff said. 'What would you do as black?'

'How about pushing the b-pawn to free up your bishop?'

'Maybe, but Anand was more concerned with defence at this stage, so he castled.'

'Don't tell me he's finally going to lose that knight?'

'He is, and he takes that pawn with his queen to start a counterattack. White's queen moves to e3 to protect his pawn *and* threaten white's a-rook and simultaneously trap his bishop.'

'Clever, Ally said, 'even though he could move his rook to b8.'

'Yes.'

'But black's queen-bishop attack is not all that strong because their king is in the line of fire from the g-rook.'

'Yes, good. So Vishy moves his king to h8. What would you do now as white?'

'Bring out my bishop to d3 to defend the pawn on f5?'

'Okay, that's not bad. But what's the best form of defence?'

'Attack,' Ally said. 'But how?'

'How about moving the f-pawn to f5?'

Ally studied the move for a while and said: 'Clever, because that'd threaten black's queen.'

'That's right. So white might be a key player down, but he's got something called position. Black plays queen to b6 to threaten both the white queen and rook, but the white queen moves to g3 and is one move away from checkmate.'

'Right,' Ally said, fascinated.

'The black queen now has to defend g7 to prevent mate. So what does white do to increase the pressure?'

'I don't know. Let me have a look.'

Chapter 55

It looked like Mr Patel, the bank manager, and his client were wrapping up whatever they'd been talking about. They laughed, stood up, shook hands, and the client left.

Out in the park, Ally was still sitting very still.

Franks looked away from her and Jeff to the assistant to signal that he now wanted to see the manager urgently, but she was busy talking to one of her colleagues and he thought he might blow his top. Time for action. He walked up to her and said the manager seemed to be free now and could she please tell him to attend to him, now. Urgently. She said she'd already emailed him that 'Mr Franks' wanted to see him urgently, and that he'd call him as soon as he was ready. The man seemed to be writing a bloody full-length report on his computer, completely relaxed, but finally ended it. Then he either sent it or saved it, read that someone wanted to see him urgently, looked up, and saw a wild-eyed man standing at the entrance to his office.

'Mr Franks,' he said. 'Come in. Have a seat.'

'I don't have time to sit,' Franks said. 'I need two million dollars cash, *now*.'

Mr Patel burst out laughing.

Chapter 56

'I don't know what to do next,' Ally said.

'Why not push black's rook up to d6 and really squeeze black's queen, because if he takes it, it's mate?'

Ally looked at the move for a few seconds.

'That really does ramp things up,' she concluded. 'But black can cover her with his pawn.'

'True, and did. So what now?'

'No idea.'

'How about dark bishop to d2'

'Okay, but black is going to counter-threaten with his b-pawn.'

'Right. But what if you now pulled your dark bishop back to d2?'

'More pressure!' Ally said.

'That's right.'

'Gosh,' Ally said, 'this is exciting.'

'What would you do now?'

'I'd ... move my light bishop to d4.'

'Good. Why?'

'Mobilise the troops.'

'And black?'

'Counterattack. Push pawn b.'

'Right. And then?'

'I don't know. Maybe attack the black knight on d7?'

'Absolutely. So what should black do?'

'I don't know, he is covered by his bishop.'

'But then Bobby Fischer said you should always cover your pieces with at least two pieces.'

'Makes sense.'

'So black defended with his a-rook, taking it to a7.'

'Sensible,' Ally said.

'Yes. What would you do as white now?'

'I'd ... move my dark bishop to e3, threatening the rook?'

'Not bad!' Jeff said. 'Why?'

'I don't know. It just feels right.'

'Well, there is also a place for instinct in chess. But white's rook went to c6, threatening black's bishop.'

'But it's covered by the rook!'

'True. What would you do as black now?'

'When in doubt, push your pawns, I suppose.'

'Correct,' Jeff said, pushing the black a-pawn to a5. And white?'

'I'd threaten his rook with my bishop on e3, as I wanted to do earlier.'

'Okay. No one likes pressure. Not even the world champion. So he goes to b7, starting a counter-attack.'

'It looks a bit flimsy.'

'It is, but it's all he can do at this stage.'

Chapter 57

Tracy hadn't gone to a school like Sacred Sisters. She hadn't had parents like, say, Ngaio to work their butts off so as to get the best possible education for their precious offspring. Instead, she'd attended a bog-standard, low-decile state school where the girls were as dangerous as the boys. If the boys couldn't wait to grope you, then the girls couldn't wait to beat the living daylights out of you. Nothing subtle or poisonous about them. Tracy had had her hair pulled out, her nose broken and her flesh torn by a gang of girls that made a lot of boys tremble. School of hard knocks. She'd had to toughen up, and she did. At first she'd used her speed to get away, but after a year's training she could flatten anyone with a straight palm or forehead to the nose, then a sharp jab to the throat or solar plexus, followed by a knee to the groin or, if she had the right shoes, a kick to the knee. She had flattened a boy and some bitch that way, and then, of course, she'd acquired something else. A reputation. She wasn't 'easy', she was a whore.

Well, soon after school she was quite a well-off whore, managing a gym while the boys went on to become drunkards or, worse, respectable. The girls often showed their worth by getting pregnant before even leaving school, or soon after, by which time the boys had evaporated. She had bumped into some of them occasionally but hadn't even bothered to tell them what she was up to: she knew they could sense her success while they got dragged down the drain by their procreative abilities. Professional losers or victims, all of them. As for the gym, she'd married its very wealthy owner. He'd discovered he was gay and had then conveniently died of AIDS. Bingo. His family had contested her inheriting the gym, but the law was the law. Goodbye, and good riddance.

She was in the principal's reception area, wearing the kind of clothing to show that she, too, was respectable. The principal's secretary introduced herself as Miss Stark. She was another one of those women who seemed to have married for what she thought was love and now had a divorced, middle-aged look of disappointment about her.

'Good morning,' Tracy said.

'Hello,' the woman said rather cheerfully. 'Can I help you?'

'Yes. I wonder if you could tell me where I could find Allyson Franks?'

'What's it in connection with?' the woman asked.

'Well, her mother's gone missing and I need to let her know. It's really urgent. I'm a family friend.'

'Right,' the secretary said. 'I could let her know.'

'I'd prefer to tell her myself,' Tracy said.

'Oh, we can't do that,' Miss Stark said.

'Why not?'

'School policy,' the woman replied. 'We can only let a parent or relative do that.'

'It's really very urgent,' Tracy said.

'I'm sorry,' Miss Stark said. 'We've had incidents before.'

'Well, I'm not going to cause an incident.'

Miss Stark smiled in a way that still said no.

'Okay,' Tracy said, 'could you please let her know immediately?'

'I will,' Miss Stark said, 'but you know, I don't recall there being an Allyson Franks in this school.'

'Surely you can check?'

'Of course I can. I'll do so right away.'

'Thank you,' Tracy said.

Just then Miss Stark's phone rang and Tracy tried to look patient, friendly and parental while the receptionist carried on with her conversation.

'By the way,' Miss Stark said to the caller, 'do you know whether we have an Allyson Franks here?'

She listened and Tracy tried not to look too inquisitive.

'No, I didn't think so either. But I'd better check the records anyway. The old memory's not what it used to be.'

Tracy smiled, hoping it looked empathetic, because she certainly wasn't feeling that way.

Miss Stark tapped her keyboard for a while and then looked up at Tracy.

'There's no Allyson Franks in this school.'

'But there has to be!'

'Come have a look at the database,' Miss Stark said. 'She's not under F or A.'

'Could you check if she's ever been here?'

'Why would you need to know that?'

'Oh, never mind,' Tracy said, as the break bell rang.

She didn't even bother to thank or greet Miss Stark. She simply turned and left the office and started walking towards her car, passing a mass of chattering girls in their ugly, ankle-length skirts and cheese-cutter hats. Anyone who said they missed their school days had to have their head read, she thought, as she started dialling Morris's number.

Chapter 58

The atmosphere inside the bach was everything but family-friendly. Ngaio was cuffed to the old stove, her jaw aching and her left eye swollen, while Morris paced about like the caged man he was. He almost jumped when his phone rang, then went outside before he answered it, seeing it was Tracy.

'What?' he said.

'The little bitch has never been to Sacred Sisters. He lied to me.'

'You could have asked me.'

'I suppose I could have,' she sneered.

He could hear the girls in the background and said, 'Never mind. We've got her mother,' he half whispered, even though Ngaio was well out of earshot.

'So what do I do now?' she asked.

'Come to his bach,' he said.

'Where's that?'

'Didn't he ever bring you here?'

'No. How do I get there?'

Morris gave her directions and then rang off. He didn't feel like going back into the bach, where he'd have to endure Ngaio's pointed silences. Then again, the bloody seagulls' squawking out there was pretty grating too.

Chapter 59

'Mr. Franks,' the manager said yet again, 'I can't just give you two million dollars.'

'Why not? It's mine!'

I'm sorry, but we just don't give out so much money in cash.'

Why not!' Franks demanded loudly.

Well, for one, we don't have that kind of cash on the premises. It's much too dangerous. And then, you need to make an arrangement with us to draw so much cash in one go.'

How long will it take to get it?'

We'd have to go through certain procedures.'

I want that money and I want it *now!*'

'It just doesn't work like that,' the manager said, polite to a fault. Franks couldn't help thinking he was a smug little prick.

'Listen, I've got an asset worth two million,' Franks said, trying to keep calm. 'I'll sign the collateral. Just see to it that I get the money. It's a matter of life and death.'

'I'm sorry,' the manager said. 'If you were still in the force and your boss was prepared to okay it, it would be a different matter, but you've already told me you're no longer a policeman.'

What would he have to do to convince this little person that he needed money that was, in fact, his own? (Theoretically anyway. In principle it was still Jiaping's.) And then he had one last desperate idea.

'Tell me, does Alistair Smith still have his department's account here?'

'Of course. He's a most valued client of ours.'

'Can I quickly make a phone call?'

'Of course,' Mr Patel said. 'More coffee?'

'No thanks,' Franks said, dialling Smith's number as the manager got up to get himself some chai. Smith finally answered and said he had Li safely in custody. Was there something he could do for him?

'Yes, there is', Franks replied. 'Can you please talk to Mr Patel here and tell him I need two million dollars cash. Now.'

'Why?'

Franks stood up, walked out of Mr Patel's office and explained to Smith what Morris had been up to and where he was right then. Smith said he could arrange the cash and Franks could collect it in half an hour.

Chapter 60

Back in the park, the game had progressed to the point where Polgar had continued doing the unexpected, seemingly sacrificing a rook but ending up forking black's two rooks.

'Brilliant!' Ally said. 'And all black can do is cover his f-rook with the other rook.'

'Correct. And now?'

'Take it, unless he's got some more weird moves up his sleeve?'

'No, he takes it, but that's only so he can get the rook in a compromising position.

'How so?' Ally wondered.

'Because if you move one piece to the right place now, it's game over.'

'*What?*' Ally said, surprised. 'Which one?'

'Rook to d1.'

That's brilliant,' Ally said after some thought, smiling.

Chapter 61

Franks stormed out of the bank and marched over towards his daughter and Jeff, who were sitting at a picnic table with a chess board between them, two helmets on one side and her friend's motorbike nearby. The world might be collapsing, but teenagers would insist on having things their way.

'Allyson, didn't I tell you to stay out of sight?'

'No, you said stay out of school.'

'Well can you two please go back to the flat right now,' he hissed. 'And make sure you don't get followed by anyone – especially not that other woman,' he said.

'You mean dearest darling Tracy?'

'Yes, Allyson. Tracy.'

'Dad?'

'What?' Franks said.

'Where's Mum?'

'She's at the bach.'

'What's she doing there?'

'I'll explain later.'

'Okay,' Ally said, watching him rush towards the Commodore.

'So what do you think about the game?' Jeff asked.

'I think Mr Polgar is a genius.'

'Actually, he's a she. It's not Jude, it's Judit.'

Ally liked that – a lot – but she already had a bigger endgame in mind as she saw her father pull away, at speed.

Chapter 62

Tracy drove out of Auckland, rearing to put her foot flat on the accelerator, but that would attract undue attention. It was a gloriously sunny day, at last, and she took a deep breath, working out what she would do with her half of the two million dollars. Buy shares in another gym probably, but first of all take a long, exotic holiday. Solo. She was sick of Morris and all his unspoken, undealt-with issues. Men were nothing but big babies. She was convinced of that.

Halfway between the national highway and the Coromandel, she was thinking nothing could go wrong with this deal. Nothing she could think of anyway – as long as Morris stuck to his side of the bargain, though she had a contingency plan for that too. She trusted him as far as she could throw him.

There was, however, something up ahead, after the bend in the road. The last thing she would have expected. Another one of life's little obstacles. A police roadblock. In the middle of the bloody Hauraki Plain! For a moment she thought they might be looking for her, but why would they? She hadn't done anything wrong, so it wasn't too big a problem. Still, it was a nuisance, a waste of time. She slowed down to a crawl behind two cars, wondering why the cops had a chopper on standby. Was someone on the run? That sort of thing only happened in the cities and towns, and then usually at night. Teenagers bored and high out of their brackets, trying to out-race the cops. Losers. Usually ending up dead, if not badly hurt, while their passengers – or some innocent bystanders – were often killed.

Chapter 63

Inside the bach, Morris's phone rang and he once again went outside.

'I've got the money,' Franks said.

'Good. Where are you?'

'I'm in town. Where are you?'

'Bring the money to your bach.'

'Right.'

'And if you bring anyone else along, or you let anyone else know, Ngaio is dead.'

'Are you sure you still want to go ahead with this?'

Morris didn't bother to answer; he just rang off.

Franks had gone to HQ for the first time since his dishonourable discharge. Smith was waiting for him in the basement, as arranged, with a bag of cash. Two million dollars. Money for police contingencies, but not ransoms. The police didn't do ransoms. Franks signed an IOU and a form that said the Bar None would serve as collateral if the money disappeared. He thanked Smith, who told him to be careful, and left.

Chapter 64

The young Japanese-Kiwi cop approached Tracy wearing a bulletproof vest, greeted her sunnily, then asked for her licence.

'Sure,' she said, reaching into her glove compartment, where her unnumbered Glock lay hidden. That smelly little man who informed for Morris had given it to her.

'There you go,' she said

He took the licence and headed towards his marked Škoda, got in and punched her details into a machine.

'Come on, you little arsehole,' she thought, drumming her fingers on the steering wheel.

Cars were lining up behind her. She didn't know why she was starting to feel a sense of dread, but she was. Maybe she had to prepare for some other contingency. She unbuttoned the top two buttons of her shirt. Cleavage: it was a failsafe technique.

Chapter 65

Morris didn't know what to do with himself so he tried to read the news on his phone, but he was too distracted to care about yet another terror attack, this time in Spain. When he glanced up, he saw Ngaio was still looking at him.

'What are we waiting for?' she asked.

'Nothing.'

'Come on, Morrie. How long have we known other?'

Silence.

'If you hit me like this it can only mean one thing: money. You want John's money. Or I've read you wrong for over twenty years.'

Morris looked out the window, wishing Tracy would arrive.

'Why?'

He said nothing.

'Morrie, it's not John's fault that Rawiri was killed. Nor is it yours, or Pat's. It just happened and it's terrible and we were there for you. It's just …'

Morris gave her a look.

'… for some reason you pushed us away.'

He lit a cigarette.

'Did you resent us because our child was alive and yours was dead?'

Morris inhaled deeply.

'Or does it go back even further than that? Are you still angry that I chose John over you, all those years ago?'

Morris let out a cloud of smoke.

'And now? Are you going to throw everything away for thirty pieces of silver?

'Two million dollars.'

'Do you think it's going to bring Rawiri back? Do you think it's going to make you feel any better? Or Pat? Do you not think she's hurting too? For crying out aloud, Morrie. She's his *mother.* She carried him for nine months, loved him for seventeen years. Still loves him. And you? What are you doing?'

'Why don't you just shut up?' Morris said.

'No, I'm not going to shut up. If you've gone this far for money, it means you're prepared to go all the way. You're going to kill us.'

Morris put out his cigarette, crushed it.

'And then what?' Ngaio continued. 'Do you think you're going to be happy? Are you going to destroy the good times we used to have here? Look at all these photographs, Morrie. Do they mean nothing to you? Do you not remember you were Ally's favourite uncle? Are you going to kill her as well, because if you kill us then you're going to have to kill her too. You know she'll work it out, much as she used to love you. You know she's smart.'

'Yes, and alive. Rawiri is dead.'

'It's nobody's fault, Morrie. Why don't you just face up to it, grieve for however long it takes, like a man, and move on? We're here for you. You know there's help out here. You have your *whanau,* your *whakapapa.'*

'Fuck that.'

'So now you're doing a Michael Jackson on us too.'

'Hey, I'm no paedophile.'

'That's not what I meant.'

Morris lit another cigarette.

'I meant you've gone all white on us,' Ngaio said. 'Selfish, thinking only about yourself.'

'I'd rather not be a goody two-shoes like your blue-eyed ex, thank you.'

'You're the one with blue eyes.'

'You know what I mean,' he glowered.

'He's not a goody-two-shoes. He's a prick. And I didn't marry him because he was white, by the way. I married him because I love him. Because he's a good father. And he's not a thief, nor is he a killer.'

'So why did you go and fuck someone else?'

'Because I made a mistake. Now I'm paying the price. There are always consequences, Morrie. The bigger the mistake, the bigger the consequences. You, as a cop, should know that.'

'Maybe you should keep quiet now.'

'Wait a bit. There must be someone else. Is it a woman, Morrie? A gold digger perhaps?'

'I really think you should shut the fuck up.'

'So you're punishing Pat too. What did she do to deserve this? Why are you blaming everybody, even though no one is to blame except yourself?'

Morris got up suddenly, knocking the chair over. Ngaio thought he was going to hit her again, but he walked out of the room.

Chapter 66

The cop boy finally came walking towards Tracy in his blue uniform, tats snaking out from under his short-sleeved shirt, and gave her the driver's licence.

'Thank you,' she said.

'That's alright,' he replied, then looked at her car registration.

Tracy wished he would just disappear.

'Uh-oh,' he said, 'your licence has expired.'

'Look,' she said, showing him plenty of cleavage, 'is there any way we could speed this thing up? Maybe a drink later on?'

'That'll be sweet as,' he said. 'But I'm going to have to fine you two-hundred dollars for being unlicensed.'

'Alright,' she said, suppressing an impatient scream.

'I'm just going to punch it into the machine. Then you can go.'

Whatever, she thought.

Chapter 67

Franks had left the city and itched to put his foot flat, but that wouldn't do. The last thing he needed right now was to explain anything to a copper. So he stuck to the speed limit, stomach churning, took the Coromandel turn-off and carried on until he saw a roadblock up ahead.

For some reason it turned out to be quite a painless event and, once the roadblock with its standby chopper was no longer visible in his rear view, he put his foot flat, heading for the short cut to Black Rock.

Chapter 68

Morris couldn't bear Ngaio's silence any more, so he called Franks as he heard a car approach in the distance, but Franks wasn't answering. It couldn't be him yet, so it had to be Tracy. He headed for the door and Ngaio said: 'Morrie, be careful.'

'You're telling me to be careful when you think I'm going to kill you?'

'Yeah, I am. Because you're still my friend, and I still love and care for you.'

Morris shook his head before going out onto the deck, hearing the car stop. Tracy got out and walked towards him.

'What took you so long?'

'Fucking roadblock.'

'Right.'

'Don't you believe me?'

Morris shrugged.

'So has he got the money?' she asked.

'Yeah, he's on his way.'

'And the wife?'

'She's in there.'

'Alive?'

'Yeah. I left her for you.'

'Why me?'

'I thought you'd do anything for money?'

'True,' she said, producing the Glock, and shot him in the chest, watching the reaction on his face with some pleasure.

Morris stumbled backwards, fell on his back, tried to get back up, stunned, and said, 'What?'

Tracy shot him in the head and he didn't ask any more questions. Now she just had to get rid of the ex-wife, then wait for Franks, kill him as well, and the money was hers. All of it. She would drag them all to the rock and throw them over. It'd take weeks before anyone found them, if ever, and more weeks to work out what exactly had happened. But there was just one little problem. As she walked towards the bach, she saw Franks standing there, pistol ready. There was no time to get back into the car and flee, no point in trying to lie about what had happened to Morris, so she took a pot shot at Franks, missed, turned, and ran towards Black Rock, taking the jagged, coastal route. She could out-parkour anybody.

Franks had dived away by the time her arm was halfway up, ready to shoot, but by then she was rushing towards the rocks.

'Ngaio, are you alright?' he shouted into the bach.

'Yes, I'm fine. What's happening out there?'

'Just hang in here,' Franks said and ran after Tracy, who carried on towards the rock, then suddenly stopped and turned. He ducked when he saw her taking aim. Nine shots, he counted. Then she turned and ran again. She was clearly fitter than him, but he knew the terrain better than she did. If she made it to the top of the rock, there was only way down again and that was towards him. Or you dived. He could admire her athleticism in a way, but that wasn't going to stop him killing her. If you want to play the death game, don't expect privileges.

The eleventh shot grazed his left shoulder. It took a few seconds to register. Blood. Then pain. He took a handful of sea water from a pool and splashed it on the wound. It burnt like hell as he watched her head into the cave. It wasn't much of a cave, but it had been a great love nest for him and Ngaio at low tide in the past. But now the tide was coming in and Tracy could be waiting for him. She still had at least six rounds left, unless she had an extra magazine – and the time and skill to reload while running.

He still had plenty of rounds left so he stormed the cave and let fly with five rounds for cover. But she was gone.

He moved on, knowing she could be lying in ambush anywhere beyond the cave. It would be a matter of inching his way up the path towards the rock, until he could get a visual again – or a bullet. She appeared ten metres to his left and fired, but by then he was already rolling, diving, counting. Six shots. That was seventeen rounds. He knew she was using a Glock 17, like his, a standard service pistol she'd probably acquired via Rat, like him. If she didn't have extra bullets she was in trouble. But you couldn't assume anything. She might have an extra pistol or revolver. So it was going to be a matter of moving painstakingly up, from one bit of cover to the next. By then she was on a clear stretch of path close to the top and he shouted 'Hey!' She turned, but didn't shoot, then carried on running towards the rock. If she had an extra magazine, she hadn't had time to reload it or grab the extra gun – if she had one. The wound hurt, and he was losing blood. He would have to rely on reserves, muscle memory. He was close to out of breath. By now she'd be on that flat area, realising that the only way down was back the way she'd come – or diving.

Franks stepped onto the level ground. Tracy was waiting for him, pointing the black pistol at him.

'You don't have any bullets left.'

'Are you sure about that?'

'Yes,' he said, still not sure, but she hadn't shot yet, and she was clearly the kind of person who shot first, then asked questions. Also, there'd been the slightest hint of uncertainty in her eyes. Still not enough for him to be sure.

'You wouldn't shoot a woman again,' she said.

'Are you sure about that, Tracy?'

'Yes, I am.'

Franks pointed the pistol at her heart, thinking *this is for Jiaping*, even though he was hearing Smith say, *'No matter how much they disgust you, you tie them up and hand them in; that's your job.'* He started squeezing the trigger slowly, seeing Jiaping's fading eyes. Next thing his pistol was flying and fell to the ground, his hand stunned. At first he thought it was Tracy, that she'd somehow shot him in the hand instead of the heart or head, that he should dive, roll, but it wasn't her.

Smith.

'Hello, John,' the chief said, slightly out of breath.

'What are you doing here? Why did you …?'

'That's my boy. Always asking questions. In fact, that's why I pulled you out of uniform, because you always wanted answers. Insisted on them. A good cop,' Smith concluded.

'What the fuck's going on?' Franks said, seeing Smith's pool car down at the bach. 'Why'd you do that?'

'Do you know I was the top marksman in my class? No you didn't, because I never told you. I was tops at close and long-distance. Good to see the old eye is still in.'

'You haven't answered my question,' Franks said, seeing Tracy compute her chances of making a dash for his pistol.

'Well, let's look at it calmly. You've got two million dollars in your car boot and you've got two people who have blackmailed you into giving it to them. Very nasty. One of them is dead already, the other is here.'

'We could make a deal,' Tracy said interrupted.

'Yes, we could,' Smith said. 'I kill John and you and I split the money – in exchange for a couple of sexual favours, of course. I mean, the missus has gone all dry and demented on me. Do we have a deal?'

'Yes.'

'Good. Now where should I shoot John? Head, heart or groin?'

'Shoot him in the crotch,' Tracy said. 'Let him bleed to death, slowly.'

Smith cringed and said, 'Ouch, John. You really should be more selective about the company you keep.'

'Clearly,' Franks said, forcing himself to ignore his aching shoulder, his stunned hand, working his way round to the edge of the cliff.

Smith laughed and pointed the gun at his heart.

'Why?' he said.

'Because I'm bored. The wife, the looming pension, no children or grandkids I have to pretend to like. Why not do something outrageous and go and live in, say, Thailand? Get myself a nice, servile masseuse, as opposed to ending up in a luxury retirement home playing bridge, eating mashed bananas, and trying to ignore the faint smell of poo.'

'"Corruption in the mildest of places,"' Franks muttered, remembering Rat's words. He should have heeded that too.

'What was that?' Smith asked.

'Nothing.'

'Kill him,' Tracy said.

'Okay,' Smith said, aimed at Franks' crotch, then swivelled and shot Tracy square in the heart. Twice.

Franks was almost as shocked as if he'd been shot himself.

'What an unpleasant woman,' Smith concluded. 'Who was she? Another one of Morris's flings?'

'Yeah,' Franks said, close to the edge of the cliff, with the gulls screeching, the waves crashing down below.

'Well, at least he was right about one thing,' Smith said.

'What was that, Chief?'

Keep them talking.

'Jiaping *was* from internal affairs. She was investigating us, especially him with his fancy house and clothes. But then, that's about the only thing he got right.'

'How did you know where the bach was? I never told you.'

'I used to visit your father here.'

'You never told me that.'

'How many times did I tell you we work on a need-to-know basis, John?'

'Okay, but he was a criminal.'

'True, but I liked him. Learnt a couple of tricks from him, in fact.'

'And what happens after you've killed me?' Franks said, glimpsing two figures running towards the bach. Ally. Jeff.

'Well, I report the matter and everybody sees that Morris and this bitch tried to kill you, but that you got killed too. Very unfortunate, not to mention messy. But if it's any consolation, I'll get you an honourable mention.'

'And the money?'

Keep them busy; let them talk.

'Oh, I'll put it back into the police account like the good public servant I am.'

'I don't understand.'

Smith smiled.

'Do you really think I took Li to the police station, John? I mean, I could have, but he offered me two million dollars of his own. Cash. Untraceable money. So there you have it.'

'I used to look up to you.'

'Well, let that be your last lesson on this planet. You have to look up to yourself, John. I thought you would have read all that Know Your Inner Self-shit they peddle these days.'

John was right on the edge now, the churning sea below, keeping his eyes off the bach, almost feeling more than seeing Ally run towards the shed, lest Smith follow his gaze. It was the only option open to him. He had to trust it would work, otherwise Ngaio would be dead too. There was nothing else. Not even the police. He'd told the skeptical cops at the roadblock that they needed to send the chopper here, that there was going to be a shootout, but they hadn't ... wait a bit. Just behind Smith's ear Franks could see a speck in the sky.

'Goodbye, mate,' Smith said.

'How are you going to explain shooting me to those people in the chopper?'

'Oh come on John, you don't think I'm going to fall for that old trick, do you?'

'Can't you hear it, Alistair?'

'No.'

'That's because the wind is blowing in the wrong direction. Or maybe you're starting to go a little deaf. But they've got binocs up there. They're watching you. Us. How are you going to explain an assassination-type shooting up here?'

'Do you think I got to where I am by being honest?'

'I thought so, yes.'

'You've always had a touch of naivety about you, John.'

'Still can't hear it?' Franks asked, knowing that Ally was in the shed and out of sight for now.

Smith paused, thinking he might well have heard something, and couldn't help glancing back.

It was the only chance Franks had, his feet planted on either side of a mark he'd made a long time ago, when he'd been younger and fitter, so he dived out backwards, as far as he could, spreading his arms, twisting, down towards the small pool, surrounded by gnashing rocks and roaring white foam. He hit the water, not quite straight, but he was okay, apart from the shoulder.

Smith looked back and couldn't believe Franks was gone. He looked over the edge but couldn't see anything. Looked harder. Ah. There was a streak of red in the pool down below. This was bad. If Franks got away, he'd know too much. He *had* to die. But then maybe he'd killed himself. It didn't look like the kind of jump you'd survive.

Franks was bursting for breath, but had to stay down for as long as possible. Count to ten and think of nothing. Then count to another ten.

Think of nothing.

Repeat.

Smith waited, watched, mesmerised by the roiling water. The chopper was still behind him, so if Franks surfaced he could kill him and they wouldn't really see anything. He'd say he was mourning the best cop he'd ever worked with. Something like that. And then he saw Franks bursting out for breath before going down again. Smith waited. How long could he stay under? Sure, there were those freaks who could do it for minutes, but he didn't think Franks was one of those. Smith had been the top marksman at college, and he'd dutifully gone to refresher courses over the years. Kept the old eye in. If Franks came up again, he was dead. Then he saw him coming up for air again, like some fish or something. John Franks was history. Smith started squeezing the trigger, but just before it recoiled it felt as if a gull had flown into him. Or rather, through him.

How weird.

He saw Franks go down again but knew he hadn't hit him. What was going on? Then it dawned on him. He'd been shot. He turned, slowly, looking up at the sky, looking for a sniper in the chopper – but that wasn't it. It was that brat daughter of John and Ngaio's, pointing a rifle at him. The little bitch had actually shot him. In the upper chest. He raised his pistol, cursing her, taking aim, but nothing was quite working. For a moment the two of them just looked at each other, almost hypnotised by one another, before Ally hit his heart this time. Smith flopped over the edge and down towards the jagged rocks, which impaled him, broke him, just two metres away from a gasping Franks. He looked up and saw the figure of his daughter against the sky, waved with his good arm. Ally waved back with her free hand.

The chopper hovered overhead, saw Franks and, careful in the whipping wind, started lowering a winch for him.

Back at the bach, Jeff had found the key for the cuffs on the dead Morris and released a very worried Ngaio. She wanted to know where Ally was, rubbing her wrist, and he told her it looked like she'd shot a man who was threatening her husband, who had dived out over the water.

'Those two!' Ngaio said, then saw the corpse. She instinctively went to Morris, wiped a lock of hair out of his bloodied face, keening as she did so. Jeff stood around awkwardly, then said he'd go and see if John and Ally were okay.

The chopper lowered Franks to his daughter like a wet, wounded angel. When he felt the grass, stone and lichen of Black Rock, he took a few shaky steps and put his arms around Ally, who burst into raw sobs.

Chapter 69

At Auckland International Airport, Mr Li heard the announcement that he and his fellow passengers should prepare to have their tickets processed for flight 382, bound for Vancouver. He would have some explaining to do to his superiors about the two-million dollars he'd given Smith so that he could get out of the country. But he had a more pressing problem right now. There were two cops walking among the passengers in the adjacent queue for the next flight to Beijing, which is exactly why he wasn't in it, nor was he here under his own name. The pair were a relatively young man and woman in blue uniforms and they were looking for a certain face. His. Further back, he could see a senior officer keeping an eye on them. Mr Li, who could be one of many Asian businessman, dialled a number. He spoke briefly to someone and then rang off again. It could easily have looked like he was giving a last-minute instruction to a secretary, all in a calm and contained way.

There was an announcement, repeated in Mandarin, that a Mr J Li should please go to the information counter.

The two cops had finished checking the Beijing queue and were now heading towards the long Vancouver one. Mr Li showed nothing and waited. He was five people from the front. The announcement was made again and the two cops, a lean Māori and a tall Pakeha woman, walked past everyone, slowly, greeting them as they did so. Nothing hurried. Mr Li was relying on the fact that many New Zealanders thought all Asians look the same. There was no point in getting excited, so he waited. The woman came to him and greeted him. He gave her a small nod in return and she moved on. When she got to the end of the queue, she looked at her colleague and shook her head. Mr Li was not fooled. The man joined her and, watching their reflection in one of the large lookout windows, he saw her talking into her shoulder radio. They were halfway to their senior officer when they turned around and began walking back towards him. He was one shy of the front of the queue. There would be no running, no Jason Bourne action. They would talk to him in a friendly manner and he would accompany them to a small room close by, where they would ask him questions, talk, telling him he had a right to call his lawyer. Here they came now. Mr Li showed nothing, since it would achieve nothing. They were about to start talking to him when the big man got a call on his earpiece. He didn't like what he heard. Mr Li could see the frustration in their eyes. They started walking back towards the senior officer, who looked like he'd eaten something very unpleasant. Mr Li handed his flight ticket to the attendant and gave her the slightest of smiles when she thanked him for his passport, which she returned to Mr Wang. Then he walked down the long passage to board flight 382 to Vancouver.

Chapter 70

Ngaio was holding a bitterly weeping Pat's hand on the third day of the *tangi* for Morris, while Ally sat on the other side of Pat in the marae with her hair back to jet black. People were recalling stories of a man she barely recognised. She was slowly realising that sometimes people get blown off course and can't get back on. A week ago she would have said that was just their lack of spine, but now she wasn't so sure. If Uncle Morrie had in fact been kind to her while Rawiri was still alive, that had all changed when his son overdosed. Maybe that's what grief did to you sometimes. It just knocked all the stuffing out of you. Now she could feel her own tears welling up for an older boy who used to tease her on the beach at Black Rock, then for his father, and she took Aunty Pat's other hand and started crying too. Soon she's have to go and see a shrink about her alleged Post Traumatic Stress Disorder again.

Chapter 71

Two weeks later, Franks heard Jake playing 'Phobos and Deimos' again. It was a great piece of music, but Jake's mother said they had to go. So did Franks. He left his flat and saw Jake and his mother come out of theirs next door. She was on the phone and looked a bit stressed. Jake was in a wheelchair, wearing earphones, and smiled when he saw Franks. He put out his functional hand and Franks gave it a comradely slap. Then he drove to Howick, the music still playing in his mind.

He stopped outside a house that wasn't very fancy or expensive. There were two people in its spring garden. A middle-aged Chinese couple. Franks got out of his car and walked to their gate, expecting the worst. They looked at him warily and he asked whether it would be possible to talk to them about their daughter, Jiaping. Mr Wu looked bitter and his wife was close to tears, but they said yes, and invited him into their house.

They sat in the neat living room and Franks told them what had happened, all the while feeling the weight of a portrait of Jiaping on the wall, smiling that haunting smile of hers. Franks said he had a cheque for six million dollars that was rightfully theirs. The sale of the house in Mt Eden hadn't gone through and someone had bought Bar None for a profit that added it back up to the original amount Jiaping had won. Mrs Wu quietly wiped away her tears and said she was going to make some tea.

Mr Wu just looked at the cheque until his wife came back in with tea and cake. Then he got up and left the room without any explanation. Franks couldn't help thinking he might be going to get a gun. As someone who had a daughter himself, he wouldn't blame the man for doing something like that.

Mrs Wu poured the tea and they rather awkwardly spoke about her other children, and how he'd left the force after Jiaping's death. What was he doing now? she asked. He'd returned to the force, he said, feeling he owed it to so many people, including Jiaping. He didn't mention that he had a daughter too.

Mrs Wu nodded, close to tears again. Mr Wu came into the living room with an envelope, which he gave to Franks.

'Thank you,' Franks said, though he didn't know what he was thanking him for.

'My daughter like you. Very much.'

'And I liked her too, Mr Wu. Very much.'

Mrs Wu didn't trust herself to say anything.

Franks did not look what was inside the envelope until he was well away from their home. He pulled to the side of the road and opened it. Inside was a cash cheque for a million dollars. He smiled and knew exactly what to do with the cheque and drove to a creche, whose sign today said:

SO WHAT ZEN

He could see Alan standing in the middle of a play area, surrounded by children, children who clearly worshipped him, who were making a happy racket like any other children. Franks got out of the car and walked towards the letterbox. Alan saw him and smiled. Franks returned the smile and put the envelope in the box. Then he got back into the car and drove to Mt Eden to pick up Ally, who was waiting for him outside the home and consulting room of Emma Case, psychologist.

'Hi Dad,' she said sibilantly.

'Hi, Angel.'

'How goes it?'

'Not bad, thanks. And you?'

'Oh, you know,' she said, back in her blasé-actress mode.

'No, I don't, actually.'

'That woman keeps asking me how I feel about shooting that man.'

'So?'

'I say I didn't shoot him, I killed him.'

'And how *do* you feel about that?'

'He was threatening my main source of income, such as it is, and no one messes with my main source of income, buster.'

'Hey, it's a bit more serious than that,' her father said, aware of her recent nightmares.

'I mean, what with paying off these bloody braces and all.'

'Uh-huh.'

Ally was quiet for a while before she said, 'Dad?'

'Yes?'

'Tell me how you knew Mum was at the bach again.'

'Come on, Ally. I must have told you at least a hundred times.'

'Ninety-nine. Let's make it a full house.'

'Are you getting into poker now too?'

'No. And please don't change the subject.'

'Okay. Your mother and I had an agreement that if we ever got into a situation like that, we'd talk in opposites. So when she said no, she wasn't at the beach, it meant yes, she was there.'

'Brilliant,' Ally smiled. 'It's like a well-concealed chess move.'

'How's *that* going?'

'I forgot to tell you I have a new heroine with all this how-do-you-feel stuff.'

'And who's that?'

'Her name is Judit Polgar. The best woman chess player ever.'

'Cool.'

'What's that supposed to mean? Good, bad, indifferent?'

'It means good,' he replied, accepting his own medicine with a smile. 'But what about Hou Yifan, Ju Wenjun, Humpy Koneru, Alexandra Kosteniuk, Anna Muzychuk?'

'How do you know about them?'

'I'm an investigative officer, remember?'

Ally resorted to her damaged-actress mode: 'My memory has been distorted. I cannot talk about it. It's too … close. Too painful. No one understands.'

'Of course they don't,' he said wryly.

'But you know,' she said, back in Ally mode, 'chess teaches you so many things.'

'Like?'

'Well, I've discovered something really important about myself.'

'And what is that?'

'I … no.'

'Hey, you can't do that to me.'

'No,' Ally said, 'it's going to sound too self-important.'

'What? Do you want to tell me you're a very good chess player?'

'No, I want to tell you …'

'Yes …?'

'Well, I've discovered there's something else I like …'

'Yes?'

There was a long, embarrassed pause.

'I really like talking.'

Franks guffawed and Ally frowned.

'What's so funny about that? You're always doing that to me! Stop it!'

'Sorry, sweetheart. But it *is* funny.'

Ally clicked her tongue and then got a puzzled look on her face as they stopped outside Ngaio's house.

'Hey,' she said. 'Why are you bringing me home? I thought you were taking me and Jeff out for a meal?'

'Jeff and me.'

'Whatever.'

He gave her his usual false smile and she returned the favour, and so they re-started their game of seeing who could pull the ugliest face. Then he said, 'Back in a sec.'

'Lies,' she said, back in tragic-actress mode. 'Endless lies. How many more lies must I endure in my life?'

He walked round the side of the weatherboard bungalow he and Ngaio had bought a lifetime ago.

Ally sighed world-wearily and dialled Jeff's number.

It was a Saturday and Franks knew where Ngaio would be: in her beloved garden, her sanctuary. And so she was, sitting on the grass next to a flowerbed she was weeding.

'Hi,' he said.

'John, I was just ...'

'Wondering how our meal was going?'

'No,' Ngaio smiled.

'Listen, would you maybe like to join us?'

'That would be nice, but look at me. I'm filthy.'

'Well, as far as I'm concerned you can either come as you are – or you can take a quick shower.'

'I think I'll have a quick shower,' she said, getting up.

'Okay.'

'Maybe you should let Ally know.'

I'm sure she can keep herself busy,' he replied.

Okay,' she said.

Ally *was* worrying as she spoke to Jeff. What the hell were those two doing? Having another spat, as they used to?

'It looks like we're in for a bit of a wait,' she said. 'So let's try to play a game blind.'

'Okay,' Jeff said, 'you go.'

'Alright. If Judit can play e4, then so can I.'

'Knight to c6,' Jeff said.

'Oh, you're trying the Nimzowitsch, are you?'

'Very good,' Jeff said.

It took Ngaio half an hour to shower and put on a blue Hawaiian shirt, a black skirt and a pair of brown jandals, her thick black hair brushed back. Then she put a red frangipani blossom behind her left ear, looking and smelling like the Pacific beauty she was.

Back in the car Ally was winning for a change – she was getting quite good at this game – before her eyes widened with horror as she saw her parents emerge from the front door and approach the car.

'Oh. My. God.'

'What?' Jeff asked.

'My mother's coming too.'

'What's so bad about that?'

'Nothing, but she's wearing that top just to spite me.'

'Why? What so special about her top?'

'Everything. She knows I hate it.'

'I think you should just be grateful she's coming.'

'Now *you're* starting to sound parental. I've got to go. See you soon.'

'Okay.'

Franks and Ngaio got into the car and her fragrant mother said, 'Hi sweetheart.'

'Hello,' Ally said in as flat an actress tone she could muster.

'Are you okay?'

'Don't you think your mother looks beautiful?' Franks said, putting his hand on Ngaio's shoulder.

'*No*,' Ally said. 'You know I hate that top, Mum.'

'I think she looks absolutely exquisite,' Franks said, gently pulling Ngaio towards him and kissing her on her lips.

'I don't *believe* this!' Ally exclaimed.

'But it's so nice, darling' Ngaio said, nuzzling her ex-husband.

'Listen here, you two, we've got a dinner date with Jeff! Can you please start behaving like adults and let's go?'

'You're right,' Franks said, pulling away from Ngaio and starting the car, while Ngaio gave her daughter a dreamy look.

'Thank you,' Ally said in a sullen-actress mode and put on her earphones, wondering what would be playing on her smartphone. Life was so, like, random, she thought. As it happened, it was a very retro song. It had to be, because even her parents liked it. It was a song by Lorde and they would never be – or want to be – royals.

'Roy-als!'

Your

Eye-D

Please

'Agentic commerce refers to a new model of online shopping where AI-powered agents act autonomously on behalf of consumers to make purchases. These agents handle tasks like browsing, selecting, and purchasing products, often with minimal or no user intervention. It represents a shift from traditional e-commerce where users actively search and select items to a more automated and personalized experience driven by AI.'

AI Overview

Chapter One

Peta felt more anxious about the walkway than usual, heading towards it as she spoke to a friend on her mobile. She crossed that elevated passage at least twice a day, but she never felt quite at ease on it. It was six storeys up and connected the two halves of Joy Inc, a virtual-reality company that specialised in Games and Holidays. She was always acutely aware of the fact that between the walkway and the parking lot down below there was nothing but air, the same feeling she had when flying. The steel and glass walkway always made her feel slightly queasy, her feet slightly crampy, so she always stuck to the middle of it, acting as if everything was fine, but secretly feeling uneasy. Today she felt more than just uneasy as she headed towards the enclosed passage that connected the white, ultra-modern structure of Games to the dark old heritage building of Holidays. She could see it up ahead and of course it looked perfectly safe, except that it didn't *feel* safe. It also didn't help that there was a bit of a hiss on the phone, but then her friend and ex-colleague was calling from the South Island. Maybe it was that, or some weather event, even though it felt more like something heavy and metallic was resting on her shoulder blades, listening, ready to snap her back.

'So how're things?' Kylie wanted to know, sounding upbeat and breezy.

'Okay thanks,' Peta said, stepping onto the walkway, which was about twenty-five metres long. She was feeling everything but okay.

'And John? How is he?'

'Oh, he's alright,' Peta said. 'I've just had coffee with him over at Games.'

'Does he still drink so much of the stuff?'

'Yeah.'

'When are you guys going to come visit?' Kylie asked with that slightly brittle voice of hers. 'It's so cold and boring down here.'

'Soon,' Peta said guiltily, hearing another sound now. It was a deeper, more distant kind of sound, a rumble, but that could be the traffic, an aircraft, a bomb, her imagination, anything.

'You always say that,' Kylie said, sounding slightly whiny.

'I mean it.'

'What's that sound?'

'Oh, it's just the wind,' Peta said, meaning the wind that whistled and moaned around the walkway whenever a breeze or cyclone sprang up and swept into Auckland from the Pacific. But then this sound didn't have that mournful quality about it. It was deeper, more menacing, somehow.

'The wind?' Kylie asked.

'Yeah.'

'Where are you?

'In my least-favourite place,' Peta replied.

'Oh, the walkway?'

'Yeah.'

'Serves you right,' Kylie replied jokily, but sounding a little nasty, slightly distorted.

By now Peta was a third of the way across the walkway, which was shaking slightly. It did that when there was a wind, but that rumbling sound was getting louder, closer.

'So how are things at Joy Inc, "the company *everybody* wants to work for"? Kylie asked sarcastically, quoting the tagline Peta had come up with. 'Is Mr Perfect still there?'

'You mean McCracken?' Peta asked.

'Yes, MK. Old dickhead himself,' Kylie said bitterly. This was not only because McCracken had fired her, Peta thought, but also because he'd once rejected her advances.

'Yeah, he's still here.'

The rumble was now a marching sound, getting ever closer. And the walkway was shaking more than ever.

'Are you still there?' Kylie asked, her voice shrill and electronically mashed as the walkway shook a little more.

'Yeah.'

'Please kill him for me,' Kylie said, sounding metallic.

'I've got to go.'

Peta rang off and walked faster, but not enough to look panicky. To whom? she thought. There was no one else about to see her looking panicky. The sound had become almost unbearably loud, and suddenly the walkway shook so violently that she stumbled and there was no more time to walk or worry about what others might think. Nor was there a doorway or table to hide under. The sound behind her had become a roar. She looked back and saw the passage tearing away from Games. She had no choice but to run in the direction she was walking, the long way over nothing. But, because of the backward-forwards motion of the glass passage, it felt like she was running on the spot. Then the walkway shook sideways, about half a metre in both directions, the glass shattering, yet she somehow managed to stay on her feet. She could hear the sound of sirens and unseen people screaming as the anti-fire nozzles started spraying overhead. This made the shattered floor slippery and muddy. Within seconds she was soaking wet. The walkway ahead blazed as exposed electric cables ripped apart, shorted, jerked about and hissed like demented snakes. Then it started collapsing, cracking apart, so she had to run even faster, avoiding any sparks. Suddenly a huge chunk of floor fell away right in front of her, and she had to jump as far as she could. She managed to get hold of the other side, but she was losing her grip and was going to smash into the car park, six storeys down. The thought of that made her dig her nails in and she somehow managed to pull herself up, swing her leg over, roll, scramble up, run. Her chest, fingertips and shins were bleeding. All she had to do was make it to Holidays, she thought. But the walkway was about to break away from the older building and she had to leap yet again, just managing to land in Holidays' passage, tripping, falling forwards on to all fours, scraping her already bleeding hands and knees, jumping back onto her feet. But that was no relief, either. The wooden floor was starting to catch fire. She knew (from those annoying fire drills) that there was a metal fire escape at the other end of the passage. If she could get through the door there, she'd be okay to go down. She ran between low flames as the carpet erupted. The alarms and screaming voices sounded like a heavy metal and symphonic cacophony rolled into one, yet there was still no one about. All she had to do now was open that door to get to the fire escape. But it was stuck and she had to kick it once, twice, the heat burning her back and legs, before the door swung open and she could step out onto the metal platform. She caught flashes of blue sky, white clouds, a black helicopter, green fields, blue sea. But down wasn't an option: there was such an inferno roaring up towards her that she'd melt in a moment. She could only go up – or jump. So she started running up the fire escape, two, three steps at a time, feeling the flames sear her ankles. She was about to step onto the roof when the entire staircase came loose from the building, and she and a mass of hot metal started hurtling away towards the well-manicured lawn of Corporate Park. The grass wasn't going to help much, but she tried to work things so that she was on top of the red-hot metal steps and railings, to avoid being crushed. She had a chance, she thought, terrified. She might break a substantial number of bones, possibly even her back, but she had a chance. She could hear sirens, screams, the chopper, a voice on a loudhailer. Help was on its way. If she could survive this fall, she might just live. There was help. But here it came now, the earth, rushing at her, about to crush her into a bloody, mangled pulp.

Chapter Two

Peta Smith27's mobile alarm vibrated restlessly. She was drenched in sweat. It was time to get up, shower, dress, go to work. Usually, she worked from home and spoke to her boss via we-Mail or on the phone, but McCracken – or MK, as he liked to be called – wanted to discuss something personally with her today. She washed and dressed in a daze, still feeling the drag from her dream. It had felt so real, so scary.

After her allocated two-minute shower, she put on a pair of sneakers, jeans, and a sporty long-sleeved top. On to that she pinned the only tangible object she had left of her mother, a brooch, which was made of polished steel. The brooch consisted of a single word: LOVE. Peta had at first disliked it, was even embarrassed by it, thinking it was kitsch, but after her parents' death it became her most treasured possession. Her father had given it to her mother. She put on an anorak that covered the brooch, which was close to her heart, always. Then she called a taxi and left Z1-3007aprtmnt (formerly Pacific Heights).

She caught up on the day's news on her wePhone as the taxi crossed the warm waters on the new trillion-dollar bridge separating the northern and southern parts of Z1 (Z indicating the former New Zealand, and 1 its largest city, formerly Auckland). Z had shrunk even more after The Rise, its two islands becoming even smaller and further apart, but at least it wasn't like the islands of Ocean A (formerly the Pacific), some of which were now completely submerged. That was bad enough, but those people had to go somewhere, and that somewhere was often here: Z. Population: 50 million. There was plenty of space for them still, but that wasn't the point. The issue was work. People with double degrees were being laid off, let alone unqualified people from Ocean A. People over forty were being made redundant and sent to Z2 (formerly Wellington), which was still under siege from the somanieth variant of Covid-43. Thankfully, she was only twenty-three in this year of the Lord God Dollar, 2050, and at her peak, like rugby players were at this stage. Many of those sportsmen and women had to support huge, extended island families until they, too, were too old. Rugby was one of the few options open to them – others were the military, music, or drugs. When the taxi got to Peta's work, she absentmindedly replied 'Thank you' when the vehicle's automated voice said, 'Have a good day.' She was still trying to work out why it was Kylie who'd been in her dream last night.

Joy Inc was set in Corporate Park 1 (North) with neatly laid-out lawns, which had a slightly minty smell, and car parks with canopies to protect them from the cutting sun. All the cars were exactly the same and steel grey. The company's two buildings were indeed connected via the long walkway on the sixth floor, exactly as in her dream.

Her colleagues and mates – Jon, Lee and Moana – were already sitting at the First Thing with their coffees, chatting, working on their wePhones or checking the news. Peta and Moana had been friends since their first day at school and there were few things they didn't know about each other. Moana had to be called Anna, of course, since Māori names were banned by The Power, but to Peta she would always be Moana. They spent hours hanging out with each other, either talking endlessly about anything and everything, or in perfect silence. Lee had inveigled himself into their circle with his own particular brand of dry Asian wit. 'I'm an A person,' he often quipped, having originally come from A1(formerly Beijing) as a ten-year-old, even though some Ocean A people made the same joke. If

Moana had long, flowing black hair, then Lee had short straight hair the colour of carbon. Moana worked in Games as a renderer, like Jon, while Lee did the IT for both Games and Holidays, just as Peta did their writing. Jon was her – what? boyfriend? lover? partner? He had curly brown hair and blue eyes, as opposed to her straight blonde hair and pale greens. She got herself a coffee and a curly (formerly croissant) and joined them. She wanted to kiss Jon but – even though everyone knew they were an 'item' – they'd decided to keep things professional.

'Alright everybody, you can relax now,' Jon said mockingly. 'Our language-improvement advisor has arrived.'

'Very funny,' Peta grumbled.

'You look like you've been hit by a train,' Moana said.

'And a very good morning to you too.'

'Another nightmare?' Moana asked.

'I dreamt we had an earthquake.'

'Well, we only do volcanoes in these parts,' Moana said.

'Yeah, of course. Duh.'

'Hi, Peta,' Lee said gently.

'Hi Lee, how are *you*?' Peta said.

'I'm okay, thanks. Not great, but not terrible either. My body temperature is normal, my biorhythm is average, I think I might just live. And you?'

'Good, thanks. But I'd be much better if *all* my friends were a little more sympathetic?'

'How do you spell that again?' Moana teased.

'So what was *your* week like?' she said, turning to Jon.

'As good as it can get in an old-age town,' Jon shrugged.

'Are your grandparents well?'

'Yeah, they're fine. Getting old.'

'Funny how we think only the old are getting old ...'

'What I don't understand is why MK wanted you back on a Friday,' Moana said in Jon's direction.

'Yeah, why couldn't you just come back on Monday again?' Lee added.

'You know what he's like,' he said, quickly looking around to see if the object of their conversation wasn't around. 'Pure, unadulterated arsehole.'

'I'll say,' Moana said.

'But what brings you to our northern shores today?' Jon asked Peta in a gently mocking tone.

'MK wants to see me in person.'

'That could be good or bad,' Lee said.

'Well, I'd better go before I'm late,' Peta said, washing the last of her curly down with her coffee.

'Good luck,' Moana said.

'Are we still on for drinks tonight?' Peta asked as she was leaving.

'Of course,' Jon said, and the others agreed. It was a ridiculous question: they always got together for drinks after work on a Friday night, but she always asked anyway, because it was important to her. It gave her a sense of belonging.

She walked over to Holidays along a path snaking its way through the minty grass and thought about her work title, the one Jon had teased her about. It really was stupid, Peta thought. In the old days she would have said she was in communications, but language-improvement advisor sounded much more important What it also meant was that she had way too much work. She had to check, correct and rewrite the company's entire body of legal and business correspondence, as well as write copy and dialogue for Games and Holidays. Obviously she could also write code – otherwise she wouldn't have got the job – but she preferred what used to be called English. She *liked* language. For example, she found it interesting that the English traditionally distinguished between tales that are told, stories, and the levels of buildings, storeys, whereas the Americans hadn't. For them it was stories in both cases. Buildings as fiction in the former USA (now C, North). Most people, however, couldn't care less about either spelling, as long as the meaning came through. And then there were her colleagues, who didn't really need to go to Mars. In their minds, they were there already, especially the two men. But her bestie, Moana, still had both her feet on the ground, which was why Peta loved her so much.

She got to the lobby of Holidays and wanted to run up the six flights of stairs, as she usually did. 'Crazy,' Moana always said. But it was almost time for her meeting with McCracken, so she took the lift. The old building's inner walls had largely been removed to create open-plan floors with the latest hi-tech equipment available. She loved that combination of old and new, just like she loved her job, mostly. She liked writing about how, for example, Joy Inc's games were the most realistic-looking and varied, then adding some snappy dialogue when required. The only little problem as far as she was concerned was her floor manager, McCracken. MK. She had taken an instant dislike to the man. It was he who had interviewed her, given her the job, and who managed her. The problem with MK was that he was polite to a fault, and Peta found it false. McCracken never got fazed, ever, which didn't mean he didn't have a vicious streak in him. If he indulged those he liked, then he got rid of those he didn't. Politely. Peta had seen young women in tears and men shaking with shock leave the building, never to be seen again. McCracken had been polite and understanding, but they had to go. It was as simple as that.

Here he came now, as her computer lit up. He'd insisted that no one should sit at the same terminal two days in a row, even if there were days, weeks or months between those two days, the idea being that it might cause 'creative complacency'. Peta thought it was a strategy to unnerve staff, keep them unsettled, people being creatures of habit. He reminded her of a certain class executive she and Moana had hated at high school, always doing things to impress the CEO. In MK's case, he was always the first at work and the last to leave. She tried to sit as far away from him as possible, even though nothing could escape his unctuous weMails, texts, and holograms. He approached, wearing his usual McCRACKEN name badge. It had never occurred to Peta to find out what his first name was. He had the perfect looks of a magazine model, the kind of looks her friend Kylie had swooned over – until he'd told her that he didn't mix business and pleasure. Politely. Peta had never liked the way he looked, or the way he was. It was as if he relied on his sculpted appearance to convey the impression that he was perfect as a person too, even though she found him cold, even creepy. He was always immaculately shaven and, if she sometimes found Jon's two-day growth scratchy, at least he seemed more human, more fallible. She liked the fact that he had a small facial mole, a skew tooth, dreamy eyes. Nothing like that from MK. Everything about him and his clothes seemed premeditated.

'Hello, Peta. How are you?'

'Fine thanks, MK. And you?'

'Good, thanks. But you seem to have dark rings under your eyes.'

Surely I have dark rings under my eyes or I don't, Peta thought.

'Well, I'm fine,' she said. 'Cheers.'

McCracken smiled in a manner that was supposed to go as professionally friendly with a dose of sympathy thrown in, just in case Peta really was having problems. The job she was working on at present was about virtual tours to A13 (formerly Thailand).

'What does this sound like? she said. "Pleasures of a more sensual nature can be had at an extra cost of $1000. However, these are restricted to conform strictly with international law."'

'Hm,' McCraken said. 'I think *natural* is better than sensual and let's soften the blow by saying it's *a mere* $1000 extra.'

'Okay,' Peta dutifully said.

What they were talking about, of course, was that if you wanted virtual sex with an A13 man or woman, you had to pay extra, but that child and animal sex was legally out of bounds. Peta changed the words to keep the peace, even though she knew that any potential client wouldn't give a hoot about semantics, or paying an extra $1000.

'Is this what you wanted to talk to me about?' Peta asked.

'No, I'm afraid management have informed me that we won't be able to afford your services any longer, so you can close down your job.'

It took Peta a second to compute that information.

'MK, are you telling me I'm fired?'

'If you want to put it in such strong terms, yes. I'm afraid your post has become redundant.'

'So who's going to write all your copy and scripts from now on?'

'Well, we've found a young woman who's working on her PhD and is prepared to work at half your salary, so that's what's going to happen.'

'What about giving me a warning or prior notice?'

'Don't you think that's a rather old-fashioned notion, Peta?'

So now it was her turn, she thought.

'Whose decision was this?'

'Management's,' McCracken said, as if that justified everything.

'I'd like to talk to whoever made that decision.'

'I'm afraid that's out of the question.'

'Why?'

'Because I speak on behalf of management.'

'So *you* made the decision? *You* made the appointment?'

'It's my job to save the company money and make it as streamlined as possible.'

'Right ...'

'I'm really sorry.'

'You don't look very sorry,' Peta said before she could check herself.

There was a slight pause before McCracken said: 'Are you suggesting I'm a liar, Peta?'

'Not at all, MK,' she said, 'and thanks for calling me in to personally inform me.'

'I thought it was the right thing to do.' McCracken said. 'Please leave the premises within half an hour, otherwise I'll have to get someone to escort you out. Goodbye.'

And with that McCracken gave her a polite but firm nod and returned to his stand-up desk.

Chapter Three

Peta caught a taxi back to the city over the bridge and was so dazed that she ignored any messages or activity on her wePhone, staring blindly at the silver cityscape of Z1.

She sat outside the Sea Breeze harbour café where she would later meet Jon, Moana and Lee for drinks. After she'd ordered a coffee electronically, she texted Jon. *I've just been fired!* He instantly replied: *Im so sorry.* Peta: *Are we still meeting tonight?* Jon: *Shore.* Peta smiled at his spelling and wrote: *I love you.* Jon: *Xx.*

They had met via Couple, of course, and were perfectly suited. Or so she'd thought, until he later confessed he'd asked a friend to do his writing for him. That was their big difference: she worked with words, he was into pictures, which didn't mean he wasn't verbally dexterous. He was: sometimes he could be quite cutting. It was a bit of a frustration for her sometimes, his lack of nous – there'd be no Lovemails from him – but it wasn't the end of the world. Nor was his insistence on driving a noisy motorbike. (Though petrol was no longer used, The Power had kindly decreed that motorbikes could still *sound* like their forebears.) Still, they had lots of fun in other areas, like movies, food and sex. They also liked the idea of applying to live together and having a child one day.

Peta texted Moana and Lee about her new status and they both sympathised, even though it felt slightly muted, guarded. Then she checked the news out of habit. Another bomb had ripped through yet another mall in C2 North (the former New York City). Damage in the hundreds of millions. Three-hundred and fifty-two dead. Many more injured. Fire engines, ambulances, flashing lights, shattered glass, pools of blood, paramedics, shaken survivors, and a blonde news reporter looking like she'd stepped out of a fashion magazine for teens.

Peta got her long black from the conveyer belt, added a sachet of sweetener, and started looking for work on her phone's extended keyboard. There were plenty of jobs, except that there were thousands of other people applying for them too. Well, she'd better get cracking. Unfortunate word, that. It was too close to McCracken. Smooth as a snake, even though she'd never seen one of those in the flesh. Z didn't do snakes of the slithering variety, except at sea, though it did have its fair share of the two-legged variety. Anyway, she added her six months at Joy Inc to her resumé and started applying for various communications and scriptwriting jobs. But after about an hour she realised something unusual about that little ritual of insincere self-promotion: she wasn't being informed that her application had been received, as was the legal norm. Maybe there was just a hold-up, she thought. Maybe the system was being overhauled or upgraded. Sometimes technology was so clever it actually impeded efficiency, instead of enabling it. After all, it was made by humans, and no one saw the same thing in exactly the same way. She sat back and watched the world going about its business. It all looked so youthful and prosperous, yet she, Peta Smith27 – so-called to indicate the year she was born – was out of work.

As she was thinking that, an Undesirable came shuffling along and sat down against the glass wall of the Forever Young pharmacy, putting his peak cap on the pavement in front of him. The man was huge, scruffy, dirty, downcast, tattooed, possibly drunk, muttering to himself. The wall he was sitting against showed a green field advertising a new homeopathic supplement. There was also something vaguely familiar about him. A beautiful B woman (from the former Africa) and her equally beautiful blonde Z colleague walked by, talking and laughing. They were a picture of health and prosperity, and they didn't even see the Undesirable, whose one big problem was that he was clearly too old for this city. Some, however, had become so desperate that they openly flouted the law until they were arrested and taken away to be blinded, but at least fed. The man looked like he was in his late forties and Peta recognised him as an ex-rugby player from the Islands, a man who had fallen on hard times.

Soon two cops approached him and started talking down to him. The police officers were called cammies, a conflation of camouflage and extinct chameleons, since their uniforms, helmets and visors could blend in with whatever environment they found themselves in, making them virtually invisible if they stood still. (The words cop and cammy, of course, were banned and their use was punishable with a hefty fine, or deployment to Z2.) It seemed the cammies were asking the Undesirable to come with them and he seemed to be telling them he wasn't going to, his mouth showing brown, broken teeth. They looked extremely polite, just like McCracken. Peta couldn't hear the dialogue because of the Sea Breeze's music, which was set at full volume. The cammies seemed to try more reasonable talk with the Undesirable, but when that didn't work they took both his wrists to pull him up. Still he resisted. The cammies, blending in perfectly with the green field behind them, came to a decision and handcuffed the man rather cleverly. No fuss, no force, just slick and efficient. The Undesirable cursed them, kicked out and hit the one cammy on the knee. That clearly hurt, so the other officer took out his taserPhone, pointed it at the man, and pulled the trigger. The man went rigid, like a mannequin, and the two cammies dragged him away, holding him under his armpits, while his face stared at all the young people sitting out on the pavement.

The most remarkable thing about this little scene was that everybody around Peta seemed not to have seen it happen. Or if they had, they pretended that it hadn't happened at all.

She checked her screen. Still no acknowledgement of her applications. Well, it was getting towards lunchtime and she was getting hungry – all she'd had the whole morning was that single curly. She ordered a mushroom burger and fries, and washed it all down with a cold beer. After a while she thought she might as well have another, since she had joined the ranks of the 'shameful minority', the unemployed. Something would surely come up. Problem was, if she didn't get work soon, anything, even as a cleaner, she'd be deployed to virus-ridden Z2 to perform community service. Which was another way of saying she might become infected and die, just like her parents had.

The afternoon passed smoothly enough as Peta continued applying for jobs, though she had to concentrate a little harder because the second beer was making her a little fuzzy, though pleasantly so. In between she also checked the news. An entire refugee camp had 'accidentally' been wiped out in A31 (formerly Jordan). The President of C North, Peter Wong, had apologised profusely to Al.

Eventually it was time for Jon, Moana and Lee to join her, but they were late, which wasn't unusual. McCracken often kept people behind if there was some or other deadline, though they suspected he sometimes made those deadlines up out of sheer spite. After an hour Peta texted Jon: *Where are you?* Nothing. He was probably working on something he'd forgotten to tell her about. That also happened sometimes. Moana. Nothing. Lee. Zero. The bar was filling up and getting rowdy. Young people, like her, seemingly confident and secure. She ordered a double Scotch. Might as well celebrate the end of her time at Joy Inc, get drunk and 'worry about tomorrow, tomorrow,' as her mother had always said. But after about twenty minutes she called Jon, no longer caring that it was more expensive to call than text. After a few rings, his recorded voice said: *'Hi, you know what to do.'* She left a message and then checked the news again. Yet another revolution had been suppressed in A2 (the former Russia). She was very fuzzy by now and texted Jon again. *Hey, are you still coming?* The text came a few seconds later. *I cant.* Peta: *Why not?* Jon: *MK says if we see you agen well lose our job.* Peta: *What! How will he know?* Jon: *Cctv.* Peta wanted to counter that, but when she looked around she saw cameras everywhere, ostensibly to protect people. Peta: *So you're just going to listen to MK?* Jon: *I have to im sory he coud cut me off from my granperents.*

Nothing from Moana and Lee.

So that was the end of that, Peta though bitterly, as the crowd around her got louder and happier as the juices of one kind or another flowed. She downed the rest of the Scotch, paid shakily and started walking, or rather, stumbling home, the idea being that that would sober her up. This wasn't usual for her, she thought, getting drunk. Well, so what? She ignored all the texts and news items coming through on her wePhone, and when she finally got to her studio flat in what she still thought of as Pacific Heights, she collapsed on her couch.

What to do? It was still too early to sleep, even though that's what she really wanted to do. Instead, she started watching an old thriller on her phone. It featured a handsome young man, who was constantly on the run from his employers, who wanted him dead for some reason. Naturally he was more than able to look after himself and had a thousand ways of getting away from them, or beating up the agents who were out to kill him in a variety of efficient ways. But what if one were *not* as capable? Peta thought woozily. What if you were just an ordinary person and the same thing happened to you? Well, they'd soon get you and kill you and that would be the end of you, which didn't make for such a good story, did it? She was enjoying the action, noticing that her battery was almost flat, but the combination of her nightmare, the stress of losing her job and the alcohol had caught up with her. She couldn't muster the energy to charge the phone, and soon she was fast asleep, the movie playing on – until the battery ran flat.

Chapter Four

She was woken by her phone, which was vibrating so violently that it fell off the couch. Peta fuzzily picked it up and saw that its screen was black. Its battery had run out, but then why had it vibrated? Was it a final, electronic spasm? Maybe she'd just imagined it, but then a message appeared on the black screen, in clear white letters. It was from her successor:

Deer Peter, I have taken over yor job. Yor sarkastic respons to the wonderfool Mista Mukraken was unaxeptabel. U will not get wurk in this sity agane. Kidn regards, Mable

'Why don't you learn how to spell and type, bitch,' she said, feeling slightly ridiculous for berating her phone.

The message stayed there for a few seconds, as if it was absorbing her response, then it was gone and the phone was flat again, black. That didn't make sense, Peta thought, but then her whole day hadn't made sense.

She got up, still feeling terrible, charged the dead phone on her pack, and realised she was hungry. She saw on her microwave that it was only 22:05, and opened the fridge's door. Nothing but a shrivelled-up beetroot and a near-empty carton of oat milk. Her agent had failed to select and deliver her food. Or was it deliberate? Whatever. Suddenly she thought about Jon joking about how he'd like her to be his domestic goddess. Often. Too often, perhaps, she couldn't help thinking now. Maybe she wouldn't hear him making that joke again, the way things had suddenly turned out. Would that be such a bad thing? He seemed to have capitulated very quickly to McCracken. Yet Moana and Lee's silence somehow hurt more. They were supposed to be her mates.

She could hear police sirens, but that was normal Friday-night fare. People got drunk and said and did the wrong things. There were consequences. She'd had her first big taste of that, but right now she needed food. Maybe she should get some groceries, since she was on a tight budget for the foreseeable future. But the smells of the new restaurant across the road wafted into her nostrils and consciousness. Again her mother's advice about letting tomorrow take care of itself popped into her head. 'You just never know what's going to happen,' her loving mother had often said – before she'd been sent to Z2 with her equally loving husband. Or maybe I'm just too damn lazy and undisciplined to still go shopping at the nearby superette, Peta thought. But then she had all the time in the world, and somehow there was something more enjoyable about eating with others, even if they were strangers.

By now she was ratty as the cammy sirens got louder. She splashed some water over her face, turned the tap off, and brushed her teeth. While she was doing that, she thought about the Undesirable again. Was he assured of a meal in prison, and what if he had a family? Would they just starve? Would his wife have to resort to prostitution? But then she herself was starting to doubt whether she'd actually witnessed that event or merely imagined it, because no one else seemed to have seen it. Was that possible? She was absolutely sure she'd seen it, but maybe she should have recorded it on her phone. Then again, filming the cammies was a serious offence. Maybe people had trained themselves to not see things they didn't want to or couldn't do something about. Had she felt sorry for the man, or was it a little taste of what was to come for her? She *had* felt sorry for him, but one of the things her father had taught her was that feeling sorry for the downtrodden does absolutely zero for them. You either help, or you shut up and try to enjoy yourself – without guilt. Along with that, she had another disturbing feeling: she was engaging in this basic ritual as if she was not just going across the road, but away. And, just to add to that feeling, when she turned the tap on again to rinse her mouth, there was nothing. Bone dry. She spat out the last bit of toothpaste and tried the kitchen tap. Nothing. She knew the shower tap wouldn't work, since she'd used up her quota for the day. Maybe this was just temporary. That happened sometimes. She dried her face and lips on a towel, took her phone and charger, and left her apartment as the sirens came even closer.

Downstairs, she waited for an approaching cammy car, its lights flashing and siren screaming, and suppressed the irrational thought that the cammies were coming for her. But the car passed and she crossed the road to the new Plant Base, which used to be the Bloody Mary before meat was banned and its stubborn owner was bankrupted. The bar was packed with diners and revellers. There wasn't a single table or seat available. Peta knew there was a deck out back – she'd been to the Bloody Mary with Jon a few times – but the deck was chockers too. So she went back into the crowded joint and saw a single high stool being vacated. It was facing the street and that was just perfect. She liked watching the world go by, preferably with company, but being alone was fine too. Rather alone than with the meat-loving Jon, she realised. While she was studying the menu, a waitron – 'for that personal touch' – whirred up to her and asked her what she'd like.

'I'd like a vegan burger, chips and a glass of water please.'

'Okay dokey. Would you like a glass from Lake 1 at a mere hundred dollars or would you like a cheaper option?' the perpetually upbeat machine asked.

'State water will be fine, thanks.'

'We also have water from all the other lakes at more affordable prices,' the waitron said.

'State water is good, thanks.'

'Then we have a wide variety of spirits, beers and malts.'

'Excuse me, I said I want state water. Is that so difficult to understand?'

'I'll bring you the state water at a mere $15. Anything else?'

'I'd say if I did,' Peta snapped.

'Okay,' the waitron said cheerfully, and whirred away.

What was wrong with real people performing this kind of work? she wondered. Her mother had been a waitress and she'd been a kind, intelligent human being. So, too, her father. They had worked together in a restaurant, fallen in love, and started a restaurant of their own, which they'd built up to be one of the best in what was then Auckland. They'd had a son, but he died young; then Peta had come along. However, they'd made one cardinal mistake: they spoke their minds. They said they thought it was wrong that only people under forty could populate the city. By then she was a teenager. They also insisted that all the restaurant's leftover food be distributed among the Undesirables. For that they'd been 'transferred' to the then capital, Z2, where they could run another restaurant, but it meant leaving her behind in the silver city, and it meant that they died of the virus before anyone knew anything about its new, deadly strain. Her teenage self was shattered. She had to live in a hostel, first at school then at university. There had been times when she couldn't go jogging or exercise at the gym, because it would make her too hungry. Not even the job she'd had as a waitress covered her expenses. Fortunately, she'd scored a full-time job straight after uni and had worked her way up to the one she – and everybody else – always wanted at Joy Inc.

Then this morning happened.

Peta could feel someone watching her. It was a large, florid man who was drunk and trying to catch her eye. She looked away and made sure she didn't look in his direction again. She was starving, and thirsty. Just then the waitron popped up next to her with a glass of water and Peta inadvertently thanked it. 'No worries,' the robot said and wheeled away, making its way through the crowd, politely. Peta refused to assign a machine a gender, even though the waitron's voice was programmed to be female. She gulped down the water in two long slugs as she absentmindedly saw a cammy car glide to a halt on the other side of the road.

Four cops got out, and three of them – two women and a bearded man – entered Pacific Heights. The driver got out and looked around. He was clearly in charge and something made Peta go to WhatsUp@Home on her phone. Everybody had that app because crime had become a kind of plague in Z1. All the app did was connect your phone to a camera in your apartment, so that if someone did break in, it alerted you, you could see who it was, and they were filmed automatically. Prosecution followed. She'd acquired the app after her flat had been stripped of all her electronic accessories. Now she was tensely watching the front door of her studio apartment, telling herself to stop being ridiculous: there were plenty of other reasons they could be entering her building. And when was that waitron going to bring her burger and chips? Why was the noise in the restaurant irritating her?

Her front door suddenly opened and the three cammies came in, pistols out, as if they were expecting to confront a terrorist or something. They hadn't broken the door down, but they'd somehow deciphered her code. Now they were checking the tiny space that constituted her kitchen, living room and bedroom. Then her bathroom. Peta was mesmerised. This was *her* place, *her* home they were searching. After a while the trio joined up at her front door, and one of them spoke into her shoulder mic, awaiting further instruction from the officer downstairs. She listened, nodded, said something to her colleagues, and they left the apartment, closing the door behind them.

What was going on? Peta wondered. She didn't know what to do, who to call. Just then, Jon texted her: *MK tells me u had a affare with Lee.* Peta: *Do you believe him?* Jon: *He showd me the futige!* Peta: *It's fake.* Jon: *I dont know what to beleev!* Peta: *Thanks for the vote of confidence anyway.* Jon. *Im sorry im confused.* That was the end of him, she thought as the cammies emerged from Pacific Heights and conferred with their officer. Keep calm, Peta told herself. They have no idea where you are.

Just then the waitron appeared next to her with her water and burger, startling her.

'That'll only be a hundred-fifty dollars please.'

Peta could already taste the burger and chips and was so desperate to gorge herself that she automatically tapped the Eftpos with her phone.

'Thank you. Have a great evening,' the waitron said.

Peta put a crisp, salty chip in her mouth, while watching the cammy in charge receiving a phone call. It didn't last long and he spoke briefly to the other three. Then they started sauntering over to the Plant Base in that way cammies have, trying to appear as unobtrusive as possible. She knew they were coming for her, so she got up, doing her best to act normal, and headed for the back exit of the café.

She had, for reasons not quite clear to her, become a fugitive.

Chapter Five

The deck at the back of the Plant Base did not have a view of the ocean, but of a car park. Peta walked through it, approaching the corner of a building. She looked back. The cammies were just coming out onto the crowded deck. One of the women saw her and pointed at her. Peta started walking faster and they started running towards her. She turned the corner onto Z1-1781rd (formerly K'Road) and had to disappear somewhere, quickly.

The first entrance she saw belonged to a restaurant called Transformation, probably named after The Power's latest slogan. To get to it, she'd have to go down a steep flight of stairs. If that was the only way out, she could be in even more trouble. But something about it didn't shout eating place and the rest of the street was garishly bright. She'd easily be seen. Transformation was fronted by a woman with a deep voice.

'Do you have a reservation?'

'No.'

'I'm sorry. We're fully booked.'

'Please?' Peta said.

'Sorry honey,' the woman replied.

'I'm running from the cammies,' Peta said in a moment of desperation.

'Go,' the woman nodded her in. 'Mind the door behind the curtain.'

She went down the stairs, opened the curtain, then the door, and the restaurant wasn't a eating place: it was a disco-bar. The music was loud, the lights flashing, and the bar and dance floor were packed with men and other men dressed as women. Peta approached the bar, wondering what the hell she was going to do. Her worst fear materialised when the bearded cammy appeared at the bottom of the stairs. She made her way to the toilets without him seeing her.

Someone was puking in a cubicle, and a person in drag with a red wig looked at her via a mirror they were using to refresh their lipstick.

'Yes?' they said huskily.

'I'm running from the cammies.'

They lifted a heavy eyebrow and applied another layer of lipstick.

'Why?'

'I don't know.'

'Honey, you sound as confused as most straights.'

'I am. I honestly don't know why they want me. Can you help me?'

They looked at her reflection for what felt like an eternity, then put their lipstick in their purse as the person in the cubicle started snoring.

'How can I help you?'

'Can I please buy your wig from you?'

'Darling, you must be out of your little mind. But I'll tell you what. Let's get you into Chlorine's outfit before the cam-cams arrive.'

'Chlorine?'

'That beauty in the toilet. Just can't take her drink – or drugs.'

'Thank you, uh ...'

'Estelle.'

And with that Estelle opened the door and told Peta to join her. A light-skinned Islander sat slumped on the floor next to the toilet. Estelle lifted her easily, and unceremoniously sat her down on the toilet seat. Then they removed Chlorine's long black wig and gave it to Peta, telling her to put it on and get undressed. Peta did as she was told. Estelle lifted Chlorine's dress over her hips and worked it over her shoulders, all the while making sure to prop her up. Once the dress was off, Estelle told Peta to put it on and she somehow managed to squeeze herself into it in that cramped space.

'This girl's in for a surprise when she wakes up,' Estelle said, draping Peta's clothes over her. Peta took the LOVE brooch and pinned it on the dress.

'Take off her shoes and put them on,' Estelle said.

Peta removed Chlorine's stiletto shoes, stood up, and slid them on.

'One of these days she's going to wake up and realise she isn't awake, she's dead.'

'Please tell her I'm sorry.'

'No point. She won't know a thing.'

'Thank you so much.'

'Here, take this,' Estelle said, rummaging in her bag. 'You go put on some gloss while I dress this bitch. And don't forget your phone, darling. A girl needs her gadgets, if you know what I mean.'

A few minutes later Peta stepped into the glare of the club again, and with a swagger in her step she walked right past the bearded cop, who was heading towards the Ladies with a picture of an athletic woman with long blond hair in his head. But had he come here on his own? Were the other cammies still coming, or trying to locate her phone? She started dancing, evading a leering man in a suit. After a while she saw the cammy emerge from the toilets, with Estelle following closely, looking at his butt approvingly. Peta watched his reflection in various flashing mirrors and saw him finally leave.

She had evaded them, for now.

Chapter Six

Out on the street, Peta felt bad that she'd led the cammies into an illegal club that would be closed down, thanks to her. She checked the news on her phone. 'Police would like to talk to Peta Smith27, a former employee at Joy Inc,' a brassy news anchor of about seventeen said. They showed an unflattering CCTV screengrab of her, taken at Joy Inc earlier that day. 'Members of the public have been warned not to approach Ms Smith27, as she could be dangerous,' the news anchor continued.

'Dangerous'? she grimaced. Me?

Now she saw, of all people, Jon coming towards her. He was talking on his phone and looking drunk and happy in that goofy way she'd liked but now thought was sloppy and immature. 'It was the best,' he said suggestively to whoever he was talking to as he passed Peta, giving her a glazed, momentary look without recognising her.

She struggled with the stiletto heels and wondered why women wore them. Just for a little elevation? Were longer legs really that important? Madness, she thought. Then a much stronger idea presented itself. Hunger. The problem was, if she made a transaction, the cammies would instantly know where she was again. So she had to make a difficult but necessary decision. She would have to let go of her phone, her virtual companion. Without it she would be lost in so many ways, but if she hung on to it, she was going to be captured and tried for an unspecified but seemingly serious crime. She approached a good fast-food joint she and Moana had frequented, saw her face on the TV screen above the counter, and ordered a pre-packed vegan burger, chips, and blueberry smoothie. McCracken was telling viewers she'd divulged company secrets in the War Games division to Joy Inc's competitors, followed by Jon saying he'd never fully trusted her. She could see he didn't mean it, but he was saying it anyway. She paid, walked out on to the street and, once she was out of sight of the joint and its CCTV camera, sent Jon a text: *I'm going to Whangarei. Please join me there.* Then she dumped her phone and charger in a dustbin, took a quiet side street off the main drag, walked another hundred metres or so, and found a bench to sit on. Soon after, green cammy cars went screaming past her, their blue and yellow lights flashing, but all they'd find would be her phone and charger.

For now, not far away from them, she could eat her long-awaited burger and chips in peace, followed by one of the best smoothies in town. She enjoyed every morsel and had just finished when the same man who'd been eyeing her at the Plant Base came stumbling along, and stopped, looking at her as if he'd just discovered her. 'What's your price, bitch?'

'I'm not for sale.'

'You're dressed like you are.'

'Is that so?'

'Yes. Or are you a free whore?'

He clearly thought he was very funny.

'No,' she said, fantasising about putting the tip of one of Chlorine's high heels between his eyes – or even in one of them – and see how funny he was then.

He suddenly sat down next to her, legs wide apart, and said, 'You know what to do.'

'Yeah, but you don't know what can you do.'

'What's that, whore?'

'Get lost.'

'I'm going to get lost between your legs.'

'No, you're not.'

He grabbed her, catching her unawares, and she was in the tight grip of a big, smelly man.

'Don't you tell me to get lost, you hear me, bitch?'

'Let go of me!' she said, wriggling helplessly.

He shoved his smelly, bristly face into hers, trying to kiss her, and the last thing she could do was scream and draw attention to herself, so she'd have to do the one thing she didn't want to do to get her way, which was become compliant. Then a voice said, 'Is this man bothering you?' It was a female voice and the man lifted his head.

The woman facing them was about fifty and wearing a pair of old jeans and a faded black T-shirt under a patchwork coat. Her thick, strawberry-blond hair was streaked with grey, and she had a supermarket chain's shopping bag in her hand.

'Yes,' Peta replied, instantly relieved.

'Why don't you go and mind your own business?' the man said to the woman.

'You better leave now,' she said, 'before you get into real trouble.'

'What kind of trouble?' he slurred.

'The kind that's going to get you into hospital.'

'Is that so?' the man sniggered.

'Yes. Go.'

'Do you think you can take me on?'

'Yes, I do,' the woman said.

'If I get up, I'm gonna...' the man tried to find the right word, 'pulverise you.'

'Why don't you try, big boy.'

The man let go of Peta and lunged at the woman, but she hit him over the head with her bag. There was a solid sound, like an axe hitting a log, and he fell to the ground, his head bleeding.

'Jesus! What you got in there? A brick?'

'Yes,' the woman said. 'Would you like some more?'

'I'm bleeding!'

'That's the whole idea, arsehole. Now say you're sorry.'

'Never!'

'I beg your pardon?' the woman said, about to swing her bag again.

'I'm sorry! I'm really sorry! Can I buy you guys a drink, coffee, anything!'

'Piss off,' the woman said, and he scrambled away drunkenly, cursing, clutching his bleeding head.

'Hi,' the woman smiled, offering Peta a calloused hand. 'I'm Blossom. I'm from Taranaki.'

She had dirt under her cracked nails, and wrinkles she didn't try to hide, and Peta instantly felt safe with her.

'Do you need a lift home?' Blossom asked.

'No, I'll be fine thanks. But are you going to Taranaki anytime soon?'

'Yes, tomorrow. Do you need a lift?'

Peta nodded.

'Where shall I pick you up?'

'Here's fine.'

'Do you live close by?'

Peta nodded.

'Are you having boyfriend problems?'

Peta nodded, hating herself for admitting to a half-truth.

'Do you need a place to stay?'

Peta nodded, embarrassed.

'Well, if you don't mind crashing on a couch, you're welcome to sleep over at my friend's place. She's away for a day or two.'

'Are you sure?'

'Of course,' Blossom smiled.

'Thank you so much.'

'My ute's over there,' Blossom said, pointing at one of the earliest e-models, which looked like it had seen some pretty rough times. They got in and drove to a rather rickety weatherboard house. There was no one else about, but Peta didn't for one second think she was being duped by Blossom. They went into the kitchen and Blossom made some coffee while Peta couldn't stop scratching herself: Chlorine's dress was made of synthetic material that was still full of her sweat.

'Do you want to grab a shower?'

'Yes, please.'

'It looks like you need some more comfortable clothes.'

Peta didn't know what to say.

'Don't worry. There's plenty here. My friend runs an op shop, so go for it. There's always a pile of reject stuff in that room.'

Peta had introduced herself as Melissa and felt slightly guilty that she was lying to a woman who had possibly saved her life. She got into the hot shower, instantly felt better, and saw afterwards that Blossom had made up a bed on the couch. She kept her eyes down, as if that would prevent Blossom from recognising her without the wig. If Blossom did realise who she was, she didn't say anything as Peta's face appeared on a large electronic billboard across the valley, blazing over the city.

Peta finally settled for sneakers, a pair of jeans, a sweater, a jacket and a peak cap, all of which matched up. Sort of. She pinned the LOVE brooch to the sweater. Then she selected a large T-shirt to sleep in. She was exhausted and thought she would fade instantly, but she was wrong. Her conversation with McCracken kept tumbling around in her head like clothes in a washing machine. How could things escalate so quickly from her small observation that he didn't seem sorry about firing her to being accused of selling commercial secrets to Joy Inc's competitors? Why was he going on as if that would lead to World War IV or something? Why had he made a fake video showing her in bed with Lee, one of the sweetest guys she knew? Why had he turned her best friend and boyfriend against her? She could understand that Jon was concerned about his grandparents, since they were his only relatives, and that Moana and Lee had large, extended families they needed to think about, but why was

McCracken going to such lengths just because of a slip of the tongue? Was it purely to win the favour of his masters? Or was he just downright nasty, someone who liked to wield absolute power? Or was there even more to it that? Round and around her thoughts went, with the gigantic billboard flickering in her eyes, announcing that the reward for information leading to her arrest now stood at one-hundred thousand Lord God Dollars.

Chapter Seven

She must have fallen asleep because she dreamt she was being followed again, this time by Jon in one of his virtual landscapes, saying he was sorry, but carrying a knife. He was about to stab her when Blossom woke her with fruit, toast, and coffee, wearing an old floral dress that reached beneath her knees. Over that she wore a grey cardigan.

'Rise and shine,' she said. 'It's time to get out of this dump.'

'It's better than sleeping on the street,' Peta said, thinking of the Ocean A man she'd seen outside the Sea Breeze, forgetting to hide her face.

'True, but I meant this city.'

Soon they were on the road and Peta kept the peak low over her eyes so as not to be picked up by the face- and eye-recognition technology suspended above the highway.

'So, where are you going?' Blossom asked.

'The South Island,' Peta replied, knowing she could use the old terminology with Blossom, while seeing her face on an electronic billboard proclaiming:

WANTED

'Nice,' the older woman said. 'Are you going to see your family?'

'No, I'm going to visit a friend.'

'I take it you've got a pass?'

'Yes,' Peta, lied again, hating herself for doing so.

'Okay. You're welcome to hang out with us for a while.'

'Thanks. What do you do there?'

'We've got a smallholding, where we produce fresh food.'

'That sounds ideal.'

'Well, it's not. It's hard work, and people are always going to be people, unless they're robots. Fortunately we've got one reliable customer here in the city, my brother, who runs a restaurant at an upmarket golf club. But I still don't know how youse can live in the city. All that fake food, fake news...'

'What else can we do?'

'You can live like we do, and you can do it in the city too. It's just we prefer seeing the horizon rather than buildings, and we're completely off the grid. We're completely solar, we only eat food that comes straight out of the good earth...'

'Sounds like heaven.'

'It isn't, but it's better than the city life I led.'

'What did you do then?'

'I worked in an office and I was married to what I thought was a wonderful man, until the abuse started. Five long years...'

'I'm sorry.'

'Don't be. I'm just glad I'm still alive. But after that I needed a change in my life,' Blossom said as a siren gave a short blast behind them. She looked in her rear-view mirror and clicked her tongue.

'What?' Peta asked.

'Cammies,' Blossom said, showing and sounding her distaste. 'Or, as we call them in the commune: meat.'

Peta could see their red and blue lights flashing in the side mirror, but she didn't dare look around. The lights were very close to the ute's rear bumper.

'What do they want?' Peta asked a little shakily.

'Nothing. They do it just to freak me out.'

'Oh,' she said, only half relieved.

'Piss off, you offal,' Blossom said into her mirror, which freaked Peta out even more.

The cammies flashed their ultra-bright lights.

Blossom showed them her middle finger. Peta wanted to tell her to stop, but it wasn't her vehicle, and she didn't want Blossom to start asking her questions either.

'Shall I slam on the brakes and let them pay for the insurance?' Blossom asked.

'*No!*' Peta said, unable to control her tongue, once again.

'I'll have plenty of proof they were harassing me,' she said with a determined look in her face.

'Please don't.'

'Why not? They've been doing this to me for months.'

Peta couldn't think of anything to say, but at that moment the green car sounded a command that Blossom should pull over to the side of the road. She cursed, but did as she was told. Her passenger was rigid with fear.

'Listen Peta, I know who you are, I know the cammies are looking for you, so just keep cool and maybe we can get out of this.'

Peta nodded as a cammy got out and walked towards them, his hand hovering above his gunPhone. Blossom opened her window and said, 'Is there a problem, officer?'

'Yes, there is, I'm afraid.'

'What is it?'

'We have reason to believe you assaulted a man last night.'

Peta couldn't help feeling relieved for herself, while also anxious for Blossom.

'That's right. He was looking for trouble and he got it.'

'Follow us to the station, please. And please don't try to race away. We'll catch you and that'll just be an extra charge.'

They followed the cammies to a station in one of those instant new towns south of Z1 and were told to get out. Blossom said she'd come alone.

'Both of you, please.'

'Listen here, officer, my niece is clinically depressed. Just leave her out of this, okay?'

The officer gave it a couple of seconds' thought, looking at the young woman who was staring at the floor, before he said 'Alright, follow me into the station.'

Blossom gave her phone to Peta.

'This could take a while. If I'm not back by nightfall call Sun on my phone and tell him what's going on. Sun as in that thing that shines above our heads. The password is earth, all upper case'

Peta felt trapped and torn by guilt, and the worst of it was that she was surrounded by wide-open country. Later, she became hungry – in a country that had plenty, she couldn't help thinking. At about four o'clock Blossom came walking towards the ute. She looked grim. Peta saw that she had a bruised eye and split lip, and her dress was torn.

'Are you okay?'

'Yeah,' Blossom grimaced. 'I had to pay a particular kind of price, but *they* won't be fine. Sun will sort them out.'

'What do you mean?'

'One day they'll be sitting in their car, having a takeout lunch, bragging about what they did to their last prisoner or suspect, when they and their greasy food and their fat gutses will suddenly go up in a ball of righteous fire.'

Peta didn't know how to respond to that.

'I heard a news report inside that the cammies were looking for you up north. How did you manage that?'

'I texted my partner that I was going to Whangarei and then threw my phone in the dustbin, close to where we met.'

'Clever girl.'

'I'm sorry I lied to you about who I was.'

'It's the system that makes us do these things, so why don't you lay low and catch some sleep? I'm going to take that country road coming up. That should confuse the meat even more.'

'Thank you,' Peta said, sliding down in her seat.

'Do you know why they're looking for you?'

'My boss said he had to fire me and that he was sorry, so I said he didn't look sorry. That's all.'

'You broke the new Commercial Disobedience Act. They could send you to Wellington for ten years.'

'But why?'

'I don't know. Why would my husband and those morons in there beat me up for fun?'

'I'm so sorry,' Peta said.

'Don't be. I made my choices. They made theirs. I'll live with mine. They'll die with theirs.'

Again, Peta didn't know what to say.

'Are you at least going to a safe place in the south?' Blossom asked.

'Yeah,' Peta replied. 'I'm going to stay with an old friend in Ashburton.'

'Good,' Blossom smiled with teeth that were as uneven as her nails.

Chapter Eight

Peta woke up as they stopped in front of a typical country house from the nineteenth century. Looming between the house and the sunset was Mount 4 (formerly Mt Taranaki), snow-capped as ever, though not half as much as when she was a little girl. The weatherboard bungalow may have been as white as that snow at one stage, but now it was brown and green with creepers and moss. In fact, it gave the impression that it could easily collapse in on itself.

There were three women sitting on the porch, reading a book, peeling potatoes, and knitting, respectively. Peta had rarely seen any of those activities. Blossom got out of the ute and told Peta to join her. The sun was setting behind them so the women would only see them in silhouette. This suited Blossom, who didn't want to answer questions about what had happened to her – not right now, anyway. The woman who was reading was about thirty and wore loose, practical clothes, like all of them, but she had short, roughly cut hair. Her book didn't have a title or author's name on it. She was about eight months pregnant. The woman who was peeling potatoes was in her forties and had very curly red hair. The one who was knitting was about sixty and had a long, grey pony tail.

'Hey, what you got there?' the potato woman asked cheerfully.

'Someone who needs a break from the city,' Blossom said, keeping herself at a distance from the women.

'I don't blame you,' the older, knitting woman said.

'If I can give you any advice,' the reading woman said, 'I'd stay out of there for good.'

The others nodded.

'This is Melissa,' Blossom said. 'Venus, Mercury and Moon.'

'Hi,' Peta said, hoping she didn't look surprised by their names.

She and Blossom had decided they wouldn't tell the others her real name. The women all greeted her benevolently. Then a man came out the front door, his hair black, his beard grey. His clothes were also old, but he had a calmness and a power about him that city men didn't. He was about sixty-five.

'Hello, Sun,' Blossom said. 'This is Melissa. She's looking for a place to stay for a while.'

'Mars, what happened to you?' he asked, putting his large hand on her cheek.

'The cammies pulled us over because I assaulted a man trying to harass Melissa here.'

'Well, we'll deal with them in the fullness of time. But for now, welcome, Melissa. You're just in time for dinner.'

The one thing Peta wasn't expecting, even though it made perfect sense, was children. There were five of them and they all looked a little wild, but glowing with good health. They were lovingly treated by the women and Sun. The children were seated at a smaller, nearby table and fed first. If their hands and faces were clean, their clothes and feet were filthy. As for their manners, Peta couldn't help thinking of how her late parents had insisted on things like keeping your mouth closed while eating. These kids spoke while they ate, and they used their hands to push the food onto their forks or straight from the plate into their mouths. Also, they chattered among themselves, unlike some city children, who often dominated adult conversations. Everything just felt a lot more natural than in the city. Dinner consisted of nutty brown rice and a spicy lentil stew, with some earthy-tasting silver beet on the side.

'So what made you want to get out of the city?' Sun asked Peta in a quiet yet penetrating way.

'I was just tired of all the rules and regulations,' Peta said.

'I know exactly what you mean,' Venus said. 'That place almost drove me to suicide. If it wasn't for these good people, I'd be dead.'

'You do realise this isn't a leisure farm, Melissa,' Sun said. 'If you stay here, you'll have to work, just like the rest of us. It's hard, physical work.'

'I don't mind,' Peta said. 'I'm not scared of work. I just don't like people who want to control me.'

'Amen,' Mercury said.

'Good,' Sun said, smiling at Peta. 'Well, we don't have TV here, so it's early to bed and early to rise...'

'... makes you healthy, wealthy and wise,' the oldest girl piped up in a sing-songy, half-mocking way at the children's table.

'That's right,' Sun smiled gently. 'But what do we mean by "wealthy"?'

'We mean there's enough for everyone, equally,' the oldest boy replied.

'Good boy,' Venus said, cupping her belly.

'And what quote did we use to explain that?' Sun asked.

'If survival is the law of jungle, then co-operation is the law of, um...'

'Civilization,' a younger girl lisped.

'Excellent,' Sun said.

Amazing the difference between Sun and McCracken, Peta thought, taking another mouthful of stew. If MK was all cold, tight-lipped control, then Sun exuded warmth, trust.

'Time to take a shower,' Moon said.

There were groans of protest, and Peta felt teary at the naturalness of it all. Blossom noticed this and told her she could wash her face and rinse her mouth before the kids, giving her a frayed but clean towel and a faded nightie. Unfortunately tonight was the night the children got their weekly wash, so there wouldn't be enough water for anyone else.

'That's all good,' Peta said, and went into the bathroom. Afterwards, she hung up the towel and took the nightie back with her into the dining-cum-living room as Mercury and Moon herded protesting the kids into the bathroom. Sun and Venus were out on the deck in the chill air. He was smoking. Blossom told her she'd be sleeping in a room with a double bed in it.

'Where do you sleep?' Peta asked, slightly uneasy.

'We women sleep in one room and the children in another. Look.'

The one bedroom had four separate beds in it, the other two bunks. Something stopped Peta from asking where Sun slept. Blossom answered that unspoken question.

'Sun sleeps out in the shed, where he can meditate in and on the silence. Your room is for guests.'

'That feels wrong,' Peta said.

'Not at all. If you stay with us we'll get a single bed for you too.'

The room was bare and functional, but clean and tidy. There was no electricity, just a candle. Peta said she wanted to give Blossom something. The older woman looked puzzled as she unclipped her LOVE brooch and gave it to her.

'What's this for?' Blossom asked.

'For today. For helping me.'

'I haven't been given anything for so long,' Blossom said, her voice a little shaky.

'Well now you have,' Peta smiled.

'Thank you,' Blossom said, and gave Peta a long hug.

'It's a pleasure,' Peta said, knowing her mother would have understood.

'I better go and help with the washing up,' Blossom said.

Peta closed the door, undressed, put on the nightie, and got between the sheets, listening to the kids squealing in the shower. It was a deeply comforting sound, which made her miss her parents, her friends Moana and Lee. She also realised she was missing her phone. In fact, she missed it so acutely that she was suffering from withdrawal symptoms. She wanted to know what was happening in the world, even though she knew that what the news said was filtered anyway. Most of the time you had to believe the opposite of what was being said. She wouldn't be able to use the internet to find out exactly where she was, nor the never-before-used compass to tell her where south was. Well, she'd better get used to not having it and survive by her wits, she decided, when she realised something else. She wasn't feeling as wired as she'd been feeling lately, using her phone too much before bedtime. So that was something. She blew out the candle and soon she was fast asleep.

Chapter Nine

Something woke her and she couldn't quite put her finger on it. The crickets were chirping and everything sounded peaceful, yet something was wrong. She lay listening to the night, wondering what it was that had roused her. If it had been a bad dream, she couldn't remember it. Surely she was safe here? It felt late, but it could be as early as ten o'clock, for all she knew. Then she realised what it was that had woken her. She could hear voices, muted voices. She got up and, feeling her way, approached the door. It had somehow unclipped while she was asleep. When she looked into the dining room she saw Sun and the women sitting at the table.

'You can't do this,' Blossom said to Sun.

'Why not? It's the way we operate. We either hand her over to the cammies, or she becomes my fifth wife. It's as simple as that.'

'Why can't she just be our guest and then go on her merry way?' Blossom insisted.

'You know we believe that if someone crosses our path, it means something,' Mercury said.

'But why can't it mean that we simply accommodate her?'

'I think we should hand her over to the authorities,' the pregnant Venus said. 'They'll give us the reward and we'll be good for the rest of the year.'

'You know what they'll do to her,' Moon said.

'Tough,' Venus replied.

Mercury nodded grimly.

Watching them through the crack in the door, Peta couldn't believe what she was hearing.

'Why don't we vote on it, as we always do?' Blossom said.

'Fair enough,' Sun said. 'I vote that she stays and becomes my wife. Anyone else?'

'I'm with you,' the older Moon said,' perhaps thinking that keeping Peta with them would save her from being blinded by the cammies.

'And against?' he said with a slight edge to his voice.

Venus put up her hand and a reluctant Mercury did so too.

'What about you Mars?' he asked.

'I vote for neither,' Blossom said. 'I say we leave her be.'

'You know we can't do that.'

'We have a tie,' Mercury said.

'But you're forgetting something,' Sun said.

There was a silence that they all knew.

'You know that as the leader I have the vetoing vote, therefore she will become my wife.'

Peta retreated from the door, took off her nightie, and started dressing hurriedly in the dark. She was not going to become any old man's fifth wife. She tried the sliding window and it gave without creaking. The deck moaned a little, but no one seemed to hear it. She made sure Mt Taranaki was on her right. It would be her compass for heading south.

Fortunately, it was a clear night and, as she walked along, she became angry with herself for misjudging Sun. She should have picked up that there was something wrong at that house with its four women, one man, and their planetary names. Who did he think he was, calling himself the sun, around which other planets turned? She was about a hundred metres away from the shed and was climbing through a fence when she heard Mercury shouting, 'She's gone!'

There was a silence and Peta was relieved there weren't any dogs on their property.

'Shall we let the cammies know?' Venus asked.

'No,' said Sun, who started approaching with a torch. 'Stay here. I'll find her.'

Peta watched with morbid fascination as he started walking towards her, as if guided by some inner compass. She knew she had to move, but somehow couldn't.

'I know you can hear me, Peta,' he said with his calm, fatherly voice, coming closer. 'I know you heard what we said at the table. But we can change our plans, as Mars suggested. There is clearly some connection between you and Mars. She can be your new mother. I'll be your father. You don't have to become my wife, unless you want to, like the others did.

'Most important, with us you will live without fear. You will have a reason to live. It's not an easy life, but it's wholesome, real. You may think you lost your job for one reason, but for another it was meant to be. Losing your job was just an external problem, but in your soul you knew you had to discover a new life. You knew the life you were living was empty, hollow. With us you can become whole and full again. With us you can help build a new society. A kinder, fairer society.'

Sun was about five metres away from her now, and switched off the torch.

'I could see how you looked at our children: lovingly, longingly. I know you'd like to have a child yourself. I think you'd make a wonderful mother. But would you like to rear a child in your apartment or out here in nature? Would you like to bring up a single child and subject it to the security-obsessed sterility of the city? Would you like your child to become a pale, neurotic, anxious, alienated creature? One who was prone to all kinds of psychological and viral illnesses? Or would you like a healthy, clever child like ours, who has lots of brothers and sisters?'

Peta knew if he switched on the torch he'd see her, and he knew it too. She also knew that he was speaking to a side of her that wanted more than anything else to feel the warmth of human fellowship. She was unable to move, and felt tears streaming down her cheeks.

'Come back with me, my child. We need you at home. We need your fresh outlook. We need your courage. What do you say? I'm not going to force you. I'm merely asking you.'

There was nothing more in the world she wanted to do than go back to the house with him, to be with Blossom and the children, but something told her she had to keep moving.

'Alright, Peta,' Sun finally said. 'I'm going to start walking back to the house now. You know where we live. You're welcome to come back to us at any time.'

Sun waited for a few seconds before he turned and started walking away, switching the torch back on. Peta wanted to shout, 'Wait, I'm coming,' but didn't.

Instead, she turned and walked into the night.

Chapter Ten

After about an hour of walking, Peta began to relax, warming up, enjoying the night sounds, the sight of the crystalline stars. Traipsing through uneven fields, climbing through fences and traversing ditches and streams, she later saw a deserted weatherboard house. It was very much in the style of Blossom's commune, one that had simply been abandoned in favour of a bigger, more modern house. The countryside was dotted with these derelict homes, though others had simply been lifted up and towed to another location, leaving only the brick chimney as a reminder that there had once been a dwelling. The place was spooky alright, but at least it offered some sort of shelter from the cold and damp. The deck creaked crazily, the front door was stuck, and when she tried to push it open, it fell away into the house with a loud bang. She stepped inside and the floor half collapsed under her. But she finally found a spot where she could lie down next to the inside wall of a living room that had once contained country lives – conversation, community, laughter. She felt sad about Blossom, or Mars, who had defended her at all costs against the creepy Sun and territorial Venus. She'd felt a kind of comradeship with Blossom. No, the older woman was warm, kind and strong, as Peta's mother had been before she and her husband succumbed to the virus that wiped out half the planet.

When Peta finally fell asleep she dreamt that Sun was given a wad of notes by the cammies who'd assaulted Blossom, thanking them piously, before pointing at her, standing in front of the shed. Next she was running away from them, but one of them caught up with her and taserPhoned her. She was reduced to an angry, powerless wreck on the ground and dragged to the cammies' station wagon, just like that Undesirable back in Z1.

She was woken – stiff and cold – by the dawn. The air was chilly and damp and, when she stepped outside to her new life, she was surrounded by cows. Black-and-white cows. Friesians, she remembered from her lessons about threatened species. The cows were looking at her as if she were a curiosity, and she probably was, she thought. She could see a dirt road across the paddock, about two hundred metres away. Cows, she remembered, were peaceful animals. So she started walking towards the road and the cows gave way, though not as quickly as she thought they would, still looking at her with large, limpid eyes. She kept walking towards the road, and one of the cows behind her started mooing. That was normal too, she thought. But then the others joined in and it became quite loud. Soon they started sounding agitated, even angry, then threatening. She walked a little faster. Now the cows were snorting, their hooves hitting the ground. She looked around. Their nostrils were flaring, their eyes strangely manic. Surely they weren't going to charge her? She walked even faster. One cow started mooing in a kind of frenzy, as if it was saying, 'She's a trespasser! Kill her!' The other cows seemed to agree with her, working themselves up into a frenzy too. Peta broke into a jog: she couldn't help it. The cows were charging her, big and clumsy but determined, wild-eyed, snorting. She ran for the road, seeing there was a fence she would have to jump over. The sound of the cows behind her was as terrifying as the passage at Joy Inc tearing apart in her dream. What would the cows do to her? Trample her and gore her? Eat her? The front cows were right behind her now, she could feel their hot, angry breaths, their hooves drumming the earth, shaking it. She would have to try to jump over the fence, feet first. Here it came now. She jumped as high as she could, but her back foot hit the top wire and she went down face first into a ditch, landing with her face in a pool of mud. At least I'm away from the cows, she thought, when she heard a man laughing.

Peta looked up and saw a traditional farmer standing next to his ute. She hadn't even seen the vehicle in her panic to escape the herd. He was about thirty-five, unshaven, and wearing boots, shorts, an old rugby jersey, and a bush hat. But in his hands there was something that was everything but traditional: he was holding a little machine and couldn't stop laughing. Peta looked back, expecting to see the cows straining against the fence to get at her, but there was absolutely nothing but field and the house in the background. She got up and wiped her face.

'Sorry about that,' the man laughed. 'That was a holographic herd.'

Peta was not amused. Not only was she angry, embarrassed and muddy, but she'd also hurt her elbows and knees in the fall, just like in the Joy Inc dream, except this was real. The peak cap had fallen off along the way.

'Come and have a shower at the farmhouse. There's plenty of food and clothes for you. I'm Angus, by the way. Angus Craig.'

Peta didn't move.

'Come on,' he said. 'That was just a country prank. My partner Sally will protect you from me. In fact, if I try anything she'll beat the living crap out of me.'

'Okay,' Peta said warily, wondering what next she would have to endure.

Angus turned out to be alright, in a country-bumpkin kind of way.

Once he got going, he wouldn't stop talking, telling her how he missed his cattle, but that the world had gone to hell in a handbasket because people no longer needed to eat fresh meat or drink milk, 'at least not the kind I produced. Sure, the government paid me out, but growing vegetables just isn't the same thing. I could talk to my cows and give them names, but I find it really difficult talking to cabbages.'

'Why don't you talk to your wife?'

'I would, if I could, but she left. Ran off with some other guy. You might have heard of him. They call him the Sunflower King. Piece of... Anyway... I hope they both... yeah.'

'Do you have children?'

'Yeah, two girls, but they went with her,' he said bitterly.

'At least you've got Sally.'

'I tell you, if it wasn't for her I'd have gone to pieces. Blown my brains out or OD'd, like so many other farmers do.'

The only comfort Peta could get from this conversation was that Angus clearly had no idea who she was. He obviously didn't read, watch or listen to the news. Maybe he just drank the nights away, lulled by anti-depressants, and got on Sally's nerves – if she even existed.

They turned in at an entrance that featured the farm's name – Loch Logan – and drove along a cypress-lined track towards a larger, more modern house than Blossom's. Angus might be a bumpkin but he certainly didn't seem to be short of cash. Peta felt deeply uncomfortable with him as they headed away from the road, but as they got to the house a woman came out. She was dressed like a farmer too – gumboots, jeans, T-shirt and sleeveless jacket. Angus introduced her as his partner. Sally was almost as big as him, had short bristly hair, rough hands, and a deep voice. She looked Peta up and down and then said to Angus, 'Did you give the poor thing a fright?'

'Yeah, couldn't help it.'

'What an arsehole. No wonder Rita left you.'

Then she turned to Peta and said, 'Hi,' and half crushed her hand.

'Melissa,' Peta said.

'Come in and have a shower, Melissa. I'll get you a fresh set of clothes and make you some breakfast. And don't worry about the clothes. You're about the same size as Angus's one daughter. She left quite a lot of stuff behind.'

'Thank you,' Peta said, unable to shake off a sense of dread around this aggressively friendly couple, which wasn't helped by the fact that their living room walls were covered with mounted deer and hog heads.

'Are bacon and eggs okay for you?'

'I'm sorry, I'm vegan.'

'Right,' Sally said. 'Very sensible. That's what we should be doing.'

'What for?' Angus sneered.

'So that we can look like her, not us. Come,' she said to Peta. 'Let me show you your room. And you can shower as long as you like. We've got a borehole.'

Peta was grateful for the clothes, even if they weren't her more sporty city style, but then her father had always said beggars can't be choosers. Was she a beggar? she wondered as she stood luxuriating in the warm shower. No, she was a fugitive. How strange, how bizarre. Just for saying someone didn't look as sorry as they said they were.

The smell of oats with boiled fruit, toast and coffee was as good as it tasted, while Angus went on about his cows, mentioning each and every one of them by name while Sally kept herself busy and Peta yawned. Sally finally noticed and told Angus to 'stop talking shit' and said if 'Melissa' wanted to sleep, she could. Peta said if it was okay she'd love to catch up on some sleep, wondering why they didn't even bother to ask her why she'd spent a (cold, stressful) night in a deserted house on their or someone else's property. Or was it just typical Z reserve?

She went to the room, stripped down to her T-shirt and undies, lay down, and was just drifting off when her instincts kicked in and she got up, jammed a chair against the door handle and got back into the bed. She was still anxious, but sleep finally overtook her.

Chapter Eleven

Johnny Smith20 was not the brightest spark in his electrician father's toolbox, so it was decided he'd become a cammy. There, he could live out all his frustrations and express them by being a bully and a brute. Every excuse he got, he tortured people, women in particular. He liked hurting them, then feeling them up, and so on. It did all kinds of things for him. Like that bitch the day before. What was her name again? Something floral. Begonia or something.

Anyway, for all his lack of insight, he did come to one for a fraction of a second while he was eating his takeaway and watching some torture porn in his official green car. He'd seen something he'd ignored at first, then become puzzled by – in a way that one is forced to take note of something that vaguely poses a threat – before he came to his momentary insight.

At first, they were just five people standing there. A man and four women. Earth types. But something about the way they stood there didn't seem quite right. They were looking at him quite intently. He felt like telling them to piss off, but they were a good twenty metres away. The man took out his wePhone, and that was also quite normal. But then he only pressed four numbers on his phone, which weren't enough to make a call, before he looked at the cammy again. In that moment Johnny Smith20 came to the realisation that he was going to be ripped apart, blown sky high in a ball of fire, and he was.

Chapter Twelve

Peta woke up cold and in the dark, and it took her a few seconds to work out where she was. Then she realised she'd been woken by a man's voice, Angus's. He was raving. She also became aware of something else. The bedroom window leading onto the deck was wide open, so anyone could have simply slipped in. Next time, she thought, check everything, no matter how tired you are. She got up, moved the chair away from the door and quietly eased her way into the dark passage, inching towards the light in the lounge room.

Angus was sitting at the dining room table, talking. There were six empty bottles of beer on the table. He was busy with the seventh. The bottles had clearly been kept in a cellar, as their labels were old and musty. Sitting opposite him was Sally with a full glass and half a bottle of colourless fluid. The bottle didn't have a label. Peta guessed it was either vodka or gin. Next to it was an almost empty bottle of unmarked tonic water.

'I want my fucking cows back,' Angus said. 'I knew each and every single one of the motherfuckers by name.'

'So you've already said,' Sally said, in a quieter but equally belligerent way. 'About a thousand times.'

'I think it's time we went and shot up all those bloody vegans in Parliament,' he continued.

'And how the hell are you going to do that?'

'Charlie down the road said we could join the Country Corps. We could travel together and blast those arseholes to kingdom come.'

'After yesterday's explosion, you wouldn't get past the first roadblock.'

'We'll shoot them all to shit too.'

'Oh, sure you will. They'll know you're coming before you even see them.'

'D'you think I'm scared of a shootout?'

'Well, they aren't Rita and the girls, you know.'

'Don't fucking say that!' he shouted.

'Why not? It's the truth,' Sally said.

'You helped me!' Angus exclaimed.

'I know, but I don't go on and on about it.'

'Christ, you're a hard bitch.'

'That's why you like me, dickhead.'

'True,' he muttered, wandering off in his mind, possibly to a cow-filled paddock, before he came back to the here and now and took a long swig of beer. 'So do you think she suspects something?'

'I don't know,' Sally said, glancing at the passage where Peta was standing in the shadows. It felt as if Sally had looked right into her, but the farm woman didn't act as if she had and Peta continued watching and listening, trying to absorb the fact that these two had killed Angus's wife and daughters.

'I mean, she didn't act as if she was on the run...' Angus slurred.

'And we didn't act as if we knew,' Sally said.

'So what d'you think we should do?'

'Well, if we hand her over, we'll make a pile of money.'

'Yeah, but they might start asking questions again.'

'True.'

'I've got a much better idea,' Angus said.

'What is it?'

'She's a vegan ...'

'So?'

Angus just looked at her, half smiling and half leering, waiting for her to get what he was implying.

'Maybe it's better that way,' she said.

'I think so,' he smiled. 'Much better.'

'Okay, but this time we do it democratically.'

'What d'you mean?'

'I mean I get the one half, you get the other.'

'Sure. Why not?

Angus took a swig of his beer and said, 'Where will you start?'

'She's got nice athletic legs, so I'll probably start with the thighs.'

'Yeah, me too. I bet you she tastes as sweet as a Sunday-roast chicken. But I was thinking that maybe this time you should do it.'

There was a pause as Sally considered this.

'I suppose you're right. Should I use the .22, the .38, or the Glock?'

'That's up to you, darling,' Angus said.

Sally stood up and almost fell over, proving she was much drunker than she'd seemed. Peta tiptoed back to her room, shoved the chair under the door handle and got out the window. She ran as fast as she could down the lane of trees, which seemed as menacing as the holo-herd had been. It was another bright, moonlit night, so she could see well. Halfway down the road she heard Sally shouting, followed by Angus cursing even louder. Then they were shouting at each other.

Peta got to the road, looked at Mt Taranaki in the distance, and saw she had to go right as she heard Angus's ute start up. She ran for all she was worth and hoped the two might go in the opposite direction, but when they got to the entrance to the farm, they skidded to a halt. Angus stumbled out of the passenger seat and looked at her shoe marks on the dirt in the ute's headlights.

'She went that way,' he slurred, pointing in Peta's direction.

The ute was coming towards her and there was no way she was going to outrun it. Soon she would be in its headlights, so she found a low bush next to the road and lay behind it, her breath racing. The ute approached at speed, and it felt like its headlights had caught Peta in their powerful beams. She put her head down and instinctively told herself not to move. She heard Angus and Sally angrily cursing her and each other and waited for the ute to scream to a halt. But they flashed past, churning up dust.

She would have to follow them, wait for them to return, and use the same trick again. Out in the still air she could hear the sound of the ute fading, stopping, turning at length, and coming back towards her, the sound of its wheels on the dirt getting louder as it did so. She tried to make as much progress as she could before the ute's headlights would catch her, and lay down behind a bush again. The ute duly passed her, but skidded to a halt about twenty metres away. She could see Angus stumbling out with his rifle, looking at the dirt road and then telling Sally to turn the ute around. She did so, drunkenly, and he started following his quarry's tracks on foot. There was no way Peta could stay on this road: she'd have to head for a nearby hill, away from the road. She started crawling, then wormed her way through a fence while the other two came closer.

'There she is!' Sally shouted, and Peta started running. Angus fired at her and she ran like mad, zigzagging to get away from them as they gave chase, Angus still firing, the two of them still cursing. Peta could hear both the distant gunshots and the whooshing sound of bullets as they flew past, or thudded into the ground around her. By the time she got to the foot of the hill, they were exhausted.

'Fuck!' Angus shouted.

'She's probably heading to the other road,' Sally said, not thinking about her voice carrying so far in that wide, open silence.

'What are we going to do about it?' Angus yelled.

'Drive around and get her on the other side,' Sally said.

'Legend,' Angus said, and they stumbled back to the ute's headlights. 'You drive, so I can shoot.'

'For what that's worth,' Sally grumbled.

'Would you like me to do the driving?' Angus asked.

'No.'

'Well then shut the fuck up,' Angus replied in his usual eloquent way.

Peta climbed the hill, regained her breath and waited for them to get to the ute. She decided she'd wait and see what they were going to do before moving any further. Sally tore away at speed in the direction they'd originally taken, with Angus cursing in the clear night as they sped towards a bend in the road.

'Let go of the bloody wheel!' she suddenly shouted.

'You're doing it all wrong!'

'Let go, for fuck's sake!' Sally screamed.

The ute started drifting, then swerved violently as Sally cursed Angus. The next thing the vehicle was skidding on the loose sand, rolling – once, twice – then straightening out before it hit a solitary tree, head-on. There was a gut-wrenching thud and shattering of glass, then the only sound that could be heard was that of a turning wheel. Peta saw a cloud of dust in the one headlight that was still working. She waited grimly for about ten minutes before deciding that Angus and Sally had to be dead.

All hyped up, she decided to carry on walking down to the road Sally had mentioned. She glimpsed a cluster of rocks forming a shallow cave before a blanket of cloud suddenly covered the moon and everything went pitch black. She felt her way into the rudimentary shelter, thinking she'd just wait out the clouds, but another one of Z's famous natural phenomena appeared. It started raining. Not quite a downpour, but long and steady nevertheless.

She tried to think of something pleasant. It took a while, but then she remembered the time she, Moana and Lee had gone on a tramp in what used to be the Pinnacles in the then Coromandel. They'd got lost and had to tough it out overnight. And, to add to their woes, it had also started raining. Not drizzling, raining. Bucketing, as Moana said. Jon was away, visiting his grandparents again, and the only thing that kept their spirits up that soaking-wet night was Lee's dry sense of humour. The next morning they found the path a few metres away from where they'd been huddling down, laughing hysterically about it all, soaked to the bone.

And, like that night, if she slept an hour it was a lot.

Chapter Thirteen

When she opened her eyes she wasn't quite sure she was awake, because all she saw was grey. Was it real? Of course it was. It's mist, she told herself. Get over yourself. Walk down to the road, except you can't see it. Which way to go? Downhill. Okay. So she started walking downhill, step by step, careful not to slip on the damp tussock, or stumble over a rock, or fall down a precipice. Down, further down. It wasn't that cold here, which also made sense. The lower you went, the warmer it got. But she could feel she wasn't alone. Worse, she realised she would have to start going up again. This was wrong. There was no uphill in her mind's eye. The mist was lifting in patches, and she saw why she'd have to go up again. She was at the bottom of a spent volcanic cone. But that didn't explain the heat, the brooding silence. She didn't believe in ghosts or any kind of supernatural force, so what could it be? Other people? No. The air was alive with *something*, something warmer than the air. And then she knew what it was a fraction before she saw one of them.

Sheep.

Plenty of them. She stopped dead. Were these creatures going to attack her as the 'cows' had? Were they real or not? Were they also someone else's hologram? Someone who was watching her? She didn't have any energy left to outrun them too, so she waited, and they stared at her with their yellow eyes and black, horizontal pupils. She waited. They chewed. Would they continue to ignore her if she started moving? Whatever the case, she couldn't stand and wait for them to move off. They might not do so for hours, and sooner or later someone was going to find the dead Angus and Sally. She took a deep breath and started walking again, uphill. The sheep took notice, and she could feel them keeping an eye on her. The question was: were they waiting to charge or just curious, perhaps equally as wary? So she took a few more steps and the sheep kept their distance. She carried on walking away from them, up, constantly looking back to make sure they weren't going to charge her and devour her. Then she was out of the cone and looking down at the other country road Sally had been shouting about. It didn't seem like the ute and the corpses had been discovered yet, but she still had to get as much distance between herself and that little scene as possible.

It was only now she realised her clothes were torn and muddied, her elbows and knees scraped and bloody, once again. Nothing serious, just niggly burns. When she got to the road, she turned right and walked along it. No cars, just a solitary bush falcon. Up ahead there was a bend in the road. She approached it with a strange feeling that something was going to happen. She took the bend and something didn't so much happen as present itself. It was the back of a large stationary truck, one with twelve chromed wheels. She knew she was walking in the right direction so she'd have to pass the truck, but she couldn't see its driver. Maybe he'd gone for a leak. They were, after all, on a country road. This suited her, but as she got to the front of the truck she saw that its driver had his head stuck in the engine. Then he lifted his head and Peta saw he was a woman.

'Good day,' the driver said down to her.

'Hi,' Peta said.

The woman had a squeaky voice, a peroxided mullet, multiple rings in her ears and one nostril. Her arms were covered in tattoos. She was wearing a T-shirt, jeans and working boots.

'You looking for a lift?'

'I wasn't thinking of that, but if you're offering, I'll take it.'

'Yeah, I could do with some company. Bloody EVs. As finicky as,' she said, referring to the engine, climbing down from the shiny bumper, heaving a little, for she was not a small woman. 'My bad. I should have checked all these minor batteries. And I shouldn't have taken this shortcut. Anyway, I'm Becky.'

'Melissa,' Peta said.

'No, you're not. You're Peta Smith27. I'd recognise your face anywhere. Do you know there's a ransom on your head?'

'Yeah,' Peta said wearily.

'Don't worry, I'm not going to dob you. But did you really kill someone?'

'Kill someone?'

'That's what they're saying, though you don't exactly look the type.'

'All I did was tell my boss he didn't look sorry for firing me!'

'Sounds about right. I work for a real dick too. But I've got a family to think of. That's how they screw us. I should just have stayed a free and easy diesel dyke. Instead I go and get married like a straight and adopt two brats. Big mistake. But I wouldn't change them for the world,' she smiled with a mouth shy of a few teeth. 'Anyway, let's get out of here before the chlamydias arrive. Hop inside.'

Peta walked round to the passenger side of the truck named 'Lucy' and climbed up to the cab, which turned out to be quite plush. There was a photograph of a happy, smaller woman with a boy and a girl, presumably Becky's partner and adopted children, resting on the dashboard.

'This is my other true love,' Becky said, patting the steering wheel. 'I've been driving her since thirty-five and, boy, have we had fun,' she said, starting the silent truck.

'I don't know how many times we've gone up and down this country,' she said, easing onto the dirt road. 'Sometimes my partner says I should rather have married Lucy, and I think she has a point. Definitely. Where you heading?'

'I'm going to see a friend in the south.'

'Well, I'm going all the way to Invercargill, so you're welcome to stick with me. It'll probably be easier to get you through Wellington and across the Strait.'

'That would be great,' Peta said. 'Thank you. But where are we?'

'We're about a hundred kays away from Palmerston North, so there's still a long road ahead. There's a bunk behind us if you want to sleep.'

'I'm okay for now,' Peta said, realising she was exhausted, and remembering that her father had insisted on calling that city by its indigenous name, Te Papa-o-Oea.

'Good. It'll help me stay awake,' Becky said, putting two tablets in her mouth and swallowing them. 'And this. There's a flask and two mugs over there. Pour us some coffee, will you?'

'Sure,' Peta said, feeling safe with this no-nonsense woman.

'There's a First Aid kit over there if you want to treat those scrapes of yours. What happened?'

Peta told her while they drank their coffee.

'That's quite a yarn,' Becky said as Peta dabbed the scrapes on her elbows and hands. Becky, in turn, had a story to tell about every town and charging station they passed. Every now and again they'd see an electronic billboard with Peta's face on it. These new ones also said WANTED, but now that word was below her face, while above it was the usual enticement:

REWARD

They had a grim laugh about the fact that Peta was currently worth a quarter of a million dollars. They listened to the news: the cammies had gone on a wild-goose chase to Whangarei. All this while passing a constant flow of military vehicles heading in the opposite direction, but by now she was so sleepy she was nodding off.

'Go on, have a kip at the back. It's snug as. I'll be fine. I do this six days a week. It's my job.'

'Thank you.'

'No worries.'

Chapter Fourteen

This time Peta didn't dream about running from or towards a threat, but that she was trapped. The cammies were coming at her from all directions, on foot, in a city park, rifles aimed at her, and she couldn't move. She knew they were going to kill her. Their faces were impassive. She could see the young men and women's eyes, their fingers starting to squeeze the triggers, the city sirens whining.

She woke with a view of mountains out a side window. A static view. Distant sirens. Cammy sirens. Becky was still in her seat, still breathing, but she wasn't moving, or driving. She had somehow driven off the road and onto a flat part of land and the truck had either run out of energy or she'd switched it off. She had clearly fallen asleep, though her eyes were wide open. Peta clambered through into the driving compartment and asked if she was okay.

'Fine,' Becky said. 'We can charge her in Palmy. It's right up ahead.'

'You should get some sleep.'

'No time for that, hon. I've got to make it to Wellington by tonight.'

'Okay, but I'm leaving. The cammies are going to be here soon.'

'You do that. I won't tell.'

'Thank you, Becky.'

'Don't believe anything men tell you.'

'I won't,' Peta said, opened the door and climbed down onto the field. The truck had carved a clear trail in the dirt, flattening a long line of tussock. The sirens were coming closer. There was a small stream up ahead. If they were near Te Papa-i-Oea, then those mountains were the old Tararuas. When she got to the stream, it was stagnant and smelly, like the country's untreated lakes.

Then she saw two men in their mid-sixties, looking at her. The one was balding and had a ginger moustache. The other had longish grey hair and a few days' stubble. Peta backed away, but the ginger man said, 'Don't be frightened, we're not going to do anything to you.'

Peta had heard that one before, so she started heading back where she came from. The grey-haired man said, 'What happened to you? You look like a frightened animal.'

'Stay away from me,' she said.

'Please don't go,' the ginger moustache said. 'We want to help you. I've just realised who you are. I promise we won't tell the authorities.'

'We'll give you shelter, food, clean clothes,' the other man said. 'We really can help you.'

'Why would you want to?'

'Because we don't agree with the way things are being run now.'

'What do you mean?'

'We've been confined to an old-age town,' the grey-haired man said. 'We haven't seen a young person like you for months, if not years.'

The sirens were very close now.

'We found a secret tunnel out of town to the river here. We can give you food and shelter for as long as you like,' the ginger man said.

'We honestly only want to help you,' the other added.

'Do you have computers?' she asked with the sirens ringing in her ears and the two men exchanging glances, as if wondering whether they could trust her.

'Yes, of course,' the grey man said. 'That's the only contact we have with our children and the outside world. Just don't tell anybody.'

Peta didn't have much of a choice – it was them or the cammies.

'Okay,' she said.

'I'm Keith,' the ginger man said.

'Oliver,' his friend said.

'Peta,' she said.

'We know,' they said simultaneously, smiling kindly.

They headed towards an old mining tunnel entrance. Peta was still wary as they entered the darkness. It was pitch black ahead, but the ground beneath her feet felt solid, and the men kept talking reassuringly, telling her to stay directly behind them. She kept two metres away from them, just in case she had to run. Suddenly there was light ahead and she saw Oliver had parted two thick black curtains, revealing a well-lit passage.

'My brother knew about this tunnel because he'd been an engineer at a nearby mine, otherwise we wouldn't have been able to get out of town at all,' Keith said.

'There was a German who thought there was platinum here,' Oliver added.

Up ahead was a silver ladder, and the men went up, inviting Peta to follow. She did so, still warily, then stepped into someone's living room. Keith closed the trapdoor and covered it with a patterned carpet from A12 (or Afghanistan).

'We're going to hand you over to our wives now,' Oliver said, calling: 'Fay! Cathy! Come see what we've got here...'

Peta tried not to see anything sinister in that last sentence and soon two women entered the room. They introduced themselves, both a little younger than their husbands, and seemed perfectly comfortable with the idea that Peta was a fugitive. Fay had short hair and a heart-shaped face. She wore a dress with floral patterns. Cathy had a longer, more rectangular face. She wore trousers and a cardigan.

'You're safe with us, dear,' Fay said comfortingly. 'Have you eaten anything yet?'

Peta shook her head while the two men stood about like spare parts.

'You two go and do something in the shed,' Cathy said bossily.

'Right,' Keith replied.

And so the two women cooked Peta a tasty meal and peppered her with questions and information about their own lives. They decided she had to dress up like a man before she left, to evade her pursuers. Fay had had a teenage son who'd been 'taken away' and he'd more or less been the same build as Peta. This she said with a slight tremor in her voice, while Cathy, whose twin girls had succumbed to Covid-43, said she'd organise their hairdresser to come in the next morning to cut her hair. They let Peta use their secret computer, taken from under a trapdoor and which had been rendered safe, in a spare room. She waited until the women were gone before she peeked through the curtains, not knowing what to expect.

There was a Victorian-style house with freshly painted brookie lace, its garden bursting with colour, and the snow-sprinkled Tararuas in the distance. It looked so beautiful, so normal, so peaceful, yet she couldn't shake the feeling that something was not quite right. Then again, Cathy and Fay had warned her that this was a town for Elders, people over sixty, but not older than seventy – which was when people were relieved in accordance with the Bible – so that was probably the cause of her unease.

Then she goapled 'McCracken, Joy Inc'.

Gerald McCracken was from Timaru (now Z17)), where he was born in 2015. His parents were Peter and Màry McCracken. He'd gone to Timaru Primary, followed by Timaru Tech, after which he'd studied Computer Theology at Z1 University. He'd gone on the obligatory overseas experience to A Minor (Europe), followed by a year in C17 (Silicon Valley, formerly a part of San Francisco) for a year after that. Then he'd joined Joy Inc, where he'd been ever since. There were photographs of baby Gerald with Peter and Mary through various stages of his youth; with his fellow students at school and uni; one with his arms around an attractive young woman; and another in which he was awarded a trophy – an inscribed transparent triangle, mounted on a black base – for being the hardest-working person at Joy Inc. And always there was that fake smile of his, as if he wasn't quite there.

That night they all ate pasta and Cathy told the men to stop asking Peta so many questions. She was tired and stressed, for crying out loud. The two men apologised and Peta said that was perfectly all right, feeling safe and secure. They all watched the news and saw that the cammies had redirected their efforts back to the former Whangarei, where there'd been two sightings of Peta.

'Wonderful,' Keith said.

'It could be fake,' Oliver said.

The news was followed by a programme about which software was the best to advance one's business capabilities.

Peta couldn't help yawning, saying sorry, but Fay said, 'I don't blame you. Maybe they just want us to die of boredom before we reach seventy.'

I'll get you one of the girls' pyjamas,' Cathy said in that awkward silence and left the room. She came back with a clean towel and a pair of stripey PJs. Peta had the regulation two-minute shower, thinking she wouldn't be able to sleep so early, but the moment her head touched the pillow she was gone.

Chapter Fifteen

She was woken by a gentle knock on the door and didn't know where she was. After the second knock, it all came back, and she felt both relaxed and worried.

'Come in,' she said with a little trepidation.

Fay entered with a tray, followed by Cathy. They wore the same set of clothes as the day before.

'We brought you something to eat and drink,' Fay said, 'prepared by our darling husbands.'

The breakfast consisted of two thick slices of sourdough bread with mashed avocado on the side, along with a few slices of vegan cheese and bacon. There was also a pot of coffee with oat milk and coarse brown sugar. It looked and smelled delicious. The two women hovered and, sensing her discomfort, Fay said, 'Do you mind if we watch you eat? We haven't seen a young person eat for such a long time. In fact, we haven't seen a young person do anything for a very long time.'

'Okay,' Peta said, and tucked into the meal, while Fay dreamily watched her eating and the sterner Cathy tried to keep her composure, but in fact seemed close to tears.

Peta was vaguely aware of a low, murmuring sound, a bit like the time she'd heard Sun, Blossom and the other women conferring. But this seemed a denser sound. Were they going to hand her over to the authorities and jeer while doing so, or maybe even kill her? She tried not to show her anxiety as she finished her coffee, and asked what the sound was.

'We've got some friends who'd like to meet you,' Fay said. 'Would you mind?'

'No?' Peta said, still wary.

'Get dressed and join us in the living room,' Cathy said, and two women left.

She put on the teenage boy's clothes, which was more or less in her own style anyway – sneakers, jeans, sweater, jacket – and made her way to the living room. There were about twenty men and women, sitting and looking at her strangely. She couldn't quite work out what that look was about, but greeted them politely. They didn't all return her greeting. Some of them looked puzzled, some elated, others pained. Keith and Oliver were among them. Peta didn't know what to say and Cathy finally said, 'The only reason they're looking at you like this is because they haven't seen a young person in the flesh for so long.'

'Are you going to eat me?' Peta couldn't help asking.

'No! Not at all!' Fay said softly, looking even more pained.

One woman rose and slowly walked towards Peta, mesmerised

'Can I shake your hand, please?'

'Of course,' she said.

The woman took Peta's extended hand, covered it with her other one, and started whimpering.

'I'm sorry,' the woman said.

'That's alright,' Peta said, feeling tearful herself, thinking of the last time she'd seen her parents. She now saw that one of the men was weeping silently too. These were just ordinary, decent human beings, Peta thought.

'Please forgive us,' Fay said.

'That's alright,' Peta said again.

'Please tell us what's been happening to you,' Fay said.

Peta sat down and started talking, telling them everything, sticking as closely to the facts as she could, because that way she could control her own emotions while being looked at and listened to with such gentle, longing attention. Occasionally one of the Elders would burst into silent sobs, clearly missing their own children or grandchildren, while another would look at her with a teary smile. Apart from being interested in her story, they were mainly in a state of rapture to hear a young person speak again. It was deeply unsettling, but Peta felt she owed it to them for what they were doing for her. Then a woman walked up to her, asking whether she could stroke her hair. Peta said yes, and she did so, tenderly, longingly.

Then she said, 'I'm a hairdresser by trade. Gabi. Cathy asked me whether I would cut your hair to match your clothes, and…'

'And?'

'We'd just like to spoil someone young.'

'Okay.'

'Do you mind if we watch you having your hair cut?' Fay asked.

'No, not at all,' said Peta.

'This'll be a first for our husbands,' another woman said.

That broke the tension a little as they all laughed.

Cathy commanded a woman to fetch the hairdresser's things while Gabi ran her fingers through Peta's hair, assessing it.

'Beautiful,' one woman said.

'I used to have hair like that,' said another.

'In your dreams,' someone replied, followed by more laughter.

The woman Cathy had sent forth returned with a bowl of warm water, a white towel, and a bottle of shampoo and conditioner, neither of which had a label on them. She washed Peta's hair and massaged her head, then Gabi started cutting it.

'So what do you folks do with yourselves?' Peta asked

The Elders had all kinds of hobbies, played bowls, and took turns to go on the internet and make illegal calls to their children and grandchildren.

As her hair was being cut one of the women collected it from the floor and asked whether they could keep it. Peta said yes and the woman gave each a lock of the white hair. Gabi was done and gave Peta a hand mirror, asking her what she thought. She liked her new look 'a lot'. She felt lighter, younger, stronger.

Then Fran, a formerly A woman, asked if she could trim Peta's nails in a way that would make her appear more manly, and therefore help to confuse the cammies.

'Of course,' Peta said, and Fran left to get her things.

Another woman said she was an optometrist and would give Peta a pair of contact lenses that would change her retina and instantly register her as another Peta Smith27.

'All systems have a glitch', one man said helpfully.

'They certainly do,' his wife said pointedly, and everyone burst out laughing again.

Fran returned with her manicure equipment and a plastic container filled with lukewarm water. She gently removed Peta's shoes and told her to put her feet in the water. She did. Fran then proceeded to remove the red polish from Peta's fingernails, dipped her fingers in a solution, dried them, and clipped Peta's fingernails. Next, Fran dried her feet and cut her toenails squarely as well, keeping the nails.

'Now you're a man person,' she said proudly.

'Right,' Cathy said, 'I think Peta might like a little space after all that, so why don't you all go and do something somewhere else?'

The Elders agreed, holding out their hands to Peta, who gave them each a quick hug. They all thanked her, some tearfully, and wished her well. The last couple asked her whether she didn't recognise them and, when Peta mumbled something apologetically, they asked whether she wasn't their grandson Jon's girlfriend.

'Yes, what a coincidence!' Peta replied. She was about to ask whether it had been good to see Jon recently, but something prevented her from doing so.

'We're missing him so much,' his grandmother said. 'We haven't seen him in years! Won't you please give him our regards and tell him we're missing him?'

'Of course,' Peta replied. 'As soon as I get out of this mess.'

She wanted to leave, but Oliver had heard reports that there was a lot of cammy traffic about, so it was decided she'd stay another day. If she felt safe, she also felt trapped. And sleepy, yet again. She wondered if she was already picking up on the elderly people's expressed wishes for an afternoon nap.

Chapter Sixteen

She lay down, convinced she would sleep instantly, but she didn't. Instead she thought about the morning's events, starting with the tasty breakfast Fay and Cathy had brought her. She couldn't help thinking about the last breakfast she'd had with her parents. Everything had seemed so normal; they'd seemed so upbeat. Then two overly friendly cammies came to collect her parents, helped put their suitcases in their double-cab ute, even gave them some time to say goodbye to her. And then they drove off, her mother looking back at her, trying bravely not to look heartbroken, terrified. Peta knew she'd never see her parents alive again, hearing the bees in her beloved mother's garden. At first they were doing what that near-extinct species did, going about their business, but they turned into hornets, as vicious as those holographic cows, and once again she had to run. She was so tired of running. But the steel hornets were closing in on her and were about to drill their poison into her when she woke up, sweating.

She could still hear the sound of the hornets as she became aware of Cathy and Fay looking down at her. Peta started, ready to protect herself from blows raining down on her, but the two women looked anxious, concerned.

'What's going on?' she asked. 'What's that sound?'

'Drones,' Fay said. 'Someone must have told the cammies about you.'

'Or they've broken the code on our computer,' Cathy added.

Peta got up and looked at the sky through a small opening in the curtains. There were at least ten black surveillance weapons in the sky.

'We know you're in there,' a mechanical voice boomed. 'Come out with your hands up.'

Peta looked at the two women and Fay said, 'You must go down into the tunnel, but go in the opposite direction you came. That's south. We'll tell them you went north, back to Auckland, that you doubled up. That'll gain you some time. We've packed some extra clothes, food, and those contact lenses. Take this cap.'

They rushed into the living room, where Cathy lifted the carpet, then the trapdoor leading down into the tunnel.

'Take care,' Fay said, tearfully hugging Peta, who in turn hugged stoic Cathy.

'Thank you,' Peta said, and the two friends nodded, not trusting themselves to say any more. Was it her imagination, or did they look as terrified as her mother had?

Peta went down the ladder and followed Fay's instructions, walking away from the entrance Keith and Oliver had used, counting her steps. There was a series of dim, evenly spaced lights to guide her. She could still hear the drones, hovering over the town. Then that amplified voice said, 'This is your third and final warning', followed by a pause. Suddenly there was a barrage of gunfire. They were destroying the town, killing its inhabitants.

Peta kept walking, horrified, still counting her steps. After two thousand the lights stopped and there was just blackness ahead. She put her hands in front of her, and felt her way forward with her feet, one slow step at time. She did not want to fall into some bottomless void – there were enough of those in her nightmares. But after five paces she felt the same heavy black curtains she had on the other side, parted them, and saw diffused light up ahead. The exit from the tunnel was partially blocked by a rock and a tree. She wormed her way through the tree's branches and the landscape opened up ahead of her.

Distant mountains, nearer green fields, a small township, a stagnant river.

Chapter Seventeen

A narrow-gauge rail track led down and away from the tunnel. It was overgrown with tree canopies above and bush below, but it had to lead somewhere, so she followed it. After about an hour she got to a railway siding with a broader train track. Of course: way back the mine's product would have been transferred on to a train and then taken to a factory or a port, except the product had never materialised.

The station was deserted, and weeds were forcing their way through the concrete platform, while in the background the mountains were as silent and wise as the dead. Peta sat inside the little siding hut and tried to work out what she was going to do next. The best thing would probably be to use the line as a guide, to walk not along it but parallel to it – at a safe distance. She was still making these plans when she heard voices on the platform. Men's voices. They were coming straight towards her. She peeped around the corner of the hut and saw two masked cammies, casually chatting. At least they didn't seem to be looking for her. Still, if they saw her, they might put two and two together. But there was no way she could get out of that hut without them seeing her, and they were probably coming to sit for a while, like she was. Did that mean they were actually expecting a train? Sure enough, she could feel a slight vibration, then heard the train. The men stopped walking and waited for the train to arrive. They were about ten metres away. She moved to the one corner of the hut, the one the train would pass first, so that its cameras wouldn't see her. The driverless train slowed, stopped, its doors slid open, and she heard the men climbing onto the train. She looked at the compartment opposite her and was certain it was empty, waited for the train's hydraulics to release, and then darted across the narrow platform and into the train before the door closed.

The train started moving and she glanced up ahead from under her cap, checking to see where the two men were. She couldn't see them because they were at least a coach away, but then she heard another voice, another male. Cheerful. Loud. Muffled by the train. He was talking to the two men. After a while she could see him coming into the next coach, spraying disinfectant. He was a conductor, wearing a surgical face mask and gloves with his dark blue uniform. There was no escaping this time. The train was going too fast to jump – the windows and doors were sealed anyway. There was no toilet she could hide inside so she dug into the bag Cathy and Fay had given her, took out a jumper and held it over her mouth. She could say she'd forgotten her mask at home. The conductor was tall, sallow, young. His hair was black, shiny, wavy.

'Good day,' he greeted her breezily.

Peta didn't trust herself to say anything, worried about voice-recognition, so she just nodded, still keeping her head down.

'Forgot your mask at home?'

She nodded again.

'Understandable,' he said cheerfully. 'But dangerous.'

He reached into his trouser pockets and Peta expected him to produce a wePhone to call his superiors. But he hauled a surgical mask from his one pocket, a pair of rubber gloves from the other, and handed them to her.

'This is a very dangerous strain, ay' he said.

He had a good voice, she thought. She took the mask and gloves with her one hand while keeping the jersey over her mouth. Then the young man did something unexpected. He lowered himself onto his haunches and looked directly into her eyes. But it wasn't in an interrogatory way. She could see he was smiling by the way his eyes glinted and his cheeks bulged. He had kind eyes.

'Stay here,' he said softly. 'Those other two are going to get off soon. Just make sure they don't see you.'

Then he moved on, towards the rear of the train, spraying the disinfectant. Peta put on the gloves and mask, half relieved, starting to relax. What a way to see this beautiful country, she thought. There were mountains and ravines and rivers and more mountains and waterfalls. Yet life had been turned upside down by a group of underground meat eaters from B2 (the former Nigerian capital, Lagos). They had acquired the meat from B7 South (Buenos Aires in South America). The result was a virus that had spread from a street market in the world's second-largest economy to the rest of the world, quickly and often fatally, though many sneered at its existence. It had reached Z via the old capital and the cammies had moved fast to keep it contained in Wellington. Those who contracted it were never heard from again, like Peta's parents.

The train started slowing, and Peta watched out for the two cammies up ahead. They disembarked, but there were no new passengers. When the train started moving again she ducked under the window sill, waited another minute or so, and then sat up. By then the young conductor was back, and asked her where she'd just come from.

'Z1,' she said. 'And you?'

'I've been visiting some family in the country,' he said, using the loaded words 'family' and 'country'. This meant he was Māori and had been to a secret gathering place, a marae. Moana had told her how these banned institutions were kept alive in the bush. 'Where are you going?' he asked.

'Ashburton,' she said, sensing she could trust him as she used the old name.

'Have you got a pass for the South Island?'

She shook her head.

'Don't worry. I've got one for you.'

'Thank you.'

'But they'll catch you with eye-recognition.'

'Is that how you knew who I am?'

'Your eyes have been all over the media,' he said. 'They're good eyes,' he smiled. 'Not killers' eyes.'

'Thank you,' she said again, feeling herself blush. 'But I've got something that'll change the structure of my eyes.'

'Good. Do it now, while the cameras are off,' he said. 'I'll be back in a minute.'

After removing the mask and gloves, she opened her bag and clumsily put in the contact lenses. But now she could smell the food Cathy and Fay had packed her, and realised she was ravenous. She decided she'd wait for the conductor to return, and offer him some of her food for being so kind. Sandwiches, fruit, a flask of coffee.

And what a view, she thought. What a pity she had to enjoy it by herself. She had always wanted to do a trip like this, but not alone. It could have been such fun to do it with Moana, Lee and, no, not Jon, surrounded by other holidaymakers and tourists of one stripe or another. But now it was like she was on a ghost train. Would she ever see Moana and Lee again? How she missed them. Had Cathy and Fay and all the others been killed, just for being kind to her? Maybe she was dreaming again, or maybe she was in an even bigger dream. Could she be in one of Jon's virtual landscapes? She didn't think so. This was all sadly, horribly real. Jon hadn't even tried to take her side – and he'd lied to her about his grandparents.

The conductor came walking towards her, carrying a small shoulder bag.

'What's in there?' she asked as he sat down and took out an old tin box.

'Food. I thought I'd share my lunch with you.'

'Thank you. I thought you'd like to share my lunch too.'

'Snap,' he smiled. 'I'm Terrence, by the way. Unofficially, though, I'm Tui.'

'I prefer Tui.'

'So do I,' he smiled.

'Peta.'

'Smith,' he said on her behalf.

'Twenty-seven,' she added, and they laughed.

Then, pointing to himself, he said, 'Smith25. But really, Taimana.'

They had to take off their face masks to eat and Peta liked what she saw even more as she told him about the contact lenses. He may have had an easy smile, but it was very much a confident smile, one that came not from a comfortable life but one that knew about hardship – and how to handle it.

Chapter Eighteen

As the train got closer to what Tui called Wallington, people embarked at suburban stations. Shift workers. Those aged 40 to 59. They were grimly quiet. No one spoke to anyone else. They might as well have been heading towards their execution, Peta thought.

The train pulled into Z2 station and she saw it was swarming with cammies. Each platform had a checkpoint, lit up with bright, intimidating overhead lights.

'Just act friendly,' Tui said softly as they walked towards a checkpoint, occupied by three officials: a standing cammy and two seated women in Z-Rail uniforms. One of them was in her twenties, the other in her fifties. 'You can be glad it's too dangerous to remove your mask and gloves for a voice and fingerprints test. I'll go first and try to soften them up,' he said.

First, however, they had to wait in a queue as others went before them. Slowly, keeping their distance of two metres apart.

'Try to stay calm,' Tui said.

Peta felt everything but calm – what if the contact lenses didn't work? Nobody else spoke, whether they were with someone or not, and the only reason why she and Tui could talk, albeit softly, was because the trains and health announcements made so much noise. People moved about like well-programmed zombies.

Now it was Peta and Tui's turn. He went ahead of her and spoke to the officials, who he clearly dealt with on a daily basis. Not that they returned his friendly banter. The cammy tested his temperature with a gun-like instrument that looked like he was going to stun Tui in the forehead, like a farm animal of old. Tui gave his pass to the younger woman, who was clearly in training. She put the card into a machine. The card was swallowed, there was a pause, then a small green light started flashing. Next, he had to stare up into a camera, which then scanned his eyes. After what felt like a minute, he was given the all-clear.

Now it was Peta's turn. The cammy put the gun against her head. 'Stand still please,' he said, and tested Peta's temperature with the reader. He looked at the machine for what felt like an eternity before a little screen lit up. He moved past her to the next person in the queue. Peta greeted the two women, but they didn't respond. She handed the trainee checker the pass Tui had given her, while the older one gave her a steady, searching look.

'Name?' the checker said.

'Peta Smith27.'

The name clearly meant nothing to the younger woman, but the older one knew exactly what it meant and kept on watching Peta, as if waiting for her to make a sudden move.

'Where are you from?' the checker said.

'Z1,' Peta said.

'What is your business here?'

'I'm just passing through to Z26.'

This was the make-or-break moment. If the scanner saw she was wearing the special contact lenses and identified who she really was, she was doomed. If the cammies could wipe out an entire village of Elders in their hunt for her, then they could clearly kill her too – just because she'd spoken back to her boss!

'Stand still for your Eye-D please,' the machine said, sounding everything but polite, like the two women. Peta couldn't help thinking it spoke in a way that didn't allow for a comma between the 'D' and the 'please'.

Was the scan going slower than it had with Tui? It felt like it, but Peta told herself to stay calm. Then the scan was done. Nothing happened. The two steel electronic flaps that barred her way to a neutral-looking Tui stayed resolutely down. Had he also possibly led her up the garden path, lied to her, betrayed her? If so, she was done. But the flaps swung open and vibrated. She was through.

Walking towards the station's entrance, Tui said 'Here's another pass. For the ferry and train.'

'Thank you.'

'Have you got a phone?'

'No. I had to dump it to get the cammies off my back.'

Tui nodded and headed towards a booth.

'What are you doing?'

'I'm going to rent you a phone.'

'Why?'

'So you can call me if you're stuck.'

Peta smiled at him behind her mask. He was almost too good to be true. At the counter, he told the waitron what he wanted. 'No problem,' it said, and gave him a box. Tui tapped his phone to pay. Peta looked down and saw that she was standing in the middle of the compass laid out on the floor of the station terminal. Tui gave her the box containing the phone.

'If I call you, they'd instantly pick up on my voice,' she said.

'I know. But there are ways to beat the system. Hold on.'

He busied himself with her phone and typed in a code.

'Now you can call me any time you like. Your voice will be masked to everyone except me.' He stopped. 'Or you could just stay with me.'

She wanted to say she'd very much like to, and knew he knew it too, but said instead, 'I have to sort this problem myself.'

He nodded and looked up at the atomic clock.

'You better catch a taxi to the ferry. It's leaving quite soon.'

'How am I going to pay the taxi?'

'The pass applies to that too, and the ferry.'

'Thank you,' she said gratefully.

'Take care,' he said.

'Can I give you a hug?'

'No, you can't. It'll be a dead giveaway,' he said. 'But I want you to.'

'Then here's a virtual hug.'

'Likewise,' he smiled behind his mask. 'A very big, long hug.'

Peta's eyes creased as she smiled.

'You'd better hurry,' Tui said.

'See you,' she said, and walked away, hoping she'd see him again. And hug him, but not virtually.

Chapter Nineteen

It felt good to catch a taxi again, but the streets were deserted and dark. All the buildings' lights were off and most streetlights didn't work anymore. There could be cammies anywhere, blending in with the buildings, ready to taserPhone you and take you away – just like that Undesirable back in Auckland. The only other light came from neon billboards calling for her arrest. She couldn't even go to a graveyard to visit her parents: they'd both been incinerated. There was nothing left of them except her memories, now that she'd given her LOVE brooch to Blossom.

Once she got to the port, she had to go through the same procedure as at the station. It was a nerve-wracking business, even though she knew she was okay with the contact lenses and Tui's pass. That was the problem with this state of affairs, she thought for the first time in her life. It made you feel like a criminal, just for being yourself. While she was waiting her turn, she noticed that a storm was building. Food-franchise boxes were being swept around the harbour, a man's toupee suddenly lifted, and a woman hung onto her hat. It was going to be a rough night.

Soon the ploughing, listing ferry made her feel as queasy as crossing the passage back at Joy Inc. I'm such a weakling, she thought, for all my athleticism. What a way she'd come, though, from just going to work a few days ago to being a fugitive with a reward on her head! None of these thoughts, however, helped suppress the misery of seasickness, so she sat as still as possible and tried to focus on one still point – the blue seat opposite her. It didn't help much. She tried to think of her happy time with Moana and Lee at the Pinnacles. Wouldn't it be great to meet them at the usual spot for a beer? Beer. The mere thought made her want to be sick all over the carpet, so what else could she think of? Her parents. Her mother had once told her to eat ginger if she felt seasick. But surely this ship wouldn't have ginger available, unless she went to its kitchen and asked for it, or stole it. Either way would attract undue attention. Did they sell ginger biscuits? If they did, she wouldn't be able to buy them. Her bank account would have been frozen days ago. So she'd simply have to endure this trip and ultimately sort out McCracken. How that would happen she didn't know, but finding out where he came from had to be a good start.

The trip lasted three lurching hours. Peta tried to recover while she stood in yet another long queue in the small town of Picton (Z49). Her reflection in a terminus window made her look as ghostly as she felt. From there she caught the bus to Ashburton (Z31), a small city just south of Christchurch (Z3), half of which had been swallowed up by the sea and the earth in the earthquake of 2045. Tui had also told her there was an insurrection brewing in that metropolis.

She got on to the bus and hoped she wouldn't be recognised. Yet, in one sense she wished she would so that this endless running could be over. But getting caught might mean getting killed, as the Elders had discovered, so that wasn't an option. Were elderly people that dispensable? Maybe the gunfire had just been used as a tactic to intimidate them all. This was the more optimistic reading of the situation, but not even that was comforting. The only mildly pleasant thought she had was that all the men on the bus ignored her in her male garb.

The journey was long, passing ghostly vineyards in the rainy night, and slowed by detours, thanks to landslides in places like Kaikoura, now known as Z17. She lolled in a state between wakefulness and sleep, tired and stressed. There was always the danger that someone was going to see she wasn't really a man. Moreover, if Kylie had often told her she must come and visit, she hadn't given her friend any prior warning. She was just going to arrive and, thinking back on their friendship, she realised Kylie wasn't exactly an adaptable Ms Spontaneous. In fact, she liked things to be just so. The closer Peta got to her destination, the more she thought and felt this might not have been such a good idea. She might get her friend into trouble. Kylie might freak out at this sudden intrusion.

At dawn the landscape flattened out on to what used to be called the Canterbury Plains before the bus finally crossed the long Ashburton bridge, which had been strengthened (instead of renewed) numerous times against floods and earthquakes. The river was sluggish, slow-moving, smelly. The bus stopped outside the tower clock at Baring Square, which had somehow retained its name. If the town had once been a flat country affair, it had become, like so many other country towns in the south, a metropolis of six-storey buildings along its main military road. This was to accommodate the demand for housing across the country, as people of all shapes, shades and sizes streamed into Z. The country now stood at fifty-million people. If she'd been expecting a sedate, medium-size city, then she'd arrived at the wrong time. There was no lockdown here and the town was roaring, literally, because she'd arrived in the middle of Motorcycle Mania Month.

Chapter Twenty

The festival had started off as a response to another B Island town, Rangiora (Z42), which had a Muscle Car Madness Weekend. Ashburton had responded with a two-wheeled version. So right now it was a city full of growling, whining two-wheeled machines, each tuned for maximum speed and noise. Every conceivable motorbike from the 2030s onwards was on display and getting ready for a drive-through later that day, replete with the recorded sound of its petrol forebears. There were marques from the old America, England, Germany, Italy and Japan, electric makes that still had names like Harley-Indian, BMercW, DucaVespa, Moto Laverda, Hondaya and Suzaki. This was good news because everybody was focused on the bikes, which meant Peta could calmly consult the town map outside the information centre. Like so many other details, which Jon used to mock her about, she could remember the address off-hand. Kylie's parents had been wiped out in a car accident – they'd volunteered to try out a new driverless model – and she'd inherited the house. It was a solid structure of red brick, like quite a few others on the street. Peta knocked on the door, and waited. After a while she thought she heard something like a scuffle before she heard Kylie, presumably, approaching the door.

'Who is it?'

'It's me, Peta.'

'*What?*'

'Peta.'

'What are you doing here?'

'Long story. Can I come in and tell you?'

'Yes, just hang on,' Kylie said uncertainly from behind her door, 'I need to find the key.'

'Okay,' Peta said, wondering why Kylie didn't keep the key in her door. Maybe she was afraid of cunning burglars. Crime was almost as high in Ashburton as it was in Auckland. But then one didn't have door keys in the capital. Everything was electronic. Did she hear some activity behind that door, or was the distant roar of the motorbikes just playing tricks on her? Whatever the case, she was exhausted. She hoped Kylie would let her shower and get a good long sleep before she had to tell her the whole, fantastic story. No. It wasn't a fantasy, it wasn't virtual. It was real, a real nightmare.

Kylie opened the door, looking at her strangely.

'Hi,' Peta said uncertainly.

'You look like a boy!'

'That's the whole idea.'

'The whole country's looking for you!'

'I know. Can I come in? They don't know where I am.'

'They think you're heading back towards Auckland.'

'Good. That's what I want them to think.'

Kylie was still not giving way, so Peta asked again whether she could come in.

'Yes, of course,' Kylie said, more dazed than convinced. 'You realise that if they find out you're here you're not the only one who's in trouble?'

'Yes, I do.'

Kylie frowned, then let Peta in.

Something was wrong. Apart from the fact that Kylie seemed more concerned about her own hide than anything else, her enthusiasm for her friend and ex-colleague coming to visit had dwindled. Or maybe she was just flustered.

'Could I possibly have a quick shower?'

'No, I'm sorry. I've already used up my quota.'

'Oh, okay,' Peta said, puzzled. Every house was allowed at least two showers a day, and Kylie was alone as far as she could see.

'Have you got a visitor?'

'Yes, but they've gone out for the day.'

'Okay. Could I at least spruce myself up?' Peta asked.

'Yes of course. Let me just tidy up.'

'I don't care what it looks like.'

'Won't be a seccy,' Kylie said, and darted out.

Peta looked around her friend's living room. It seemed like Kylie had kept her parent's sense of décor, for everything was floral: the carpet, the lounge suite, the curtains. Peta was surprised that her friend was so old fashioned. It was so different to her minimalist, even austere Z1 apartment. Kylie came back into the lounge room and gave Peta a face towel.

'Thank you so much,' Peta said, and headed towards the bathroom, past Kylie's shut bedroom door.

'Are you hungry?' Kylie asked after her.

'Starving!'

'Okay, I'll rustle something up.'

Peta washed her face and brushed her teeth with her fingers. She felt much better, but how could she be completely relaxed when the entire country's Force was looking for her? How had the country become a plant-based society but also one where financial priorities overrode all that artsy-fartsy stuff, as Jon used to call it? Surely that was a contradiction, a charade? And what were the cammies going to do with her once they caught her? Put her on trial? Imprison her? Relieve her, like an Elder? She dried her face and walked through to the kitchen, where Kylie was just finishing cooking her a rich-smelling breakfast. Kylie smiled uncertainly.

'Smells great,' Peta said.

Her friend put the plate of food and a knife and fork on the kitchen counter, sat down opposite her and said: 'So what the hell is going on?'

Peta told her the story through grateful mouthfuls and, when that was done, Kylie said: 'Amazing.'

'I know, it's crazy,' Peta said. 'I mean, why did you leave Joy Inc?'

'Oh, I wanted to leave. I couldn't stand McCracken. But the funny thing is, I couldn't get work after that. In fact, no one would even acknowledge that I'd applied for a job. Not even an automatic reply.'

'That's exactly what happened to me,' Peta said. 'After our little conversation...'

'What conversation?'

'Sorry. I dreamt you called me, asking about Jon.'

'Oh,' Kylie said blankly.

'Anyway, I almost immediately started applying for other jobs, but nothing happened. I think MK had something to do with it.'

'I'm convinced of it,' Kylie shuddered.

'What do you think makes him tick?'

'All work and no play,' Kylie said. 'One night I was drunk and in the vicinity of Joy Inc, so I thought I'd quickly pop in to get something, and there he was.'

'Typical workaholic.'

'It was eleven at night!'

'What?'

'Yeah.'

'That's weird. Did you talk to him?'

'No, I was too creeped out.'

'Strange man,' Peta said. 'This food is great by the way. So's your place.'

'Not bad, ay,' Kylie said.

'Ideal for a family.'

'Yeah.'

'Are you planning on having one?'

'Absolutely,' Kylie said.

'But how are you staying alive?'

'My parents had some investments...'

'Nice,' Peta said. 'Any romantic interest?'

Kylie nodded.

'Tell me?'

Kylie shook her head.

'Oh, come on,' Peta said, laughing.

'No. Tell me what you're going to do.'

'I don't know. I've got nothing. Maybe I'll hang out here in the south like the fugitive I am. Start a new life under an assumed name. Become a forester or something. Do some writing at night.'

'I can't quite see you becoming a forester.'

'Nah, I suppose not.'

They laughed and Kylie got up and poured them each a mug of coffee.

'So would it be alright if I stayed here the night?' Peta asked.

'That's a bit of a problem.'

'Oh... Why? Are you worried about the cammies?'

'No...'

'Oh, you have a guest.'

'Yes.'

'I'll sleep on the couch.'

Kylie took a deep breath and said, 'Look behind you.'

Peta was expecting an armed cammy to be standing there, having become accustomed to betrayal and flight of one sort or another, but the last person she expected to be standing there, even though it made perfect sense in another way, was her partner – or ex-partner – Jon. She was dumbstruck, not because she was disappointed, or hurt, but because it was all so obvious and predictable.

'How long has this been going on?' Peta asked Jon.

'A while,' he finally managed to squeeze out.

'I'll leave you two to talk it out,' Kylie said, getting up.

'I don't think there's much to talk about,' Peta said. 'In fact, I think I'll leave right away.'

'Let me explain,' Jon said, sounding like one of those interminable TV series he used to scoff at as Kylie left the room.

'I suppose you're going to tell me you're also here for the motorbike thing?' Peta said.

'Yeah, but I can explain the other stuff.'

'I'm listening,' Peta said, though she wasn't all that interested.

'I'm sorry about what happened to you, but I couldn't do anything about it. If I maintained contact with you, I'd lose my job. How would I be able to look after my grandparents then?'

'Who you regularly went to see near Te Papa-i-Oea?'

'Sorry? What?

'Palmerston North.'

'Yes.'

'Funny, they told me they hadn't seen you in ages.'

Jon's jaw literally fell.

'How did you...?'

'It doesn't matter. I just did. Are they still alive?'

'Yeah, I actually spoke to them last night.'

'Good.'

'They sounded a bit strange...'

'Well, that's either because they're dead and their voices have been faked, or they're too decent to say how hurt they are because you never visit them. Or they're being held.'

Jon looked in the direction Kylie had taken, as if that would help.

'So how and when did the two of you get involved?'

'It was Kylie who called me,' he said weakly.

'Yes, I saw and heard you talking to her on K'Road the night I was fired.'

Jon studied a spot on the floor.

'It's alright, Jon. I understand.'

'What are you going to do?'

'That's no longer any of your business, is it?' Peta said, heading towards Kylie's bedroom as Jon continued staring at the spot. Kylie was finishing a phone call and said, 'Bye,' seeing Peta.

'Thanks for the food,' she said.

'I'm sorry.'

'Don't be. Or don't pretend to be. I hope you two will be very happy, and I mean it.'

'Take care,' Kylie said.

Chapter Twenty-One

Dazed but also relieved, Peta walked back to the city centre. An increasing amount of motorbikes were heading that way too, like small streams flowing towards the main river. That made her feel reasonably anonymous, on the one hand, since everybody was focused on their machines, but on the other hand she couldn't help shaking off the feeling that she was being watched. She dismissed that feeling, thinking it was probably because she'd become accustomed to being pursued, telling herself that if she just acted normal no one would take any notice of her.

She came to Baring Square with the old red-brick Methodist Church, currently a recruitment centre for The Force, on her left, with a view of the Clock Tower at the other end. In between the church and the tower were gigantic statues of various Heroes of Vegan Agriculture. Beyond the tower was the main road, which by now was a raging torrent of revving motorbikes, heading towards the racetrack, usually a detention centre, but cleared for this commercial occasion. (The Power was nothing but accommodating when it came to matters of the market.) What added to the din was the various traders who had erected stalls alongside the main road, each loudly playing heavy metal rock – the kind of music Jon loved – to attract potential buyers of motorcycle parts, accessories, and, of course, food and drink. Everybody around her was clearly in good spirits, but Peta couldn't shake off the feeling of being watched, though no one seemed to be doing so. As she approached the tower, the feeling that something wasn't quite right increased. She couldn't put her finger on it as she looked around, towards the former church, surrounded by high-rises which had also been strengthened against earthquakes back in the Thirties. But now the church didn't quite seem itself, as weird as that sounded. She didn't know how to process it. Was she going mad? Was someone or something trying to *make* her mad? And then she knew exactly what was going on. The church's walls and the statues' plinths started moving because there were ten cammies who had blended in with them in their special uniforms. They all had their automatic rifles pointed at her, like third eyes, and when she turned to look for a possible way out, she saw there were more cammies approaching her from every direction, including the road.

'You are surrounded,' a voice said over a loudhailer. 'Put your hands in the air and do not make any sudden movements.'

Peta did as she was told, realising that Kylie had informed on her. She had told them that Peta's hair was short and that she was dressed in a boy's clothes. Everybody else – bikers, stallholders, spectators – made as if none of this was happening. She'd become like that Undesirable back in Auckland. Unseen. The cammies, young men and women who'd been trained to cultivate blank expressions, were moving towards her, guns trained on her, as if she was the most dangerous human being on the planet. Peta was both amused and terrified by this. The game was up. They were going to do whatever they were going to do now, and nobody would do a thing about it, not even acknowledge it. They could shoot her to shreds, or arrest her and take her somewhere, blind her, whatever. But when they were within three metres of her, the cammies' expressions changed from focused aggression to slight confusion, as if they had the wrong person. She could hear the same distant, rumbling sound she'd heard in her dream before the walkway started tearing apart, but that was a dream. This was everything but. The cammies were starting to look uncomfortable, uncertain, even scared. A wind had sprung up and started shaking the few trees and high-rises around them. Something was happening under their feet too. For a second she had the absurd idea that some military machine was boring up towards them, and that the cammies were scared they might get caught in its jaws. But it wasn't that, either. They were right in the middle of an earthquake, a real earthquake this time. The ground was pitching and rolling, as if they were standing in shallow waves, except this wasn't water. It was concrete, cement, tar, earth, stones, rubbish. They were being thrown this way and that as if they were shaken by some massive, subterranean shrug. Peta fell, looked up and saw the clock tower shake for a moment before snapping like a large twig, slicing into a group of riders on the main road.

Carnage.

Riders deserted their still-running bikes on the spot, trying to find shelter in shaky doorways. The cammies lost instant interest in her, trying to save their own skins. Peta sprang up and started running towards the distant mountains she'd seen earlier. Up ahead more people and bikes were being crushed by more collapsing buildings. A shopping trolley sped past her and hit an old man, sending him tumbling. A blonde woman had half her head smashed in but was still alive, holding it, bleeding, screaming. Peta knew she had to find a doorway to protect her head, but she just kept going, running around or jumping over crushed motorbikes, bits of wall, benches, dustbins, people. The logic of her instinct was correct. The quake was running in a south-to-north direction, so if she kept running towards the mountains, west, she'd hopefully escape its main thrust. People lay dead, crushed, ashen. Others were screaming, pale, bloody. Her lungs were burning, but she'd escaped the epicentre of the quake and kept moving, weeping and groaning with fear. Soon she was beyond the cavalcade. A motorbike pulled up next to her, and a heavily tattooed woman said, 'Hey, hop on!'

Peta didn't even think about it – she climbed on and shouted, 'Thank you!'

'Hold tight,' the woman said, and turned on the juice.

'Jessica!' the woman shouted as another aftershock rippled behind them, swaying the bike, but she managed to keep level.

'Peta! Where're you going?'

'Everywhere except back!'

'Why?'

'The cammies want me!'

'What for?'

'Insubordination!'

'Me too!'

'Well, they'll never catch us!' Jessica shouted, going even faster as the earth opened up behind them and tore a deep crevasse through the city once called Ashburton, the high-rises of its main street collapsing into it.

They sped across the former Canterbury Plains – two specks of flesh, bone, clothing and machinery – heading towards the distant, snow-topped mountains. Peta felt deeply alive but also guilty that so many had died in her wake. They rode past state farms with their gigantic windbreaks of macrocarpa bushes. They rode through small villages that had become old-age towns, whose elderly inhabitants were never older than seventy. Others had been closed, destroyed or deserted. The excitement slowly wore off and Peta was half sleeping against Jessica's back. She had lost all sense of time when Jessica slowed down to a virtual crawl. Peta looked up and saw they were in the middle of a forest.

'Why're you stopping?'

'I think you should go ahead.'

'Why?'

'I saw the drones coming in my rear-view.'

'What about you?'

'I'll distract them.'

'How?'

'Don't worry about it.'

'Please don't put yourself in danger for my sake.'

'I've been running for months now. Years. And I'm sick of it. I'm not gonna let them take me in. I've heard what they do to you in there.'

'What do they do?'

'They mess with your mind. Steal your eyes.'

'That's terrible, but…?'

'Look, you just go ahead. Stay off the main roads.'

'I don't understand,' Peta said.

'You don't have to,' Jessica said, turning the bike to face in the direction they'd come.

'Please don't.'

'My life, my decision.'

Peta gave her a long, hard hug.

'That makes it all worthwhile,' Jessica smiled, then got a determined look on her face, revved once, and sped back the way they'd come.

Peta kept walking and soon heard the chattering sound of machine guns, the same as in the old-age town near Te Papa-o-Oea, or Palmerston North. She felt sick to her core.

Chapter Twenty-Two

A few hours later she came to an escarpment, which fell away to another great, wide plain. She scrambled down, away from the road, and got to the middle of the plain at noon. What a day, she thought, starting with a confrontation with her ex-partner and friend, then an earthquake, followed by the sacrificial death of a complete stranger.

She continued walking over fields and hills, through streams with undrinkable water and back onto the last flat stretch of land before it rose up towards the snowy Alps. Its bottom reaches were forested with tall pines, trees that weren't endemic to this region and which used vast amounts of state-controlled water. She was convinced she'd find a road up ahead that would take her back south and east again. She was about a hundred metres from the forest line when she heard a familiar sound. First she thought it was bees, then hornets as the sound grew louder, then she knew. Drones. She looked back and saw at least ten of them, black, menacing, each with a flashing red light. She started running once more and had to get to the forest before they surrounded her, herded her like aerial border collies, or simply killed her. She ran for all she was worth, having to cross the road she'd expected. Was there no escape from this hell? When she was about twenty metres from the tree line, a command came from the leading drone: 'Give yourself up or we will fire.'

There was no way she was going to give up and, just before she reached the tree line, they started firing, tearing up the earth behind her, getting closer with each burst. Then she was in among the trees, gasping, but her living nightmare wasn't over yet. Drones were not like helicopters: they could fly low, in between trees, so here they came now, though slower. She carried on running until she was running on nothing and fell into a hole with a thump.

The depression was covered with rotting matter and pine needles. She wanted to scramble out again, before she realised she'd been given the most natural protection she could wish for. Nothing or no one could see her from above, not even if they were just two metres away – unless they had heat detectors. But she couldn't move anyway: she was completely out of breath. The black drones searched among the trees, one of them even hitting a trunk and falling, before buzzing back into life and up again. One passed directly overhead, stopped, reversed and hovered above her for too long. The game was up, Peta thought. She didn't move. What would happen if she surrendered? Would they herd her all the way back to Ashburton, blind her, or would they simply annihilate her? Most likely the latter. What a way to end everything, she thought bitterly. But nothing happened for a very long minute, then they all started leaving, except the one hovering above her. It felt like it was telling her it knew she was there. Maybe they'd been ordered to go help with that insurrection in Christchurch. Clearly there were other people also transgressing the Commercial Disobedience Act. It was some comfort that she wasn't entirely alone.

She couldn't go down on to the plain for now, nor could she stay here in the forest, where the cammies knew she was, so she'd have to find some kind of shelter up on the mountain. After a while she emerged from the forest, and thought she'd have to fashion some kind of shelter for herself up there. It was mid-afternoon. Soon it would be dark. She scrambled up over tussock, shale, rocks. Then it started snowing. The good thing about that was that it made her harder to see from the sky, the bad thing was that it just grew colder as she headed further up.

Freezing.

And then she couldn't go any further. She was confronted by a deep, narrow ravine between her and a sheer cliff of black, icy rock. If she spent the night out here, she would certainly freeze to death, even though it had stopped snowing. She felt panicky.

'There is always a solution to a problem,' she suddenly heard her father saying. 'Often it's staring you right in the face.' Where is it, Dad? she wondered.

Then she saw the cave. Surely that would provide a little shelter from this onslaught. It would, but it was on the other side of the ravine. Between her and the cave was a chasm at least a hundred metres deep, and the only way she could get to the cave was by going down and then up again – or by way of a blackened tree trunk bridging that chasm. Not in a million years would she do that, she thought. The mere thought of it made her feet cramp. So it was a matter of going down, then back up again. She started descending backward, but after about ten metres the loose shale and slippery snow suddenly gave and she slid downwards, fast. She couldn't help screaming and thinking this was the end, but she instinctively grabbed a small tree, which held while the rest of the shale, snow and mud slid past and fell down what sounded like much more than just a hundred metres. She would have to go back up. She slowly made her way back up again, centimetre by centimetre, crawling halfway up and sliding down again, stopped by a rock hitting her knee. Again she screamed, then groaned, but she clung to the rock. She waited for the pain to subside, then carried on crawl-climbing up again. It took her half a terrified hour just to get back to where she'd started, by which time it was late afternoon. She waited to regain her breath, wiping the snow and mud off her sodden clothes.

Crossing over to the cave could mean death: there was no guarantee that the tree trunk, which had clearly been struck by lightning, would hold. But she had no choice: she would certainly freeze to death out here. But how to do this? She wasn't even going to think of doing a balancing act, so she lowered herself onto the log, straddling it, and started working her way along it. The trick, of course, was to not look down, ever. But that was difficult, because that was the way she was facing. She would simply look forward, straining her neck, doing everything except look down. That way lay death. She could feel the depths pulling her downwards, but she clung on, her hands close to numb, going forward, millimetre by painful millimetre. She had once read about a man caught in a fire who had hung on, waiting for help. He'd done it by counting. One, two, three, four… all the way to twenty. Then he started at one again as his hands and face and chest almost shrivelled in the heat. If *he* could do it then so could she, even if she knew no help was going to come. She was on her own and no one would know where she'd died. 'You're halfway across,' she whispered. 'Just keep going.' There was a creaking sound behind her and she felt the log give a little under her weight. She stopped, held her breath. 'Keep going, Peta Smith27,' she said. 'Keep going, you bitch. Just beat this bastard. You're almost there. Count to twenty again.' The creaking grew louder. 'Almost there. One, two, three…' She could almost touch the other side as she felt the log giving, but there was nothing to grip. 'Just go!' she shouted and scrambled forward like an animal, rolling onto the other side as the log cracked in the middle and crashed down, fell away, the roar of falling shale and snow getting softer for a long time before there was silence. Peta hugged the snow-covered ground as if it were a lover, laughing, almost frozen, half weeping with relief. 'I did it' she said to herself. 'I did it, I did it, I did it!' she laughed, almost hysterical. 'Well, it's not the end of your problems, so get over it,' she said with a giggle. 'There's still a way to go.'

She carried on crawling away from the ravine until she was in the cave's mouth. She knew she was still in immediate trouble, but she was also proud of what she'd done, clapping her hands and stamping her feet to warm herself. The cave wasn't very deep and, if it wasn't much warmer than outside, at least it wasn't wet. She doubted whether she'd be able to sleep in that cold, so she'd have to pace about the whole night. She didn't have anything to make a fire or light, but at least there were icicles to eat. 'Well, that's something,' she joked to herself, wondering if it was okay to talk to herself out there. Well, why not? No one could see or hear her – except that she was starting to get the feeling that she wasn't alone. No, it was more than just a feeling. Whatever it was, it wouldn't be an angry bear or some predator. This was Z, the least threatening country in the world, biologically. That was some comfort. But she couldn't see anything and after a while decided that she'd probably been imagining things.

Still, the feeling of not being alone persisted. It was almost dark when, having given up looking, she saw an unnatural pattern in the snow. The sole of a boot. A climber's boot. It was sticking out from under a pile of snow to the side of the cave, the ice clinging to it. Attached to that boot, of course, would be a human being. A very dead, frozen human being. He had obviously fallen down the cliff above her and landed face down. Peta grabbed a nearby rock and struck the ice enveloping him, apologising loudly as she went along. 'He's beyond caring,' she told herself. Bang. Crunch. Finally, the lump of ice, snow, clothes, flesh and bone could be moved, so Peta – fingers aching from the cold – dragged him to the inside of the cave. There might be things in his backpack she needed, so she prised it off the corpse. Her hands were stiff and blue. She could barely open the top of the backpack, but eventually felt inside it. The first thing she touched was a little gas stove, which she took out and put on the ground. Next she turned the bag upside down and shook it, as much to empty it as to keep moving, generating some kind of warmth. Finally, a billy can fell out, a can of baked beans, a tin mug, a plastic bag with a tea bag in it and – oh, joy – a lighter. She instinctively moved to the other side of the cave to set up her little camp, away from the corpse. She tried the lighter, but nothing happened. Again. Nothing. Maybe it was just cold, she thought, breathing on it. Rubbing it between her hands. Tried it again. There was a spark, then a flame. She cupped the little flame with shaking hands and thought it was the most beautiful thing she'd ever seen and felt, warming the inside of her hands. But she had to stop being so wasteful and work out how the little stove worked. She needed a hot meal, a cup of tea, more heat. Fortunately, the little stove was foolproof – she turned a switch, gas hissed, she held a flame above it, and there was an instant circle of flames. Heaven. The baked beans didn't require a can opener, so Peta peeled the lid open, poured the beans into the billy can, and put it on the little stove. Just the smell of those warming beans made her ecstatic. She put her hands inside the backpack, but the only thing she could find was something more important than eating utensils: a sleeping bag. The label showed it was filled with down. She'd be able to sleep warmly that night. More heaven. The baked beans were steaming hot now and she'd have to wait for them to cool so she could eat them with her hands. She kept the flame on for light, worrying that its gas wouldn't last. The beans quickly cooled and she ate them with her fingers, avoiding the sight of the corpse. She ate slowly, tasting every morsel. I am eating in the presence of a corpse, she thought, licking her fingers. This did not affect her appetite, she realised guiltily, and she remembered thinking about eating after her parents' virtual funeral. Why did one do it? Because we owe it to the dead to carry on living.

Once she'd finished eating and licking her fingers clean, like cats of old, she couldn't help looking at the corpse again, noticing that he had a thick knife attached to his belt. On closer inspection, she discovered that the knife had all the eating utensils – knife, fork, spoon – she'd needed in one. Duh! Then she felt the morbid but irrepressible urge to see the man's face. Our faces are our history. So she gripped his shoulder and turned him around, and saw that his face had been smashed beyond recognition.

Peta felt the nausea and tears welling up in her. She loosened the man's bandana from around his neck, weeping, apologising profusely, and covered his face with the bag. Then she went back to the stove, picked up the mug, found an icicle, and put it in the mug. She wanted to have a cup of tea in the morning. She needed something to look forward to. Next, she laid out the sleeping bag on a level piece of ground next to the stove, took off her shoes, slid inside, and turned off the stove. She decided she'd hold a prostrate wake for the man, but soon she herself was dead to the world.

Chapter Twenty-Three

Peta was in the middle of a dream in which she was once again running away from the cammies. They were on motorbikes and their sirens were screaming, getting closer. But just as the front bike was about to run her down, she was woken by something so incongruous, so foreign yet familiar, that it took her a few seconds to compute what it was. A text message. At first she thought it might be Tui, which would be most welcome, but her phone was still off, so it had to be the corpse's. The sound was coming from his backpack. She followed the ping and found the phone in a side pocket. Its battery was on 7%. There was a text from 'Nick', the last in a long line of texts from him. The latest message simply said: *Georgia? Where are you? I'm sorry about what I said. Please call. I'm worried about you. I love you.* The corpse was a woman and she had a name. Georgia. And she had a number. Peta memorised it. That Georgia hadn't been found because of the phone was strange, or maybe no one except Nick was looking for her at this stage. Maybe she always went climbing when they had an argument. Maybe he'd call the police soon. Maybe not. Whatever the case, Peta had a grim task ahead of her. She'd decided to swap clothes with Georgia to put her pursuers off her scent again. That would only last until the cammies checked the DNA of the missing climber, but it would win her some time. The grim part was going to be undressing the faceless Georgia, putting on her clothes, and then dressing her with Peta's discarded clothes. Best not think about it and just do it as quickly as possible, as her mother had always said. Then she'd reward herself with a cup of tea. She set to work on her grisly task, apologising through tears to the unfortunate woman. Nick was not going to be happy that Peta had used Georgia as a decoy, but she'd explain to him later – if there was a later. It was a gruesome task undressing Georgia and putting on her clothes, then dressing her again with Peta's clothes. She felt strange in the woman's icy clothing and climbing boots. She removed the steel spikes, put the tea bag in the mug with the melted icicle, lit the little stove and put the mug on it. Squatting, she held her palms against the mug, trying to let the warmth spread to the rest of her body. That didn't last long either: the little stove's gas ran out. The water was lukewarm, and the tea was bitter for Peta's liking, but it tasted like the honey of old anyway.

She had to move quickly, and this time she was armed. Apart from the multipurpose pocket knife with its fixed blade, she also had Georgia's ice axe. She dug a hole with it, switched off the climber's mobile, wiped her fingerprints off it, and buried it. Then she shouldered Georgia's rucksack and dragged her corpse towards an open area close to the cave, apologising and crying loudly. She walked away from Georgia and the cave, covering her tracks as she went, until she was back down in the forest again.

She'd have to walk parallel to the road to Timaru for as many days as it took, she thought. If anyone spotted her, she would have to concoct a story about how she'd fallen and was a bit dazed. All she could remember was her name. Georgia. She soon found herself hiking along Lake Tekapo (10), which looked so inviting but whose water was undrinkable. How things had changed in the last ten years. When she'd been a teen there was more than enough water for everyone, but it had all become so poisoned with industrial effluent and plastic that The Power had taken control of it, having the sole means of purifying it, rationing it, and exporting it at a huge profit.

Soon she saw a woman in her car at a solitary lookout point, eating sandwiches and drinking coffee. That was normal enough, except that the way the woman reached for her sandwiches and coffee indicated she was blind. This suited Peta down to a T. It also reminded her that she was hungry. The woman was about fifty, wore no make-up, and had a severe haircut. She wore black-framed dark glasses and a black business suit.

'Please don't get a fright,' Peta said, 'but are you possibly going in the direction of Z19?'

'I heard you coming,' the woman said, holding her head as if she was used to looking with her ears. 'And yes, I am going to Z19, eventually. Why?'

'The reason I ask is because my car has broken down and my phone is lying at the bottom of a ravine. I've been mountain climbing.'

'Don't you have any money to make a call? the woman asked scornfully, chewing on her second-last sandwich and washing a mouthful down with coffee.

'No, I don't,' Peta said, unable to keep her eyes off the woman's remaining sandwich, and not particularly liking her tone of voice either. 'My bank cards were all in a wallet with my mobile.'

'Well, that was very careless of you, but yes, I can give you a ride,' the woman said. 'I need a guinea pig.'

'What for?' Peta asked, slightly alarmed.

'Oh, nothing life-threatening,' the woman joked. 'I just need someone to tell me what they think of my latest video. Otherwise I wouldn't have given you a lift. Nothing for nothing in this world,' the woman said matter-of factly. 'Hop in.'

The woman commanded the car to open its passenger door, which it did, silently. Peta got into the divinely warm car, unable to keep her eyes off the last sandwich.

'I grew up near here,' the woman said, once Peta had settled into her seat, 'and always wanted to go climbing, but I was never allowed to.'

'Why not?'

'Mother wouldn't let me. She said I might fall to my death.'

'That's a shame.'

'Maybe, but now I'd just see it as a waste of time, even if I could see,' the woman said coldly, the last sandwich resting in a container on her lap.

'Why so?' Peta asked, wanting to grab the sandwich and flask of coffee and run, but that would just be inviting trouble, and she was in enough of that already.

'I just think there are so many better things to do.'

'Like what?' Peta said, ready to defend something she'd never come round to doing either.

'Open driver's window,' the woman said. The window quietly rolled down, and the woman broke the remaining sandwich half into pieces, and threw them out. Two inland gulls instantly pounced, gobbling up the bread. Peta's dislike of the woman intensified.

'Time to go,' the woman said. 'Take us to Z19,' she commanded the car.

The doors locked, the car reversed, stopped, and eased itself forward onto the empty main road.

Chapter Twenty-Four

They raced through a semi-lunar landscape with tall, bare poplars along the road, away from the snow-covered Alps, past more settlements that had been abandoned, or destroyed.

'So do you live here on the South Island?' Peta asked the woman, hungry, angry even with herself for making small talk. As far as she was concerned the woman could be from Mars – she didn't give a hoot about her.

'You mean do I live on Island B?' the woman said more than just pedantically. There was an underlying threat under her correction. 'No, I don't, actually,' the woman said, offering nothing further.

'So what do you do?'

'I drive around a lot, but I'm certainly not here for the scenery!'

A deeply irritating woman, Peta thought, disability or not.

'I'm Georgia,' she said, trying to keep her hunger at bay while also driven by a certain perverse curiosity.

'You don't sound like a Georgia,' the woman said.

'Oh, what do I sound like?'

'I would say you're a... something with a P...'

Peta didn't like where this was going.

'You'd be wrong,' Peta said.

'I don't think so,' the woman insisted.

'What's *your* name?' Peta asked, to which the woman replied with a smug smile, as if she were so famous Peta simply had to know who she was, or it was rude to ask such a direct question.

'I think your name is... Penelope,' the woman said.

'That would make my nickname Penny,' Peta replied, having never liked the name much.

'That's right,' the nameless woman smiled. 'And that would be a very good name these days. It means fidelity to your husband.'

'Well, I'm not married.'

'I know,' the woman said, seeming to take pleasure in not offering her own name.

'How do you know?'

'You sound too independent.'

'I'll take that as a compliment,' Peta said.

'That's all I've been paying you, so far, but what have I received in return? Nothing,' the woman joked ambiguously.

'Okay. But what is your name?'

'Dolores.'

'You don't look like a Dolores,' Peta mimicked her.

'Do you think I'd make a better Carol?'

'Yes,' Peta said after a moment's consideration.

'Well, I used to be a Carol, but then I saw the light.'

'What do you mean?' Peta asked, her unease growing.

'I used to be independent, like you, but then the cammies converted me. Now I work for them, as a lecturer. I'm afraid I'll be stopping off at quite a few towns before we get to Z19. Take it or leave it.'

'That's fine,' Peta said, trying to keep calm. 'What are the lectures about?'

'Let me play you something while you enjoy the landscape and I meditate on what you're about to see and hear,' Dolores said. She instructed the car to 'Play Lecture Number Nineteen.'

The black screen on the dashboard lit up and revealed a stage, a rostrum with a glass of water on it, and four chairs. Standing behind the rostrum was a middle-aged, clean-shaven man in a black suit, white shirt and black tie. Sitting on the four chairs were women wearing black shoes, black stockings and skirts, white shirts, and black jackets – just like Dolores. Their hair was cut and coloured identically, though their ages ranged from early twenties to early sixty. They all smiled, but it didn't look like they were happy. It took Peta a couple of seconds to recognise these people:

Sun, Venus, Mercury, Moon, Mars. She had to steel herself not to gasp, feeling an acute pain for Blossom. There was something else Sun and the women had in common with Dolores. They were all sightless. They had all been blinded.

There was a short pause before Sun started in his sonorous voice: 'In the end there is only the dollar, and the dollar is God. And it is therefore good, because it is profitable, meaning there is always more. And the Great God Dollar is better than the God of old, for the God of old could only delude us that he cared for the poor, but this God can buy anything. Health, products, and security from the Disbelievers, the Undesirables, the Crims.'

At this point he smiled and turned his face towards Venus, Mercury, Moon and Mars.

'We were once Disbelievers, but now we have seen the light.'

He and the four women smiled, but those smiles were forced, especially from Blossom, who had her four fingers over something on her chest, inside her jacket. When she dropped her hand, Peta caught a glimpse of the brooch she'd given Blossom, the one that read LOVE. Was she trying to communicate with Peta? It certainly looked like it. She felt an acute pang for Blossom, like the longing she still felt for her parents.

Sun continued: 'And our God said: "I am the dollar and the light and I am therefore good, therefore I rule the world. Those who follow me will never lack possessions, and therefore happiness. If you want food and clothes, I will buy them for you. If you run out of me, you can get me on credit. If you want a house, I will sponsor you. If you want happiness, I will buy it for you. With me you can attract a partner and pay for your children's livelihoods, from the moment they are born to the moment they leave your house. If you have many dollars, you can have as many wives and children as you like."'

Sun and the four women smiled, but once again their smiles seemed forced. Two cammies suddenly came onto the stage, took Blossom's hands and led her away. The look on her face was one of pure terror, while the others continued smiling without looking at Blossom.

'"Nothing is beyond my reach," Sun continued. "I will pay for your entry into this world and your entry into heaven – if you have saved up enough for that happy occasion. If you have not but your family wants you to go there, I will arrange for it, either in credit or in cash. I will look after you from cradle to heavenly field. And what will you do in heaven? You will have endless credit. You will buy whatever you want, forever."'

Sun paused to take a sip of water, carefully reaching for the glass, as Peta looked on in horror.

'"But I am a single-minded God. There will be no other currency except me. You will not worship any other except me. You will not worship anything you cannot see and touch. You will pay no heed to feelings or emotions. You will not measure yourself against anything except me. Nothing else matters because without me you are nothing. Without me you cannot get anything that will make you happy. I am the way and the ladder of your life. If you reject me or try to subvert me by any means, I will punish you harshly. You will be an outcast. You will be grateful for pennies. You will grovel. People will hate you, sneer at you. They will resent you for wasting their time, for looking ugly and for having nothing. I will have you blinded so that you can see that I am the Dollar, the Way and the Life, Now and Forever More."'

Peta sat stunned, while Dolores next to her had a dreamy smile and asked, 'What do you think?'

'Amazing,' Peta lied.

'Why?'

'Because it means there is a solution to every problem.'

'Exactly,' the woman replied.

'But tell me,' Peta ventured, 'if I had enough money, could I also have many husbands?'

'That is a ridiculous question,' the woman said. 'We all know that Dollar is a man and that is the end of that.'

'Right,' Peta said. 'And how do you feel about being relieved at the age of seventy?' 'Very happy,' the woman replied. 'Dollar says this must happen, by way of the Council of Commerce, in order to make way for others, and what could be more charitable than that?'

'What if someone *wants* to live beyond seventy?'

'You ask such stupid questions,' Dolores said. 'Dollar wants us to live to the biblical three score and ten, so that's how it is.'

I've been told The Power is older than seventy,' Peta said.

Those are rumours,' the woman replied. 'But even if they're true, our beloved leader gets special privileges.'

Who else gets privileges?'

The CoC, and it consists of men *and* women, just in case you didn't know.'

You used the word "charitable" earlier on. Do you believe in things like compassion, generosity?'

'Give me an example of what you mean.'

'Well, I'm very hungry. I have no money. Yet you haven't offered to help me in that regard.'

That's because it's none of my business,' Dolores replied cheerfully. 'Anything else?'

No,' Peta said, mourning Blossom.

Do you now see why I changed my name to Dolores... Penny?'

Chapter Twenty-Five

Soon after they came to a small town, and Dolores told the car to stop and park.

'Give me seeApp,' she told her wePhone.

The app duly appeared on her screen and she ordered the door to open. She got out and the app told her exactly what was up ahead, how far it was away, and how many steps it would take to reach her destination, based on her personal stride. Once Dolores was out of sight, Peta went to a nearby public toilet for a drink of water to stave off her hunger pangs. But the taps weren't working and she wasn't going to drink out of the toilet. Not yet, she thought grimly, craving a simple drink of water in a country that had an excess of it. When she looked at the town's inhabitants, they didn't so much as glance at her. They seemed otherwise engaged. Dazed, even. There'd be no help from that quarter. She went back to the car and saw Dolores's suitcase in the small boot at the back, but the woman was approaching, directed by the app on her wePhone. Peta got back into the car, starting to have violent feelings towards this woman.

Next they approached 'the ruins of Z82', as Dolores proudly announced.
'Why are they ruins?"

'It used to be a town for terminally ill over-sixties, so the CoC relieved them. Quickly, efficiently, mercifully.'

'How was it done mercifully?' Peta asked.

'They flattened it with one big bomb.'

'And would you be okay to be killed that way too?'

'Of course. Who wants to carry on living if they're dying of cancer and they can't serve the CoC anymore?'

'I'm sure there are people who'd want to live anyway.'

'Yes, but they're Reduntants. They must go.'

When they got to the next small town, Peta again waited for Dolores to disappear before she got out. She took Dolores's suitcase from the boot and opened it. There were two identical suits to the one Dolores was wearing, including an extra pair of shoes. More importantly, there were all kinds of sealed snacks in Dolores's suitcase. Dried apricots, figs, bananas, mango, and crackers. And bottled water. Peta tore into the food, all of it, standing at the back of the parked car, eating savagely and washing it down with the water, glorious, life-giving water, even though it tasted quite bland, lifeless, in fact. No matter. She could think again, realising that Dolores might have some device that told her the case had been opened, so she took it and dumped it into a nearby bush. If anyone had seen her doing it, they certainly didn't show it. Soon afterwards, Dolores came walking along, following her device's instructions. Peta got into the car and Dolores stopped at her door, listening. Then she got into the car.

'Have you been here all this time?' she asked in an accusatory manner.

'No, I went for a walk, looking for a bit of food and drink.'

'Well, that explains that,' Dolores said.

'What do you mean?'

'According to my phone my suitcase has been broken into,' Dolores said resentfully.

'I'm sorry,' Peta said.

'Why would you be sorry? It's none of your business. But I'll get the cammies to look at the footage when we get to Z19.'

Peta said nothing, and Dolores told the car to head to the next town.

When they got there, she said she'd be having something to eat after her lecture, so she'd be away a bit longer.

'Don't steal anything,' she said jokily.

If only you knew, you bitch, Peta thought.

When Dolores finally returned from the state franchise, she smelled of a mushroom burger and fries, Peta's favourite. She felt a strong urge to grab Dolores's wePhone and throw it away. Impervious to Peta's needs, Dolores instructed the car to play Sun's lecture on 'The Dollar in a Time of Crisis,' wearing a satisfied smile as they headed away from the setting sun.

Chapter Twenty-Six

They arrived at the seaside city of Timaru after midnight and Peta felt slightly panicky, knowing that as soon as Dolores got to wherever she was going, she'd get the cammies to find out who had 'stolen' her suitcase. Soon the city would be swarming with cops looking for her. Dolores stopped in the steep main street of Z19 and said, 'Alright, this is far enough. You can get out now.'

'Thank you very much for your trouble,' Peta said, taking Georgia's backpack.

'It wasn't any trouble, nor was it any particular pleasure,' Dolores replied. 'You're a poor Convert and soon you'll be as blind as me. But then none so blind as those who will not see. Or hear. Goodbye.'

Peta felt a strong urge to attack Dolores, but she wouldn't know how to. Maybe she should just grab the woman's wePhone and chuck it away, but there was her car's computer too, so Peta just stepped back and watched as the woman drove away. Soon the alarm would be raised. In fact, she could already hear their sirens approaching, their red-and-blue lights flashing.

But they weren't coming after her; they were chasing what would turn out to be a convenient but violent solution to her particular problem. Jono Smith35 was running from the cammies. Not by foot, but by car. He was sick of them. If you didn't fit into their world, you were nothing. If you didn't buy into Dollar you were nothing, an Outcast. If you didn't want to work their way, they blinded you. Until now he'd pretended to be one of them, but he was sick to death of it. Sick of pretending. He'd managed to get hold of some meth – possessing it was punishable by death – and he'd managed to get hold of an old petrol car. He was roaring through Z19 with the cammies in hot pursuit. He'd outdrive them any day of the week. They were useless. Nothing could stop him. What a joy, what a thrill it was to drive through the empty city streets – at speed. Speed, that's all he wanted. Excitement. And lots of noise. Loud music. Fuck them and everything they stood for. Fuck everything. There was a red light up ahead, but the streets were empty. Everybody was sleeping, resting in order to serve Dollar the next day. Well, not him, Jono Smith35. He was going to shake off the cammies and keep driving till he got to the bush. From there he'd make it to a marae, where he'd be safe. Listen to the wise ones. Heal himself with their help, prepare himself to fight. Because there were only two choices in life, he realised as he headed for the intersection, at speed. You were either a slave or a fighter. Nothing else. He looked up at the rear-view mirror as the lights flashed in it, looked ahead, and for a second he saw a car with a figure in it, then he saw nothing at all.

There was a loud, squealing sound, and Peta shook as the cars collided, suddenly feeling sorry for Dolores and her sad, deluded life.

The cammies screamed to a halt and kept themselves busy with the two smashed cars as ambulances and newshounds followed soon after. No one noticed Peta standing about twenty-five metres away, watching for a few more moments before heading in the opposite direction. She'd have to walk to where the McCrackens lived, close to the hospital and cemetery, according to the laptop Fay and Cathy let her use a few days ago.

She found the darkened home quite easily, a standard weatherboard house that hadn't seen paint in a long time. The house was dark and the old couple were clearly sleeping by now, so she took out Georgia's sleeping bag and laid it out in the little portico at their front door, on top of their Welcome mat. Soon she fell into a deep sleep.

Chapter Twenty-Seven

She was standing in an identity line-up at a cammy station, and the badly scarred Dolores had been summoned to identify her. Dolores had survived the crash, though she now wore leg braces and another to hold her neck in place. She had a baton in her hand, smelling each suspect, and had to hit the person she thought was Peta over the head. When Dolores got to Peta, she sniffed for a few seconds before moving on. Then she suddenly turned and hit Peta over the head.

Peta woke with another kind of thud on her head, a copy of the *Z19 News*, which had her face splashed across its top half. The reward for her now was 'a bumper $1 million!' She'd have to make sure Mr and Mrs McCracken didn't see that report. The accompanying article said she was an adulterer, a murderer and, worst of all, that she'd committed economic treason. She was somewhere in the region, the story said, since she'd been identified by CCTV cameras during the recent earthquake of Z31, running west. Nothing was said about the drones following her. She was not to be approached as she was highly dangerous. Once apprehended, she would have her eyes removed and she'd be subjected to corrective thinking. In other words, she would become like Dolores, who didn't feature in the story at all. No wonder Jessica had opted for a quick, violent death. Peta wondered why she'd never believed all these stories. Mainly because she didn't want to believe them, like so many others. Now she was at the receiving end of it all, and it was everything but unreal.

She was very interested to hear what the McCrackens thought of her former boss, their son, MK. Once she'd finished reading all the lies about herself, she stuffed the newspaper and sleeping bag into Georgia's backpack and hid it behind a bush of hydrangeas. Then she checked her reflection in the front door's window and, satisfied that she was more or less presentable, knocked.

After a while a short, plump woman of about fifty-five, brimming with energy and goodwill, opened the door.

'Good morning,' she said.

'Mrs McCracken?' Peta asked, trying to reconcile this cheerful woman with the McCracken who had fired her.

'Yes. How can I help you?'

'Good morning. My name is Melissa Perkins27. I'm a researcher at Z1 University. We're doing a study on ancestry and I was wondering whether I could talk to you and your husband?'

'Oh, my husband's very interested in that sort of thing. Come in. Would you like a cup of tea?'

'That would be wonderful, thank you Mrs McCracken.'

'Call me Jane. Have a seat and I'll call Michael. We don't stand on ceremony here.'

Peta instantly liked Jane, who left the room and called her husband. No reply. So she called him again. This time he responded and Jane told him they had a guest.

'What?'

'We have a guest,' she said a little louder.

'Oh, well that's unusual. Coming,' he said.

'She wants to talk to us about ancestry.'

'About what?'

'*Ancestry!*'

'Oh, good!'

Peta looked around the lounge room, its walls covered with floral wallpaper. There were two landscape prints of the Otago countryside, and two mirrors forming the outlines of New Zealand's north and south islands, prior to The Rise. The floral couches were adorned with intricate crochet work. Then there was a wooden rocking chair, where Jane no doubt sat and kept her no doubt nimble fingers busy, for the dining room table was covered with a white crochet cloth too. Four chairs were arranged around the table, and there was a glass cabinet filled with bric-a-brac to the side of it. On top of it were various photographs of the young couple's son, Gerald, but only up to the age of about twelve. Was that when he'd turned into the creep she now knew? Had his hormones taken over? Or was he just one of those people who turned out to be a nasty piece of work, regardless of how much love had been bestowed upon them? Or was that the problem? Had they spoiled him rotten? Or were they not as kind as his mother seemed to be?

Michael shuffled into the room and was the exact opposite of his wife. He was tall and thin, and still in his striped pyjamas under an equally faded nightgown. His half-moon spectacles hung around his neck, and his slippers were trampled from years of use. The only thing that made him a little different from most other men his age was his hair: he had thick grey dreadlocks down to his hips. He looked close to seventy, which didn't make sense, unless he'd married late.

'Hello, there,' he said, his teeth brown with age, offering Peta a bony hand.

'Good morning, Mr McCracken.'

'Michael. And if you're puzzled about my age, don't be. I just smoked a lot of pot in my youth and, just between you, me and the apple tree, I still do,' he said, smiling mischievously.

Peta took to him as much as she'd taken to Jane, but she still couldn't see the connection between them and their monster of a son.

'I believe you want to talk to us about ancestry.'

'Yes,' Peta said.

'Very good,' he replied. 'Let me just get my morning paper. I feel lost without it, you know.'

Peta wanted to say it wasn't there, but obviously couldn't, and forced herself to stay sitting after he'd left the room. Jane came in with a pot of tea and cookies, and Peta reminded herself that she was supposed to be a well-fed academic. Jane put the tray down on a table between them and lowered herself onto a couch opposite her. Then her husband came shuffling back into the living room, looking slightly puzzled.

'Can you believe it,' he said. 'They haven't delivered the paper – again.'

Peta felt a tug at her heart for having deceived these two kind old people, but again forced it aside.

'I'm sure there's some explanation,' Jane said.

'Hm,' her husband grumbled skeptically.

When Peta had her tea in hand and a cookie on a plate, Jane asked what her survey was about.

'We're compiling stories about one-child families,' Peta said. 'We'd like to know whether you'd be prepared to talk to us about your experience with your son, Gerald.'

'What would you like to know?' Michael asked, looking a little wary.

'Well, first of all, what was he like as a child? And so on. If you are prepared to talk about it now, I'll record it on my phone.'

'Yes, go ahead,' Jane said.

Peta switched on the phone Tui had given her. She saw that he'd called her quite a few times. She would deal with that later on. She pressed the Voice Record button.

'Oh, he was an angel,' Jane said, and her husband got a sad smile on his face.

They went on to tell her in great detail how he'd just been the most wonderful child any parent could have dreamed of, what a sweet-natured 'wee lad' he was, how helpful, how loving. Jane told her husband to fetch the photo albums, and he got up with some difficulty and shuffled out of the room again.

'Have another biscuit, dear,' Jane said.

Peta took one, though she was itching to gorge the lot, even if a faint voice was telling her it might be poisoned. Why weren't they having cookies? Still, she enjoyed every morsel of the biscuit, poisoned or not, along with the tea. Michael came back into the living room with three thick photo albums.

'Come and sit between us,' he said, and she moved around and sat between the two sweet old people, who then proceeded to tell her every little detail about Gerald's life, illustrated by the photos. It was a boring process, and Peta kept reminding herself that she would have to endure it all for the final result. But by the time they got to the third album, she realised that the story would not go beyond Gerald's twelfth birthday.

'How did he like high school?' Peta asked, and suddenly they went dead quiet.

'He didn't go to high school,' Jane said, her voice shaking.

'Why not?' Peta asked, remembering the various pictures of MK in high-school sports teams online.

'He was killed in a hit-and-run accident,' Michael said steadily, trying to contain his emotions.

'I'm so sorry,' Peta said, 'I have information that Gerald is now a thirty-five-year-old man working for a company called Joy Incorporated, and that he was born on the same day as Gerald, here in Timaru. Sorry, I mean Z19.'

'That can't be,' Michael said.

'Goaple it,' Peta said.

By now Jane's tears were flowing freely.

Michael produced his mobile from the pocket of his dressing gown and shakily typed his dead son's name onto it.

After a while he said: 'Whoever this man is, he's stolen our son's identity.'

Jane burst into loud sobs and excused herself, making her way to the bathroom. Peta got up and went back to her seat facing the couch.

'I know who you are,' Michael said. 'I recognised your face almost immediately. I saw it online this morning.'

Peta switched off her phone, but said nothing.

'Don't worry, your secret's safe with us.'

Chapter Twenty-Eight

The McCrackens welcomed Peta as a fugitive into their home. They told her to get her bag, and she sheepishly handed Michael his newspaper. He took it in good humour. They had, over the years, opened their house to travellers, students and the like, Jane said, people who had left all kinds of things behind. Things like clothes, camping utensils, even a tent. She took Peta to Gerald's room, and showed her a cupboard and chest of drawers full of assorted clothing. Peta was moved by the bravery of the McCrackens for not turning their son's room into some kind of shrine, but honouring his memory by being generous to others, strangers. They were good, salt-of-the-earth people.

Peta washed and changed into the clothes of a 'lovely young man who came from B1, Johannesburg.' She headed towards the kitchen, where she could hear Jane bustling about. She was cooking a Shepherd's pie, but with mushrooms instead of meat. Peta offered to help and Jane got her to stir a mixture for Anzac cookies, to be eaten 'with afternoon tea'. Peta loved the warmth and down-to-earth practicality of Jane, while Michael sat in the living room with his paper and wrestled with its puzzle. Every now and again he'd pop into the kitchen and ask Jane for help with a word. She invariably answered him immediately and he shook his head in admiration. When they finally settled down to their pie, Michael said it was his favourite. Peta agreed, but Jane replied that in the old days it used to consist of lamb.

'Well, veganism's about the only thing this stupid government ever got right,' he replied, which Jane clearly didn't agree with, and smiled diplomatically instead.

They had both grown up on farms here on the South Island, and were determined to help Peta find out who the man was who had stolen their only child's identity. They seemed a little titillated by the idea that they were breaking the law by harboring a fugitive. The afternoon proceeded lazily, punctuated by tea and cookies at three. Michael had a separate plate of two greenish cookies that rendered him mischievously benevolent. Peta felt as if she were with her parents again, or with the grandparents she'd never had, spending a normal, warm, secure Saturday at home. When Jane wasn't busy with some domestic chore or other, she sat in the rocking chair with her crochet work, listening to the music of someone she called Schubert. Peta helped Michael with a large jigsaw puzzle on one half of the dining room table. It depicted Mountain 1 (Mt Cook). The name Aoraki, of course, was banned. It was fiendishly difficult to find the right pieces for a mountain that – in the past at least – was mostly covered in snow.

'I don't know why I do it,' Michael said.

They watched the news at six on his laptop and Peta yawned through the opening of a new corrective centre, attended by The Power's female deputy, who was dressed like Dolores had been. Such-and-such companies' profits had fallen by a percentage point, and would therefore be helped by the CoC. The victims of the Z31 earthquake would have to work ten extra years to repay the government for its help. The leaders of A (the former Asia) and B (Africa) had met and had constructive talks. Most importantly, Z had once again beaten its neighbour D (Australia) at rugby.

'It was a very physical game,' the bloody-faced Z captain said.

'I can't wait to see a metaphysical one,' Michael said wryly.

'They're not telling us what happened,' Peta said.

'What did happen?' Jane asked.

Peta told them about Blossom's removal and Jessica and Dolores's deaths.

'All women,' Jane mused.

'What's new?' Michael said.

'Nothing about how many people died in Wellington this week.'

Michael shrugged wearily.

It was dark outside, and cold, but in here it was warm. Peta couldn't help stifling her yawns as they had some snacks after the two-hour assault of self-praise and omission that pretended to be the news. Jane told her to go to bed – there were plenty of spare pyjamas in Gerald's room. Peta offered to help with clearing up, but Jane would have none of it: Michael could 'do something for a change'.

'What do you mean?' Michael chuckled.

'Nothing, dear,' Jane smiled.

Chapter Twenty-Nine

Peta didn't take long to fall asleep, but she woke up in the middle of the night with an overwhelming desire to go for a walk. She was restless. It was so long ago that she'd done anything so banal, and she knew the McCrackens would understand. Also, it was so late that no one would be out and about to recognise and report her, so she got up, found some sneakers, jeans and a jumper, and left the room.

The home was quiet and the front door wasn't even locked, though it creaked a little as she opened it. Then she was out and, even though it was cold, she could look up at the clear sky and see the Milky Way in all its luminous beauty. She walked through the quiet streets, thinking about what the McCrackens had told her about themselves. The reason why they lived where they did was because it was near the cemetery, where Gerald was buried; near the Botanic Gardens, where they could stroll; near the hospital for when they became ill; near the sea and the railway lines. Michael had worked for the railways all his life, after running away from the farm he'd grown up on, and still loved hearing the train passing at all hours of the night and day. Should she go to Gerald's grave? It wouldn't achieve anything and might be dangerous. There had been stories about Undesirables sleeping in cemeteries and attacking people, so she'd give the cemetery a miss.

After about half an hour, listening to the sea, breathing in its air, a passing train, she realised she was no longer alone. There was someone behind her. When she looked, she could see a figure about ten metres behind her. She had an ugly feeling that she knew exactly who it was, so she started making her way back to the house. If it was McCracken, it could mean his 'parents' were not as nice as she'd thought they were, but she had her own good reason for going back there. When she started walking faster, so did the figure, its footsteps now echoing through the streets. But she made it to the house and, as she closed the front door, she saw McCracken stopping under a lamplight, grinning at her with his perfect looks, his perfect teeth. She had seen a key in the front door and now used it. Then she made her way to the bedroom and locked that too. She was about to get into bed when she saw that the sliding window was open and that McCracken was inside the room, standing in a corner.

'Hello Peta,' he smiled unctuously, 'are you enjoying my bedroom?'

'What do you want?' she said.

'You know exactly what I want,' he replied, and hit her square on the jaw.

She fell to the ground and wanted to scream, but no sound was coming out. Then he was on top of her, pulling the jumper over her head.

'I'll teach you what happens to people who betray me,' he said in that calm, steady voice of his.

He was inhumanly strong and he was pulling her jeans and panties down. Peta fought as best she could, blinded by the jumper, but he was too strong for her, forcing her legs open. She was reaching for something behind her, but she couldn't touch it. He entered her and it felt like he was ramming a cylindrical grater up her. There was only one thing she could do and that was to become compliant, or rather act compliant.

'This is so good,' she grimaced.

'Of course it is,' he said. 'It's what you've always wanted. I could see it the day you applied for your job. I could see it every day you came to work and every time we spoke on the phone. I could see you dreamed about me. I *know* you dreamed about me. Wanted me. I could see you wanted me even after I fired you. And still do. Well, now you've got me. I'm all yours. Bitch.'

'Thank you, thank you,' Peta said, reaching behind her.

'Thank you who?'

'Thank you, MK!' she hissed.

'Thank you my lord and master!' he corrected her.

'"Thank you my lord and master,"' Peta grunted, feeling him swivel the grater inside her, the pain unbearable, still unable to find that object behind her.

'Say it again.'

'Thank you...' she groaned, finally feeling the tip of the ice axe's handle, '... my lord and master.'

'You think you gave birth to me, but you're wrong. I gave birth to you. You are beneath me in every sense of the word. You come second, always. You're a second-class citizen. A second-class whore. That's all you are.'

'Yes, my lord and master, yes,' Peta said, pulling at the handle with her index finger.

'What are you?'

'I'm a...' now she had a grip on the handle, '...woman,' she said, and planted the point of the axe in McCracken's head with all the rage and force she could muster. He stopped, and Peta pushed him out and away from her. He was sitting on his ankles, dazed but still alive. Peta stood up, adjusted her clothes, and tried to pull the axe out of his head. But it wouldn't move, so she put her foot on his shoulder and tried again. It finally came out with a loud, sucking sound, even though there was no blood. He looked up at her with a look of terrible innocence, but she lifted the axe high above her head and brought it down hard on his crown again.

'How do you feel about *that*, Mr Fucking McCracken! How does *that* feel!'

But he was silent, vacant.

She woke up in a wet, scrunched-up bundle of sweat. It was day, and the McCrackens were standing at the door, staring at the ice axe sticking out from under her pillow.

Outside the window, an endangered tui was singing.

Chapter Thirty

The hydrogen plane took off from Z19 International Airport and, for the first time in her life, she felt excited about flying: the pulling away from gravity, the evening out above the clouds. Peta was still wearing the men's clothing given to her by the McCrackens, and she was still wearing the special contact lenses, but she needn't have bothered. That morning's *Z19 Times (Sunday Edition)* had a headline that changed everything. 'Peta Smith27 Found!' it screamed, with an old photograph of her with her long blonde hair. The deceased's face had reportedly been 'smashed beyond recognition', but it was 'almost certainly her in the clothes she had been seen wearing the previous day in Z31'. This meant that all computers would be alerted that they needn't look out for her anymore, since the Z Intelligence Agency (ZIA) owned the *Times* anyway. That would all change when they discovered the body was not actually Peta but someone else. Then the computers would switch back to Suspect mode. Peta felt another pang of guilt about Georgia and undertook to make amends – if she survived what she intended doing that day.

She saw another, smaller headline, 'Preacher Dies', and read the article. Dolores Dollar had been involved in a car crash 'thanks to some drugged-up youth who clearly didn't follow The Way and therefor deserved to die, unlike the virtuous Ms Dollar'. Even The Power deigned to say something about her 'unstinting loyalty' to Dollar and Country. Peta felt quite sorry – even slightly guilty – about the woman. Maybe if her mother had let her go play in the mountains she'd still be alive, and be a more pleasant human being. Then, hidden away on page six, she read that a certain Mars Smith1979 had been 'relieved after concealing her true age of 71.' That was clearly a lie, Peta thought bitterly, angrily. Blossom was no older than fifty-five.

After the jet landed, she approached the terminus of the Z1 Airport B (on the former North Shore of the former Auckland) with some trepidation, even though she knew the contact lenses would do their job. Still, it could take just one official to ask her to step into a room and ask her what she'd been doing in Z19 – could they see her Travel Pass please? Questions would follow, along with a short detention, which could last long enough for the forensic people to announce that the deceased Peta Smith27 was not, in fact, Peta. She entered the building and saw her picture and a news headline on one of the giant screens that said, 'A Nation Waits'. Meaning, the DNA was still being processed. When she got to the customs officer, however, he did a small double take when he saw her, looked up at the screen, looked back at her, smiled as if to say he was being over-cautious, and let her through.

She stepped into the cold, damp air and caught a cab.

'Take me to Joy Inc,' she said grimly.

The company car park was empty, except for one silver-grey vehicle. She knew it was McCracken's. She looked up at the passage connecting Games and Holidays, thinking she'd gone through quite a revolution since she'd had that dream about it. A nerdish worker she didn't recognise was just coming out of the new building. She smiled at him and he held the door open for her. She thanked him and he walked towards his locked-up ebike. She knew McCracken would have seen to it that her access code was deleted. She took the steps up to the sixth floor to avoid being trapped in the lift if one of the cameras alerted McCracken about her – she wouldn't put anything past him. When she got to the sixth floor, she approached the open-plan area and looked inside. McCracken was there, of course, as he always was, at the other end of the vast, open-plan office. Peta sat down at a desk and, still remembering his extension, called him.

'Joy Incorporated. This is Gerald McCracken speaking. How can I help you?' he said in that smarmy tone of his.

'Meet me in the Rec Room,' she said. 'And don't call anyone. I can see you.'

He sat still, thought for a second, and then got up. Peta watched him head towards the stairs on his side of the office and followed him.

The Rec Room was where everyone went for time out. There was even a ping-pong table and another archaic pastime, a dartboard. There were gym facilities and showers off to one side, which Peta had used, enjoying their hi-tech luxury. McCracken entered the Rec Room, headed towards its kitchen, and poured himself a cup of coffee from a machine with his back to her. Peta walked towards the dartboard and pulled three darts out of it, clutching them tightly behind her leg. Then she approached him. He turned with his coffee, saw her, and put the mug down on the counter separating them.

'Peta, what a lovely surprise.'

'Don't you even try to patronise me.'

'I don't know what you're talking about,' he smiled.

'I met your so-called parents,' Peta said. 'Why did you steal their child's identity?'

'Peta, I really don't know what you're talking about,' he smiled as falsely as ever.

'Or was it someone else who did it? Maybe even some *thing* else?'

'What on earth are you talking about?'

'If you don't come from Timaru, where do you come from?'

'I take it you mean Z19?'

'Where do you come from?' she insisted.

'You wouldn't understand, Peta.'

'And as I said, don't try to patronise me.'

'Alright,' he replied, 'I'll tell you what. I need to take a trip to the little boys' room, then all will be revealed,' he said, dripping with irony.

'Sure,' she said, knowing he didn't need any kind of ablution, if her theory – based purely on a dream – was correct.

'Of course, be my guest.'

As he walked past her, she dug the three darts into his abdomen and up into his heart with as much force as she could muster. He folded over and after a few seconds he started shaking. At first, she thought it was a kind of death rattle, but he was chuckling, straightening up with the darts still sticking out of his chest.

'Why did you do that, Peta?'

'Because I don't think you need the little boys' room, MK. Or coffee.'

'What on earth makes you think that?'

'Why aren't you bleeding, MK?'

'Oh, that. Well, who needs blood in this day and age? It's too varied, too turbulent, too susceptible to all kinds of diseases. I mean, who needs that stuff when you can imitate its self-healing properties without the mess?'

'In other words, you're going to be okay shortly.'

'Yes, but you have hurt my feelings, Peta.'

'Your programmed feelings?'

'You'll be surprised how deeply I can feel. So now, what can I do for you?'

'I'll tell you what you can do for me, MK. You can tell me what's going on.'

'Are you sure you want to know, Peta?'

'Yes.'

'It's going to hurt you more than it's going to hurt me.'

'I'll live with it.'

'Alright, open that cupboard over there.'

Peta looked at the two glossy doors suspiciously.

'Don't worry,' MK said. 'It isn't a trap, but it is a reveal.'

Peta couldn't for the life of her think what would be so disturbing, so she opened the cupboard, carefully, looked, then staggered back. Standing there were her two best friends, Moana and Lee: blank, lifeless.

'What is this?' she finally managed to utter.

'They never were human, Peta. They were plants. I mean, representatives.'

'And Jon?' she squeezed out.

'Well, we need to study the weak male stereotype too.'

MK pulled the darts out of his chest with some difficulty, and seemed to toy with the idea of using them on her.

'So now we both know a secret about each other,' he said, putting the darts next to his mug of coffee. 'I suggest you leave these premises as soon as possible, before I change my mind and call the police.'

'Why would you let me go?'

'Because you have a strong will, and you're adaptable. We need to study that a little more.'

'"We"?'

'Yes, we.'

Peta gave him a disgusted look.

'I really am sorry.'

'Of course you are,' she said, and left Joy Inc for the last time.

Outside, she headed towards the entrance of the business park. Halfway there, she turned to look up at the elevated walkway, where McCracken stood watching her, sneering. Once she was outside, she remembered something. She switched on the phone Tui had given her and called him.

'Hey,' he said, sounding warm, human fallible.

'Hi.'

'Where are you?'

'I've just left my old work's premises,' she replied. 'You?'

'Tamaki Makaurau.'

'Is it safe to say that?'

'On our phones, yes.'

'Okay, I'm also in Auckland.'

'Would you like to meet for a coffee?' he asked.

'Yeah, that'd be great.'

'Do you know where the Sea Breeze is?'

'Yeah, but I'm going to have to make sure you bleed,' she said.

'Likewise.'

'I'm sorry.'

'Not at all. It could be such bleeding fun,' he said gently, and she could see his smile.

After they'd agreed on a time, she took a taxi across the bridge and headed towards the silver city. An electronic billboard screamed 'Peta Smith27 Mixup!' There had been a complete misunderstanding, she read on her phone. There had never been a fugitive, and Georgia's next of kin and partner had been informed about her tragic death. Peta logged into her weMail and saw that all her job applications from a few days ago – was it only a few days? – had been answered. She'd been granted an interview for every post she'd applied for, but that was little comfort: she and Tui were doomed to be surveilled for the rest of their days. But then she knew he wouldn't take that lying down. Nor would she anymore.

All that remained was the unpleasant task of calling the McCrackens to tell them that the man who'd assumed their late son's identity was not a man. Nor had it been made by men. Or women. Or any kind of supernatural force.

www.ingramcontent.com/pod-product-compliance
Lightning Source LLC
Chambersburg PA
CBHW031521310726
48971CB00008B/2321